ICE RIFT SIBERIA

Ben Hammott

ICE RIFT - SIBERIA

Ben Hammott

Author can be contacted at: benhammott@gmail.com
www.benhammottbooks.com
Cover Design by Robert Ryminiecki

Books in the Ice Rift Series

Ice Rift Book 1

Ice Rift – Salvage Book 2

Ice Rift – Siberia Book 3

CHAPTER 1

The Kamera - Siberia

Three Russian KamAZ-53501 trucks rumbled through the gates held wide by two men and into the compound surrounded by a security fence topped with razor wire. Like a well-rehearsed ballet movement, the vehicles turned and reversed towards the largest building. With a loud hissing of airbrakes, they parked in a neat row. Men climbed out, and while some raised the shutters on the tailgates and climbed inside, two men headed for the entrance. The man spinning a key around his finger, split off, unlocked the door to the smaller hut attached to the side of the main building, and went inside. The other man halted at the main building's single door, and slipping a key card from his pocket, he stared at the dead lights on the key lock. He glanced alongside the building when the chugging of the backup generator spluttered to life, spurting dark diesel fumes from the exhaust protruding from the roof; the main generator lay inside, situated on the lowest level.

The man turned back to the key lock when it beeped. The small green light glowed, indicating it had power. The door buzzed when he inserted the card, releasing the electronic lock.

"Shall we start unloading, Director Stanislav?" asked comrade Saveliy.

Stanislav halted his pushing on the door and scowled at the man who had spoken before casting his annoyed glare at the men waiting at the rear of the vehicles with pallet trucks waiting to be loaded. "You should have already started."

"Yes, sir." Saveily turned away smartly and shouted. "What are you lazy sows waiting for? Start unloading."

Stanislav entered the building and strode over to the doors of the elevator at the far end. He pressed the call button and stepped inside when they slid open. He pressed the down button and arrived on Level 1 of The Kamera a few moments later. He stepped out into the darkness and shivered from the coldness that greeted him; it seemed colder down here than outside. The air was musty, stale, from its long confinement. Aware the heating system would soon drive away the cold and the filtration system would cleanse both when they were switched on, he crossed to a small access panel set high in the wall and pulled it open. As the elevator doors closed behind him, reducing the sliver of light seeping from the elevator, he reached for the clunky power lever. Pitch blackness enveloped him when the doors met. The winch motor filled the silence when it hoisted the elevator above ground. Stanislav pulled down the lever. A flash of sparks lit up his face when the contacts engaged. Ceiling lights flickered on along the corridor as power infiltrated through the secret facility that had been abandoned many years ago to become a storeroom for Stalinist and cold war era documents.

The rumble of pallets being loaded into the elevator filtered down the shaft. They had a week to ten days to prepare the facility for the important and highly classified task Stanislav had been charged to oversee. As he strolled along the corridor, he glanced into rooms and made mental notes as to the purpose to which each would be assigned. He had been handed a once-in-a-lifetime opportunity to impress his superiors and climb the ladder of success he craved. Nothing and no one would prevent him from succeeding.

*****

Almost three weeks after leaving Antarctica, and a journey of 10,652 miles, (17,143 km) the Russian-owned ship the Spasatel Kuznetsov pulled into port. Before it had even attached its mooring lines to the dock, a truckload of soldiers appeared and lined the wharf. A few minutes later, a black car pulled alongside the quay and sat there ominously. When the ship had been moored and steps wheeled into place, two men climbed from the car and boarded the vessel.

Captain Brusilov, forewarned of their impending arrival, met them at the top of the rickety portable stairway and placed the two alien pistols on the foam padding lining the metal suitcase handcuffed to one of the men's wrist. Without a word being exchanged between them, the men turned away and headed down the steps. Before they stepped from the ship, a small black blob slithered unseen onto the suitcase-carrying man's black shoe and mimicked the shine of its polished patent leather.

Brusilov observed the men until they had climbed back into their car and driven away, before returning to his cabin. His eyes swept the line of soldiers along the wharf. There to ensure he and his crew didn’t disembark until they had all been debriefed and interrogated about the events that had unfolded during their salvage mission aboard the alien spaceship. Only then would it be decided if their mission had been a success or a failure. The outcome of that decision would determine if they received praise or punishment.

*****

The two men in the black car—and their precious cargo—had a long journey ahead of them. Swapping charge of the briefcase when each took a turn at the wheel while the other rested, they only stopped to refuel, go toilet and grab something to eat as they drove.

After a drive that lasted four days, the car turned onto a small road that stretched into the cold, desolate Siberian tundra. After traveling for a few hours along the bumpy potholed road badly in need of maintenance, they halted at the first of the three checkpoints stationed with armed guards along the road's two-hundred-and-fifty-mile route. After a guard had scrutinized their credentials and confirmed the photographs matched the identities of the two men in the car, he handed the papers back and lazily raised an arm at his comrade beside the barrier. The guard raised the pole wound with razor wire and waved them through to continue their journey along the remote, lonely road few had travelled.

At the road's end, the driver steered the car through the gates of the security-fenced compound and pulled to a stop alongside a small cluster of unassuming agricultural buildings. The man with the suitcase handcuffed to his wrist climbed out, shivered from the biting wind that assaulted him and gazed up at the dark clouds skidding across a foreboding gloom-washed sky as he crossed to the door. He stared at the camera focused on him until a buzzing signaled the lock's release. He entered, crossed the vacant room and pressed the button set beside the elevator doors. He stepped inside, and as soon as the door closed, the elevator carried him deep below ground.

The man stepped out onto Level 1 and was greeted by a scientist wearing a white coat.

"We thought you were never coming," said Vadim. "We're excited to get started on the project."

Vadim dragged his eyes away from the man's stone-faced expression, which unnerved him a little, and focused on the suitcase chained to the man's wrist. Inside was what they had all been waiting for. "Follow me."

Vadim led the man along the drab gray-painted corridor, and after a couple of turns, they entered a brightly lit workroom where a group of white-clad scientists specializing in various fields of expertise relevant to their assigned tasks waited to receive the precious cargo.

The man placed the suitcase gently on the table they were gathered around, released the shackle from his wrist and unlocked the case before stepping back. The scientists stared excitedly at the alien weapons before one of them removed one from the case. As they huddled around the weapons, pointing at various details and giving their opinions as to what might be their functions, the man, his mission completed, headed for the exit.

*****

The black blob, the only surviving piece of EV1L, slid from the man's shoe, slithered across the room and hid in shadow while it surveyed its new, pleasantly warm surroundings.

*****

Luka Kupetsky, the animal experimentation controller, cook and maintenance technician, or general dogsbody as he would label his role, stared at the exterior camera feed on the CCTV monitor as he watched the two men who had just arrived drive away. He had been stuck in the security room for three boring hours waiting for them to arrive. As soon as they had passed through the compound gates, he pressed the button to close them, rose from the chair and headed along the corridor.

Aware the scientists, who had also been waiting for the men, would be occupied for a while with whatever had been delivered, Luka decided it would be the perfect time to indulge in a much-needed treat, but first he needed to collect a friend to share it with.

Ten minutes later, Luka peered through the small glass panel set in the door of one of the science rooms. Satisfied it was unoccupied, he entered and switched on the lights. As fluorescent tubes stuttered into life the length of the room, a chimpanzee followed him through the door.

"Shut the door, Boris," instructed Luka softly.

The chimp Luka had befriended and named closed the door gently and followed his human friend.

Luka halted at the first work bench and from his pocket pulled out two metal forks, a flip-top lighter adorned with a skull, a jar of chocolate spread and a bag of pink and white marshmallows, which he dangled enticingly in front of Boris's face when the chimp jumped onto the workbench. He yanked them from the chimp's reach when he grabbed at them.

Luka waved a finger. "Not yet, Boris, you know the drill."

Boris chattered his lips in reply.

"I'm going as quick as I can."

Luka opened the bag and breathed in the rush of escaping sweetness previously trapped inside. He placed them out of Boris's reach, picked up the lighter and looked at his impatient comrade.

"Gas please, Boris."

Boris turned the small tap set into the worktop.

Luka flicked his lighter and touched the flame to the tip of the Bunsen burner. The hissing gas whooshed into flame.

As Luka adjusted the flame to the desired heat, Boris picked up a fork and held it out expectantly. Luka fished a plump pink marshmallow from the bag and slid it onto the prongs. Boris wasted no time bathing it in the flame. Luka unscrewed the jar of chocolate spread and placed it between them before skewering a marshmallow on his fork and turning it in the flame.

The smell of toasting sweetness filtered through the room.

Boris took his treat from the flame and examined the browned, smoking morsel of deliciousness. Deciding it was ready, he plunged it into the jar and shoved the chocolate-covered treat into his mouth.

Luka smiled at the satisfied look on the chimp's face.

They had been together for a little over two years now. When the chimp had arrived with five others at his previous laboratory posting, he had realized immediately that this primate was special. They had instantly bonded, and Boris soon proved his intelligence and quick learning ability. To safeguard him against the experiments carried out on the other animals under his care, Luka had falsified an official document reporting that Live Specimen 829PRI was part of an ongoing experiment being carried out by the Experimental Resources Department (ERD) attached to the Defense Ministry. Though ERD was something Luka had invented, there were so many secret organizations in Russia it was impossible to keep track of them all, and few would dare pry too closely and bring unwanted attention upon themselves. The signature he had forged on the document also helped to safeguard his deception. It was of a well-known high-ranking official, someone few would argue with. Assigning himself as guardian and overseer of the ongoing experiment no one was aware of, Luka had been able to include Boris in the list of animals he had been ordered to bring to the remote secret facility.

"How tasty is that, Boris?"

Boris tilted his head, curled his lips back and let out a series of hoots to show his pleasure.

"Shush! You'll get us caught. You know we're not allowed in here."

Boris complied and held out a hand. Luka gave him another marshmallow and smiled as Boris speared it with the fork and held it in the flame. Boris was a quick learner and one of his only two real friends down here. He pulled his toasted indulgence from the flame, dipped it into the chocolate, placed it in his mouth and sighed with pleasure.

*****

EV1L needed to regain its strength and grow. To achieve that it needed to feed on something living. But before it could do that it needed to rest and recover from its ordeal. Its metabolism had been thrown into disarray by the explosion that had almost destroyed it. The warm environment it had been brought to was ideal for the purpose.

EV1L ignored the seven, white-clad humans it couldn't absorb in its present state and directed its senses around the room in search of an exit. Its attention focused on a vent high in the end wall. Keeping to the edge of the wall, it flowed to the far end of the room and slithered like black mercury up to the slatted grille. It oozed into the vent and headed along the small metal tunnel. Washed by the warm draft blowing through the vent, EV1L hung from the ceiling. It achieved a state of hibernation and rested.

CHAPTER 2

Alien Weapon Test

To find out how they worked, what they were made of and the nature of the power source, the scientific team spent the following two weeks methodically running a battery of non-invasive tests on the pistols. They were swabbed for alien containments, tested for radiation leakage, X-rayed, weighed, measured, photographed from all angles and scanned by laser for a 3D computer model. The latest technology they used to discover the makeup of the outer shell was a Micro X-ray fluorescence (micro-XRF) spectroscopy, a non-invasive technique that wouldn't affect the pistol. It had only been delivered to the facility the day before.

The outer shell, which seemed to have been molded around the inner workings as there were no joints or fixings anywhere over its smooth, hard surface, was, as far as they could tell, a type of tough composite plastic that wasn't too dissimilar to that used in various earthbound manufacturing processes.

When the team felt they had done all the non-invasive tests they could with the available technology the facility had to offer, they made their report to Director Stanislav Volosheninov, the man tasked to oversee the investigation and the current head of the facility.

After reading through the reports, Stanislav penned his own and phoned his superior at the Kremlin to inform him of their progress and request permission to test the weapon's firepower before they dismantled one. After a delay of two hours, which was rapid for the Russian hierarchy, his Kremlin contact rang with permission to proceed.

Keen to test the weapons, the scientific team tasked with reverse engineering the alien weapon followed Director Stanislav and the alien pistol he carried from the room. Two floors below their work room, they entered a long room set up as a test firing range.

The expectant group gathered around the table set a short distance from the door they entered through and glanced at the three, simple life-size human-shaped targets positioned at the far end of the room.

Krisztina Zolushka, the team's technical expert, moved to each of the two video cameras set on tripods, switched them on and set them to record. One focused on the targets, and the other would provide a wide shot of the room that also took in the scientists.

Director Stanislav switched on the weapon. Their previous examinations and the reading of the report Captain Brusilov had made about the use of the weapon, led them to believe the dial on the side altered the power of the light ball it fired. Starting with the lowest setting, he aimed at the target and pulled the button trigger.

Barely making a sound when it fired, the small orange ball of light grew to about twelve inches in diameter. It struck the target without causing any damage and slammed it against the back wall.

"A non-lethal setting," uttered Svetlana Chuchnova, one of the two females in the group. Svetlana specialized in the interdisciplinary field of materials science and engineering; she also had an avid interest in biomaterials.

Eager to see what else it could do, Stanislav turned the dial to the next setting and aimed at another target.

A small red ball of light shot from the barrel and left a small smoking hole in the target when it passed through. It exploded in a crackling eruption of light when it struck the far wall. Pieces of concrete blasted into the room and clattered to the floor.

Amazed by the weapon's power and efficacy, the scientists stared at the foot-deep, hand-width wide crater that revealed pieces of metal reinforcing rods.

Rarely one to display emotion, Stanislav surprised them all when he uttered, "Bay!" (Pronounced Vou.) "Wow! There was no recoil and it's so silent."

"An excellent stealth weapon," stated Vadim, the armament technician brought in to work out the technicalities of reverse engineering the weapon. With the help of the other technicians and scientists, his goal was to understand the alien technology in order to replicate the weapon and build more powerful rifle versions with greater range.

After turning the dial to the final setting, Stanislav aimed at the final target.

The bright green ball of light expanded as soon as it left the barrel. It had grown to nine inches wide when it struck the target, which disintegrated where the light struck. The light ball erupted in a shower of sparks on striking the wall. Again, lumps of concrete shot out and skidded across the floor towards the gathered group.

Amazed at the amount of power and destruction such a small weapon could inflict, the team stared at the two-foot-wide, and about the same deep, hole in the wall. Molten metal dripped from the ends of the reinforcing bars the light had eaten through.

"I'd like to see its effects on flesh," said Alexei Yenotov, a scientist with a wide field of expertise and, at forty-nine years old, the oldest of the group.

Physicist Waldemar Witte smiled. "Are you volunteering, Alexei?" sweeping an arm at the targets.

"No need to comrade, your mother has." Alexei crossed to the intercom attached to the wall and pressed the talk button linked to the adjoining room. "Luka, bring in the sow."

Alexei grinned at Waldemar when the large door at the far end of the room opened, and Luka entered with a large sow in tow.

Luka glanced at the ruined targets, the holes in the wall and the concrete debris scattered over the floor. Aware he would be tasked with clearing up the mess, he sighed.

Knowing better than to ask questions or show too much undue interest in what was taking place here, Luka led the pig to the middle of the room in front of the targets. His casual gaze at the scientists focused briefly on one of the two women, Krisztina, who flashed him a fleeting smile. Unable to return a similar expression as the others might see—fraternizing was frowned upon between colleagues but shut off miles from civilization, they had become friends, and shortly after, lovers—he knelt and tethered the large pig to one of the metal rings set in the floor.

"If you've finished, Luka..." called out Stanislav, impatient to continue.

Glaring at the man he despised, Luka noticed the unusual object Stanislav held. It looked like a gun, though not like any he recognized. He assumed whatever it was, it was why they had all been ordered to the facility in the ass end of the Siberian wilderness. He also assumed it was responsible for the destruction in the room, the excited activity that had started a few days ago, and the reason for the pig and the cow that had been brought to the secret facility a few days before. He had asked Krisztina what was happening, but she had refused to tell him. No one trusted the government not to be listening. Even though things had changed with the long overdue collapse of the Berlin Wall, the facility had been constructed in an era when mistrust was prevalent in all walks of Russian life and when listening devices were used extensively to eavesdrop on the masses.

Luka stroked the sacrificial pig's head. If there was anything left of the animal when the scientists had finished with it, pork would be on the menu for the next few weeks. He exited through the large door he had entered through and waited with the cow tethered to the rail running the length of the wall.

After turning the dial back to the first lethal setting, Stanislav handed the pistol to Vadim. "Now you've seen it in action, do you think replication is feasible?"

Vadim eagerly took possession of the alien weapon. "Its power source and charging unit will probably cause us the most headaches, but I've reverse engineered and modified other countries' weapons that have fallen into Russia's hands, so I'm confident between us we shall succeed—or share the blame for failing."

Stanislav nodded in understanding. No one wanted to be singled out to take the full brunt of any repercussions failure would bring. Stalin might be dead and the cold war behind them, but gulags and fatal punishments remained. The report he would make to his superiors after the tests should be well received. Hopefully, when they had designed and built prototypes ready for mass producing new weapons equipped with alien technology, it would go a long way to seeing his status upgraded and getting him transferred to a less remote and inhospitable location. If reverse engineering the weapons proved impossible, he would ensure the brunt of the responsibility for the failure fell on his subordinates.

When Vadim raised the weapon, all eyes in the room focused on the pig looking at them curiously. The sow grunted when the small ball of light passed through its side and skidded along the floor in a trail of bright sparks. It squealed and yanked at its tether when it felt the pain.

Krisztina forced herself not to avert her eyes from the distressing sight. It wouldn't do to show weakness in front of her comrades.

Fascinated, Alexei moved a few steps closer to the stricken pig and stared through the neat hole in its flesh. "The heat has cauterized the wound, stopping the flow of blood."

"Try the next setting," encouraged Waldemar. "Aim for the head so you don't destroy all that delicious pork."

As he returned to the table, Vadim turned the dial one click. Taking careful aim, he fired at the pig's head.

The growing green ball of light was on target. The pig's head disappeared in a bright flash when it struck. The light ball bounced off the floor in a spray of color and split up into smaller balls that sprayed holes in the targets and the walls. As lumps of concrete clattered to the floor, the headless pig collapsed on its knees.

Stanislav beamed as he crossed to the intercom. The tests were going better than expected. His superiors couldn't help but be impressed. He pressed the talk button. "Bring in the cow."

Luka entered with the cow a few moments later.

"Just leave it free," ordered Stanislav.

Luka glanced at the dead pig that emitted the aroma of seared pork. Though its head was missing there was no blood. Wondering what kind of weapon could produce such an effect, he let go of the rope around the cow's neck and left the room.

Vadim held out the pistol to Waldemar. "To witness what effects the non-lethal fire power has on something living, I've dialed it to the first setting."

Keen to have a turn, Waldemar almost snatched the weapon from Vadim. A bit disappointed he didn't get to fire a destructive shot, he aimed at the cow's side and fired. The orange blast struck the cow and knocked it off its feet. Skidding across the floor it swept targets and concrete debris aside before coming to a halt. Waldemar gazed at pistol admiringly. “I love alien technology.”

The bellowing cow, which was less impressed, raised its head feebly.

Stanislav retrieved the weapon from Waldemar. “Now we’ve seen it in action, we have work to do.” He turned to Krisztina. “Switch off the cameras, collect the memory cards and transfer the footage onto my computer so I can upload it to the Kremlin.”

“Yes, Director Stanislav,” replied Krisztina.

Talking excitedly, the others left the room.

Krisztina crossed the room and spoke into the intercom. “They’ve gone.”

Luka entered and moved to the wide-eyed cow struggling to its feet. He calmed it with soft words and stroked and patted its neck. Though a bit wobbly, it remained on its feet. He led it from the room, and returning a few moments later, he approached Krisztina.

“It’s a weapon that has got you lot excited?”

Krisztina ejected the memory card from one of the cameras and slipped it in a pocket. “You know I can’t talk about it.”

Luka grabbed her arm gently, spun her around and pulled her tight to him. “I’ve seen enough to know I’m right.”

“Then you’ve seen too much. You know how this works. Ignorance keeps you safe.”

“Don’t worry, I won’t let on.”

They kissed.

“Will you be able to slip into my room again tonight?”

Krisztina unwound herself from his arms and crossed to the second camera. “I’ll see. It depends on my work. Everyone is eager to continue with the project, so I might have a few late nights ahead.”

“You will try though?” asked Luka, hopefully.

Krisztina smiled. “Of course.” She ejected the memory card from the second camera and after giving Luka a kiss, headed for the door and left.

Luka sighed again when he glanced around at the carnage he would have to clear up. He might also be working late. He headed for the pig’s carcass. His first job was to get it to the kitchen, so he could carve it up, freeze some and then start preparing dinner. He grabbed its hind legs and dragged it from the room.

CHAPTER 3

Growing Pains

EV1L paused at an intersection in the airduct and focused its senses along the four possible routes: left, right, ahead and down. Animal noises it failed to recognize drifted from below. It dropped into the chute and crawled along the vent towards the sounds. Pausing at the grille of horizontal slatted bars, EV1L observed the creatures trapped in cages that lined two sides of the room. It slithered between the slats and dropped onto the rack of cages.

Boris, sleeping off the food prepared by his human friend, opened an eye lazily and turned his head to the faint thud on the cage opposite. Sensing the menace emanating from the strange black blob, he remained still and observed what it would do. The spider monkeys in the adjoining cage screeched aggressively at the blob, setting the other animals into a frenzy; the three beagles barked, the rabbits trembled and cowered in a group and the mice twitched their noses and tried to clamber onto the wheel being frantically rotated by the first mouse to claim it.

EV1L ignored the animals' fear and panic as it moved along the cages in hunt of a suitable victim. It halted at one of the cages and observed the small white creatures scurrying around their prison. It seeped through the wire mesh and hung from a glutinous thread until one of the long-tailed creatures passed below. It dropped onto its back and began its absorbing process. The mouse screeched and shook frantically for a few seconds before falling still. EV1L pulsed with delight as the creature's flesh invigorated its form. The other mice in the cage fell to terrified silence as they witnessed the demise of one of their brethren. Fearing they would be next, they frantically started chewing on the wire mesh trapping them. Some were so desperate to escape they broke teeth trying to chew through the metal confining them.

After a few minutes nothing remained of the mouse EV1L had consumed. No bones, blood or organs, not even a whisker remained; it was as if it had never existed. Needing more sustenance to regain its full strength and size, much more, it focused on its victims at the end of the cage as it slithered towards them. The rodents' terrified expressions and shaking bodies were reflected in EV1L's shiny, tar-like mass.

*****

Weary from his day's toil, Luka slumped into the comfortable armchair facing the television. Both were some of the few luxuries he had managed to bring with him. He glanced at the wall clock and Stalin's face behind the hands that stared at him, a clock that was once a reminder that the tyrant controlled every second of Russian life and was always watching you. It was almost time for his favorite TV program. Though the signal was lousy way out here, it was just about watchable. He aimed the clunky TV remote at the small screen and switched it on. As he reached for the bottle of vodka on the small table beside the chair, he cocked an ear at the door. Wondering what had riled up the animals, he climbed out of the chair and strode for the exit.

A few steps along the corridor, he peered through the window set into the door of the animal housing room and scanned the room lit by dim lighting. The agitated animals within his view seemed to be focused on a single cage. He opened the door and stepped inside.

"Zatknis (shut the hell up) the lot of you!"

The animals calmed on hearing Luka's voice. Unlike most of the humans they had contact with, he had always treated them kindly and fed them.

Luka crossed to the cage the surrounding animals looked at and was surprised to see the mice that should have been inside weren't there. With puzzlement creasing his brow, he checked the cage door was secure—it was—and then for any holes in the mesh—there weren't any. His bafflement increased when he noticed a scattering of rodent teeth outside one end of the cage. He glanced around the room for the missing rodents that had somehow escaped.

After walking the length of the room checking every nook and cranny, he found no sign of the mice. As he pondered the dilemma, he concluded one of the scientists upstairs must have taken them while he had been clearing up their mess and preparing their dinner. It was the only logical explanation. He fumed that they would do such a thing. Protocol bade them to inform him of their animal requirements in advance. Except when it came to the animals under his care, he didn't have any authority over the higher ranked scientists. That they dared to enter his domain and take them without his permission was breaking the rules and left his records in error. It was something that would not be looked kindly on when discovered by his superiors. Someone would pay for this affront, and he was determined it wouldn't be him. He stormed from the room to find out who was responsible.

*****

Oblivious to the problems it had caused Luka, EV1L draped its form, tripled in size from its rodent feast, around a warm pipe on the ceiling and settled down to let the nourishment it had absorbed rejuvenate its form. It wouldn't take long, and then it would return to the captive animals and feast some more. It would take some time, but when it was large and powerful enough, it would visit the humans. Soon it would be able to breed, and as soon as they were strong enough, they would find a way out of this place to feed upon more humans and conquer their world.

*****

Half an hour later, Luka returned with the first scientist he had confronted.

"I assure you, Comrade Luka, none of us have touched your precious rodents," argued Waldemar for the third time since Luka had accosted him when he stepped from the restroom. Though he had adamantly denied any of them had touched his precious animals, Luka was just as adamant they had. To placate the man, he had agreed to go with Luka to find out what had happened to them.

Luka glanced at Boris shaking the door of his enclosure and pointing at one the cages opposite. He waved an arm at him to calm down before turning to the empty mouse cage. "Then how do you explain that!?"

Waldemar glanced into the cage and then at the small door secured shut with its locking pin. "The door was closed when you found them missing?"

"It was."

Waldemar glanced around the floor. "And you searched the room?"

Luka nodded. "Thoroughly."

Waldemar stroked his bottom lip with his teeth as he pondered the mystery. "They can't have just disappeared."

"Obviously. Someone has taken them, as what other explanation is there?" said Luka.

"But who, and why? We're nowhere near ready for the radiation testing phase that would require their use." Waldemar glanced at the cages. "Are any other animals missing?"

Luka shrugged. "I haven't checked."

Waldemar looked at the man. "Maybe you should?"

Boris shrieked frantically when his human friend walked along the cages and halted at the rabbit cage he had been pointing at.

Wondering what had gotten Boris so agitated, Luka ignored his hooted calls and peered into the rabbit cage. "Two rabbits are missing."

Waldemar joined Luka and looked at the four rabbits in the cage. "You're certain?"

"Of course I'm certain, I can count. There were six earlier and now there's only four."

"Okay, okay. Check the other cages while I inform Stanislav. And shut that damn monkey up for god's sake."

"It's a chimpanzee, not a monkey. It belongs to the family of great apes," corrected Luka.

Waldemar glared at Luka. "I don't care if it's King Kong's offspring, shut it up."

As soon as Luka released the catch of Boris's cage and pulled the door open, Boris leapt onto him.

Luka smiled at the chimp as he stroked its head. "What's got you all riled up?"

Boris cooed as he rubbed his head under Luka's chin.

Waldemar shook his head at Luka. "You two make a lovely couple." He crossed to the intercom and pressed the button linking him to the laboratory. "Director Stanislav, can you come to the animal housing room as we have a situation requiring your attention?" He released the button and waited.

Stanislav's irritated voice responded a few moments later. "What is it? I am rather busy here, and I don't have time to waste sorting out Luka's problems."

Waldemar sighed as he pressed the talk button. "I really think you need to see this, Director."

Stanislav groaned. "You had better not be wasting my time. I'm on my way."

Waldemar looked at Luka. "You're certain there's no other way your animals could have escaped?"

Luka nodded. "Unless they were able to unlock their cage doors, climb out, refasten them again and somehow get out of this room that was locked from the outside, someone took them. It's the only possible explanation."

Waldemar teeth-stroked his bottom lip. "I agree." He glanced at the rabbit cage when it rattled.

Hissing at something at the far side of their cage, the four rabbits began thumping their feet in agitation.

Boris jerked his head towards the sound. He pulled his gums back over his teeth as he started screaming and thumping Luka's shoulders.

Perplexed by what could have caused Boris's fear, Luka approached the rabbit cage.

Boris screeched when he leapt onto the cages and then jumped for the pipes that ran the length of the ceiling.

Waldemar glanced at the chimp. "What's gotten into him?"

"He's frightened," stated Luka, peering into the rabbit cage at something moving beneath the thick layer of sawdust covering the cage floor.

Waldemar joined him looking at the shifting sawdust. "Could that be one of your missing rabbits?"

Luka rolled his eyes at the stupid remark. "Only if it has been squashed flat." He straightened up and looked at Boris cowering on the pipes in the corner of the room. Whatever was in the cage, Boris feared it.

When Waldemar reached for the pin holding the rabbit cage door closed, Luka grabbed his hand. “I’m not sure that’s advisable.”

Waldemar shook his hand free. “Don’t be stupid. It might be your missing mice.”

Luka stepped back. “I doubt that. They’re not Houdini mice.”

Waldemar opened the cage door. He reached towards whatever was moving and brushed away the sawdust with his finger, revealing something black and greasy.

“What in Stalin’s name is that?” uttered Waldemar.

“Nothing I think we should be messing with,” replied Luka.

“It looks like thick oil or tar.” Waldemar glanced up at the ceiling to see if anything could have dripped into the cage, but the ceiling was clear.

Luka had a bad feeling about the black sludge. “Let me remove the rabbits, and then we can quarantine the cage and whatever that thing is.”

“Stop overreacting, Luka.” Waldemar put his hand back inside the cage and prodded the black blob. “It’s soft, spongy.”

“I really think you should leave it alone,” cautioned Luka.

“I’m the scientist. Fetch me something to put it in, and I’ll take it to the lab to examine.”

Luka shrugged. “If that’s want you want?”

“It is.”

While Luka searched for a container, Waldemar brushed aside more of the sawdust riddled with pungent rabbit droppings and urine. Whatever the substance was, it was about the size of a dinner plate. He froze when the blob pulsated, sending ripples out from its middle. Confused by the movement, he prodded it again. The edges of the thing snapped around his hand like a clamshell closing. Waldemar screamed and yanked his hand from the cage.

Every animal in the room became agitated and screeched, squealed, hissed, barked and grunted.

Luka spun and rushed to the man's aid when he saw Waldemar attempting to shake the black substance from his hand.

"Get it off! Get it off!" screamed Waldemar. "It burns!"

Luka was at a loss as to what to do. He sure wasn't going to touch the black burning stuff.

The door opened. Stanislav entered and froze on hearing Waldemar's screams and stared at the black substance covering his colleague's hand. "What the hell is happening here?"

Seizing his chance to escape from the black terror, Boris swung along the pipes, dropped to the floor in front of Stanislav and barged past him into the corridor.

In agony, Waldemar ran towards Stanislav waving his hand at him. "Help me! Get it off. It's burning!"

Worried Waldemar was going to touch him with the burning black he waved in front of his face, Stanislav stepped back and kicked him in the stomach. Waldemar staggered back, crashed into the empty mice cage and toppled to the floor.

Stanislav turned to Luka and demanded an explanation. "What is that black stuff and where did it come from?"

Luka shrugged. "It was in the rabbit cage. Some mice went missing, and when we looked for them we found that...stuff, in with the rabbits. Two of them are also missing."

Ignoring Waldemar's screams and pain-wracked writhing on the floor, Stanislav continued questioning Luka. "Missing? How could your animals go missing?"

"That's what Waldemar and I were trying to discover when we found that thing." Luka looked at the black substance that seemed to be stretching up the man's arm and noticed his arm seemed too short. His hand was missing.

Shocked by the revelation, he looked at Stanislav. “I think that thing ate them. Look, Waldemar’s hand is gone.”

Stanislav took a cautious step nearer the screaming man and studied Waldemar’s arm. Luka was right, his hand was gone. “We need to seal this room, now!”

“What about Waldemar?”

“Fuck him.” Stanislav turned and strode from the room.

Luka looked at Waldemar guiltily. They weren’t friends, but he couldn’t let the man suffer. He quickly followed Stanislav though the door. He returned a few moments later with a fire axe and stood over Waldemar.

Through pain-filled eyes, Waldemar looked at the axe and laid his rapidly diminishing arm on the floor. “Do it!”

Luka raised the axe and brought it down just above Waldemar’s elbow. Waldemar screamed before passing out. Luka knocked the severed arm away with the axe before dropping it. He quickly took off the man’s belt and tied it tightly around the arm to halt the blood flow. Unable to lift the man on his own, he grabbed his ankles and dragged him from the room.

Stanislav glanced at Waldemar’s severed limb and then at Luka. “Now will you seal the room?”

“And how do you propose I do that? The most I can do is lock the door. The only rooms that can be sealed completely are on Level 4.”

Stanislav glanced anxiously into the room. “Well, shut the damn door then before that thing gets out.”

Luka closed the door and turned the key in the lock. He looked at Stanislav. “Now what?”

“We need to find a way to contain that thing. Come with me.”

“What about Waldemar?” asked Luka.

Stanislav turned, looked at his unconscious co-worker, and sighed. “You grab him under the arms and I’ll grab his ankles.”

Luka glanced at the door through which he could hear the agitated sounds of his animals. Though reluctant to leave them at the mercy of the black blob, Luka was afraid to go back in. Hopefully the scientists would work out how to kill it, and everything would return to normal.

Carrying Waldemar between them, they headed along the corridor.

CHAPTER 4

dEV1Lish

After Waldemar had been taken to the infirmary and Pechka, the elected first-aid official, was contacted to come to the infirmary, Stanislav and Luka left him to have his wound tended to while they headed for the laboratory. After informing the others of what had taken place, the scientists were shocked by what they had just heard.

"But what is it and where did it come from?" asked Vadim, finding it difficult to picture the organism just described.

"We have no idea," replied Stanislav. "But we can worry about that when we've neutralized it as a threat."

Krisztina, like the others who hadn't seen it, found it hard to believe such a thing existed, let alone here in the facility, but she trusted Stanislav's observations. The man had his faults, but he wasn't prone to exaggeration. Frowning, she asked, "How big is it?"

Luka held his hands about ten inches apart. "It was about the size of a dinner plate and flat, like a pool of thick, oily liquid."

"Then it doesn't have eyes, limbs or anything?" enquired Svetlana, trying to visualize the strange entity.

Luka shook his head. “It’s just a blob. It wrapped itself around Waldemar’s hand when he prodded it. I told him not to, but...”

“Then it should be easy to catch if it can’t see, hear or smell,” offered Alexei. “It probably reacted in defense when Waldemar poked it. If we avoid touching or aggravating it, we should be okay.”

“If we can’t touch it, how will we catch it?” said Svetlana.

“We could place a container over it, slide something underneath, turn it over and put the lid on, job done,” suggested Vadim.

“We should destroy it,” stated Luka. “Burn it or something.”

“Let’s not be too hasty,” argued Stanislav, wondering if it would be advisable to contact his superiors to find out how to proceed. However, if he did, they might send people to catch the thing, whatever it was, and claim the glory. He thought it strange it had appeared so shortly after the arrival of the alien technology and too much of a coincidence for the two not to be connected. If the thing was an alien lifeform that somehow got here from the spaceship in Antarctica, there was only one person who was going to claim the victory for proving alien lifeforms existed—*him*. “We have no idea what we’re dealing with yet or the benefits it might have for the Motherland, so no one will be destroying it.”

Luka glared at Stanislav. “Exactly what benefits did Waldemar get from it? The damn thing took his hand and would have taken more if I hadn’t acted.”

“He shouldn’t have poked it,” stated Stanislav. “As Alexei just said, the thing probably thought it was being attacked and defended itself.”

He turned to his colleagues.

“We capture it like Vadim suggested and take it below to one of the sealed experimental chambers to observe and examine. Once we have it safely contained and have more of an idea what it is, I will contact the Kremlin to find out what they want done with it."

"What about our work on the alien weapons?" asked Krisztina.

"As far as I'm concerned, this thing, creature, or whatever it is, takes priority over the weapons. I'm certain those at the Kremlin will agree when I inform them. Vadim, I understand you are about to cut through the outer shell to get at the inner workings."

Vadim nodded. "I'm about ready. I'm all set up on Level 2."

"Then you continue with that and the rest of us will concentrate on catching this thing."

"I still think you should destroy it," said Luka. He pointed at the alien pistols resting on one of the tables. "They might do the job."

Stanislav stepped to the side to block Luka's view of the weapons. "Luckily for the scientific community and Russia, that decision is not yours to make." He turned his back on Luka. "Okay, Comrades, Vadim, take one of the weapons to work on, and I'll lock the other in my office. Alexei and Svetlana, you will capture the thing and bring it below to Level 4 where Krisztina and I will have a chamber prepared to receive it."

"Good luck if you think that thing will placidly sit there while it's captured," scoffed Luka. "It reacted damn quick when Waldemar got near it."

"As this thing seems to be liquid, we could use CO2 fire extinguishers," suggested Krisztina. "CO2 gas has a temperature of minus 66C so maybe the cold will incapacitate it long enough for it to be captured."

Alexei nodded at Krisztina. "Great idea, Krisz. From the descriptions, scant though they are, it seems to be a glutinous liquid, so it should work."

"What about me," enquired Luka. "What shall I do?"

"You can catch that damn monkey you let escape," ordered Stanislav. "When the *thing* has been captured, you can return to your animals. Until then, keep out of our way."

As the others left the room, Luka approached Krisztina. "I don't like this."

"Me neither. I don't understand where this thing could have come from, but it can't be a coincidence it only appeared after we received the alien weapons."

Luka raised his eyebrows. "Alien pistols? As in UFO alien?"

Krisztina shot a worried glance at Vadim who was collecting a few tools across the room. "Shush. Forget what you've just heard, or at the very least don't let on that you know."

"I won't, but where did they come from?"

"It's all extremely top secret, but the weapons came from an alien spaceship found buried in the ice in Antarctica. Don't ask me anymore because that's all I know."

Luka shrugged. "I thought they looked strange but didn't for one moment imagine they came from a UFO."

"Technically it wasn't a UFO as it wasn't flying, but that's enough about that. We need to concern ourselves with catching this thing, alien or otherwise. Hopefully, we'll soon have it contained. Then maybe we'll find out what it is."

Glancing at Vadim across the room to make sure they weren't being observed, Luka held Krisztina's hand. "Be careful and don't get near it, even if it looks dead. And whatever you do, don't let it touch you. I've chopped off enough limbs for one day."

"I'm inquisitive, not stupid. I'll be careful."

Luka nodded and released her hand. "Good to hear."

"I have to go. Maybe I'll be able to see you later, but with all that's going on..."

"I know. And I have a chimp to catch."

He followed Krisztina out of the laboratory.

CHAPTER 5

dEV1Lry

Because EV1L still wasn't strong enough to reveal its presence to the humans, it had hidden when two of them had entered the animal room, interrupting its feeding. However, when they had discovered its hiding place and poked it, its defensive instincts had prompted its attack.

Having finished consuming the flesh, muscle and sinew from the human arm, EV1L slithered off the bones in search of additional nourishment. It needed to grow stronger quickly to survive now the humans were aware of its presence. It climbed up the side of the metal cupboards the cages rested on and headed for the first of the small four-limbed creatures that barked at its approach. Whimpering from fear of its strangeness when it entered their cage, they cowered into a corner. It would devour them all.

Having devoured the beagles, EV1L moved along to the next items on its menu. The spider monkeys screeched, hooted and displayed their teeth at the approaching menace. EV1L melted through the gaps in the wire mesh and reformed on the other side.

One of the spider monkeys attacked. Its hands grabbed at the black blob, stretching out glutinous lumps that wrapped around its small paws. Failing to break free from the rubbery restraints it tried biting through them. EV1L attacked and wrapped around its face. The monkey's terrified features were revealed in the substance covering its contours. The creature's muffled screams continued until lack of air released it from its pain. The remaining spider monkeys pressed themselves into the far corner of the cage and huddling together, trembling while they awaited their fate.

*****

Alexei and Svetlana cautiously entered the animal room and closed the door. The first thing they noticed was the lack of sounds or movement coming from the cages. Always expecting they were going to be fed, the animals normally reacted when anyone entered the room, but now there was only ominous silence.

Spying the remains of Waldemar's arm bone, Alexei pointed it out to Svetlana, who wished he hadn't. They crossed to it cautiously and discovered it was absent any Black.

Svetlana gazed into a nearby cage and stepped nearer to investigate. It was empty, and so was the next and the next. All the animals were gone.

Adjusting his hold on the heavy fire extinguisher under one arm, Alexei's head swiveled anxiously as he searched for the black blob Luka had described.

Spying no sign of it, he glanced back at Svetlana following closely and raised the thin metal rod gripped in his free hand. "Use this to search the cages and let me know if you find it."

"Have no fear on that as it's not something I'm planning on keeping secret. When you hear me scream, you'll know I've found it."

Svetlana glanced worriedly at the plastic container she held and wondered if it would be strong enough to contain the creature. It had melted Waldemar's flesh, maybe it could do the same to plastic. She opened the first cage and poked the sawdust covering the bottom with the metal pointer. Finding nothing but mouse droppings, she moved along to the next.

Alexei was searching the third cage on his side of the room when the rod snagged on something concealed beneath the sawdust littered with pungent rabbit droppings and urine. A bead of sweat dripped from his forehead as he slowly raised the object. He relaxed when part of a rabbit's ribcage lifted clear of the sawdust. He shook it off and continued along the line of cages. He paused at one of the two large primate cages at the end of the row and stared at the half-eaten corpse of a spider monkey. Flesh-cleaned bones of its cellmates lay scattered around the cage. He focused on the monkey's face. Normally they wore a cute, slightly mischievous expression, but now, abject terror was frozen on its face. He turned and clicked his fingers to attract his comrade.

Svetlana crossed to the cage and glanced inside. Moving her gaze away from the poor creature's dead, fear-filled face, she examined the wounds. There was hardly any blood and the flesh seemed to have been melted from the bones that also showed signs of being dissolved, digested. She turned to Alexei. "I wonder why it didn't finish it off?"

Alexei shrugged worriedly as he gazed around the room. "Probably full from gorging itself on all the other animals."

"Or we disturbed it when we entered," offered Svetlana ominously.

"Oh, great. It knows we're here."

"It could be a good sign," suggested Svetlana.

Alexei held the thin rod out like a sword, as if ready to stab and slice at anything that attacked. "If it is, it's lost on me."

"It could mean it's frightened, or at least wary of us."

"Not as much as I am of it. It's a puddle, it could be anywhere." Alexei poked the bottom of the monkey cage but found nothing black and dangerous.

Crouching, Alexei waved the rod under one of the metal cupboards the cages rested on. The clangs of rod striking against the legs rang through the room. He placed the extinguisher on the floor and taking a small flashlight from his pocket, aimed it along the gap beneath the cupboards running the length of the room.

Observing, Svetlana said, "You do know that if this was one of those American horror movies, something would lunge out and attack or pull you under."

Alexei glared at her. "You're not helping. Go search the end of the room."

"In horror movies, splitting up is also a bad idea."

Svetlana turned away from Alexei's glare and began searching the animal food preparation area at the far end.

After Alexei had finished searching the gap beneath the cupboards, he turned his attention to the ceiling. The pipes that ran the length of the room and branched off through the walls were too high to reach, but he saw no evidence of the creature hiding there. After he had searched inside the cupboards, he returned to Svetlana.

"We've searched everywhere. It's not here."

Svetlana wasn't convinced. "It has to be, the door was shut. It can't get out."

"It had to have gotten in here somehow, so it might have left the same way." When Alexei's eyes came to a halt on the air vent, he pointed the rod at it. "And that I believe is it."

Svetlana focused on the vent. "If you're right, it could be anywhere now."

"I suppose we had better check inside or Stanislav will only make us come back." Alexei dragged the empty cage below the vent off the table and let it crash to the floor. He then placed the extinguisher on the table and climbed up.

"What do you want me to do?" asked Svetlana.

"I don't even know what I'm doing, but be ready with the container I guess." I'll remove the grill and see if it's inside. If it is, I'll give it a blast of CO2. Hopefully that will subdue it. If it works, I'll drag it out into the container, and we rush it downstairs and let the others deal with it."

Svetlana nodded. The plan seemed simple enough. "And if it's not inside?"

"We lock the room and make our report." Alexei gripped the slatted grill, yanked it free and dropped it to the floor. He cautiously investigated the vent with the flashlight. Though it was empty, he noticed a faint oily residue on the bottom, similar to a slug trail, though less noticeable.

"What do you see?" asked Svetlana, gazing nervously around the room. She wasn't certain the creature wasn't concealed and watching them.

"Vent's empty as far as I can see, but it has definitely been here." Without thinking, he wiped a finger in the greasy slick and looked at his slightly blackened fingertip before showing Svetlana.

"Not sure that was a clever thing to do after seeing the melted remains of that monkey and what it did to Waldemar's hand."

"Shit!" Alexei frantically wiped the finger clean on his shirt.

"It's probably its saliva, if it has saliva, that does the damage, so don't French kiss it and you should be okay."

"Not something I ever plan on doing." Satisfied he had cleared the stain from his finger, Alexei stared along the vent weighing up their options before looking down at Svetlana. "You know we have to check it out to find out where it went?"

Svetlana glanced at the small opening and scoffed. "You'll never fit in there."

"I won't but you will."

*****

Stanislav and Krisztina halted at the elevator that led to level 4. Unlike the upper three levels, the lowest level hadn't seen use since the facility had been abandoned in the seventies. Luka, who had been down to power up the main generator, had been the first to walk its corridors in years.

While Stanislav unlocked and opened the hatch covering two red and green buttons, Krisztina engaged the lever on the power unit fixed to the wall. When it clunked loudly into the on-position, the green elevator call button glowed, and Stanislav pressed it.

Krisztina joined Stanislav at the door listening to the winch motor raise the elevator from the lower level and followed him inside when the doors slid open. A press of the button marked with a down arrow symbol closed the doors and set the elevator descending seventy feet. Both hesitated when the elevator glided to a halt and the doors slid open. They stared into the dark corridor lit only by the elevator's single light. Separated from the air conditioning system of the upper levels to avoid contaminants spreading, the air they breathed was stale, musty, oppressive, as if tainted with the suffering and deaths of those once experimented on down here.

Both were aware of some of what had gone on down here during Stalin's era and later. This was *Laboratory 12,* where the Soviet secret police concocted exotic poisons used to kill dissidents in hideous and (mostly) untraceable ways. When it came to murdering your enemies for political power, both at home and abroad, poison had been Russia's preferred weapon. To safeguard the anonymity of the assassin, and hence Russia's involvement, the mission of Laboratory 12 had been to devise a poison that was tasteless, odorless, and undetectable in an autopsy. To test and refine the effectiveness of different powders, beverages, liquors, and diverse types of injection and dispersal apparatuses, toxins were administered to prisoners and persons subject to execution. When a target was identified, prisoners of similar age and build were tested to identify the correct killing dosage. It often took a few attempts and the lingering deaths of a few unfortunates before the correct dosage was determined. An autopsy would then be carried out to see if any detectable residue remained. If there was, the toxin would be refined and more suitable prisoners tested until a satisfactory result was attained.

Stanislav stepped into the corridor, crossed to a power panel beside the doors and turned the power lever with a loud clunk that echoed though the level. Lights flickered into life along the corridor and highlighted the lime green paint peeling from concrete walls and the rows of cell doors lining the opposite wall.

Though neither of them had ever set foot on this level before, Stanislav and Krisztina had consulted the blueprint of the facility stuck to the wall of the security office before coming down.

Stanislav glanced at Krisztina when she stepped from the elevator. "Let's head straight for the laboratories located at the far end."

Krisztina joined Stanislav walking along the corridor. She glanced in some of the open cell doors. Each were equipped with two simple metal beds furnished with thin mattresses and a single blanket. She could almost sense their past occupants' fear and suffering. When she halted at a closed cell and moved her face to the small observation window, Stanislav's hand on her shoulder halted her.

"It's best you don't look inside. When this place was abandoned, so were any prisoners locked in their cells."

Visualizing the terrible fate of the prisoners left to die inside, Krisztina stepped back from the door. "That's horrible."

"Stalin and some of his subordinates were evil men. However, it's poetic that Stalin was responsible for the existence of this place and one of the poisons created here was probably responsible for his death."

Surprised by the news, Krisztina asked, “Is that true?”

Stanislav shrugged. “Allegedly a poison concocted here was administered to Stalin by one of his bodyguards, Ivan Khrustalev, acting on orders from Lavrenti Beria, the dreaded head of the Soviet secret police, when he feared Stalin was about to have him executed. That was the fate of previous secret police chiefs when Stalin thought they were becoming too powerful. Also, apparently, on the day he died, Stalin planned to begin the mass deportation of Soviet Jews to Siberia and the republic of Kazakhstan—an act calculated to provoke the West and start World War III. Though Stalin was confident he could win such a war and destroy capitalism, he had to move quickly before his half-ruined, half-starved country collapsed. Others in his administration weren’t so optimistic of the outcome and may have joined with Lavrenti to ensure Russia wasn’t obliterated in an all-out nuclear holocaust brought about by their country’s mad, paranoid dictator.”

“What a terrible time to have lived through, though due to Stalin’s strict and brutal regime, millions didn’t, of course.” Krisztina pointed at the cluster of glass-walled rooms at the far side of the hall they had entered. “Is that the infamous Laboratory 12?”

“It is. Laboratory 12 is the collective name for a group of twelve rooms containing laboratories, observation and control rooms, plus contaminant storage chambers for the storage of the chemicals and toxins. They were all cleared before being sealed and abandoned, so it’s perfectly safe.”

“I think I’ll avoid them all the same if possible,” said Krisztina, who lacked confidence in Russia’s track record of cleaning up contamination. She followed Stanislav into the first laboratory and glanced around the room.

Surrounded on all sides by glass walls looking into the surrounding rooms, unfortunate prisoners brought here to be experimented on could see the stages of their demise. First, they would be prepped here and strapped to one of the three metal trollies parked along one wall. When ready, they would be wheeled into the test chamber where they would be administered the poison and observed as the toxin took effect. If they survived, they would be taken to the adjoining recovery room to recuperate until they were ready for the next round of tests. If they died, they would be taken to the last room, the morgue, and dissected to study the effects of the poison and if any residue remained.

"There's nothing here suitable to contain the creature," stated Stanislav. "Let's try the other laboratories."

A short walk farther along the corridor weaving between the glass-walled rooms brought them to another laboratory. Its door led to an air lock chamber with another door opposite, a safety feature to prevent any toxins from escaping into the main lab area. When Krisztina closed the first door behind her, air rushed into the chamber through a vent in the ceiling, causing her ears to pop as the pressure increased.

"Positive pressure to prevent anything from escaping when the lab is entered or exited," explained Stanislav, unnecessarily.

Krisztina was surprised. She thought such precautions were only required when working with contagious substances, such as diseases, or chemical weapons. It made her suspect it wasn't only poisons that had been concocted down here. She glanced through the glass door worriedly at the vast range of laboratory equipment and machines spaced around the room, which identified it as a chemical laboratory, and wondered if it was safe to enter.

It seemed Stanislav had no such concerns. When the rush of air had equalized, he promptly opened the door and stepped through. He crossed to a console and pressed a button, turning off the air pressure safety feature they didn't need.

A glance around the room revealed exactly what they searched for. Stanislav strode to the far door and entered a room with a glass chamber positioned in the middle. Tubes and wires led off from the top, and two sets of gloved, corrugated arms were positioned on either of its longer sides.

"This is perfect," he stated, running a hand along the top edge.

Krisztina walked to a side wall and into an adjoining room surrounded on two sides with metal, glass-fronted, cold-storage cupboards. A range of empty test tubes, glass flasks, measuring beakers and a plethora of other chemistry equipment was stored on shelves running the length of a third wall. She turned when Stanislav called to her.

"Give me a hand with this."

She returned to the glass chamber and released the catches on the lid at the opposite end to Stanislav and together they raised it.

Stanislav looked at Krisztina with excitement in his eyes. "You do realize what a momentous occasion this is? If that thing did come from the Antarctica spaceship, though Stalin knows how it got here, we will be the first to examine an alien life-form. I—we, all of us—could became famous for what we are about to do. We are about to make history."

"I understand that, but we need to take every precaution. It could have killed Waldemar if Luka hadn't acted so quickly."

Unconcerned, Stanislav ran his gaze over the inside of the lid and pointed out four nozzles. "Hopefully it won't be necessary, but these will sprout jets of intense flame when activated if we need to destroy the life-form, and this is"—he tapped the side of the chamber—"armored glass. The creature, whatever it is, won't be able to break it."

Aware of Stanislav's desire for advancement and public recognition, Krisztina experienced relief that Stanislav was willing to destroy the creature if the need arose. "As you said, hopefully it won't come to that, though it's comforting to have the option. However, first we have to capture it and get it inside."

“I’ll check up on Alexei and Svetlana to see if they’ve caught it yet.” Stanislav crossed to the internal phone attached to the wall, lifted the receiver and pressed the facility-wide communication button. “Alexei, Svetlana, we are ready and waiting on Level 4. Report your progress.”

CHAPTER 6

dEV1Lize

"No way am I squeezing in there," stated Svetlana, backing away a step to reinforce her refusal.

"It won't be so bad," argued Alexei. "You can take the extinguisher, and if it's in there, give it a good blast and scoop it up."

"And how is that supposed to change my mind?"

"Well, someone has to do it. I won't fit, so that leaves you."

Svetlana shook her head. "Uh-uh! Not going to happen. It could be in there, waiting, ready to pounce."

"I doubt it has the intelligence to set up an ambush or, lacking the limbs to do so, is able to pounce," reassured Alexei. "It's probably a simple organism with one thought—food."

"Exactly! I don't want to be its next snack."

Alexei swept an arm around the room. "Based on the empty cages, it has probably sated its hunger and has crawled into the vent to sleep it off. It has no limbs, so it's not like it's a fast-moving creature that will rush you, is it? The most it can do is slither."

"That's speculation. We have no idea what it can do." argued Svetlana.

"From Stanislav's and Luka's account of its attack against Waldemar, it only reacted when Waldemar poked it, probably a defensive response. If someone poked you, you wouldn't just stand there and take it, would you?"

"Damn right I wouldn't, but I wouldn't react by melting someone's hand."

"That's because you have limbs to defend yourself. It doesn't. It just used what it had. My point is, that if you don't provoke it, it should leave you alone."

"If spraying it with freezing CO2 isn't provoking it, I don't know what is."

"You would be incapacitating it and it's not like you'll have to get close—a couple of meters will do." Alexei glanced around the room and pointed at something in a corner. "Once you've frozen it, you can use that broom to drag it out to me and I'll put it in the container."

Svetlana glanced at the broom, the extinguisher and the vent. It seemed a recipe for disaster. She sighed. "I'm not promising I'll get very far, but I'll give it a try."

"You'll be fine." Alexei jumped off the bench and handed Svetlana the flashlight. "Hop up, and when you're in, I'll pass you what you'll need."

As Svetlana climbed onto the bench, Stanislav's voice came over the intercom.

"Alexei, Svetlana, we are ready and waiting on Level 4. Report your progress."

Alexei crossed to the intercom and pressed the talk button. "We are still tracking the creature. It seems to have gone into the air duct. Svetlana is going in to find it." He released his finger from the button.

"Understood," replied Stanislav. "Keep me updated."

Alexei turned to Svetlana. "You ready?"

"Not in the remotest, but I suppose I had better get this over with before I come to my senses." She scrambled into the vent not much wider than her shoulders and gazed along the dark passage. The light she aimed ahead glinted off the creature's slick trail. She couldn't imagine a less welcoming scenario. She turned on her back and gazed at the entrance when the extinguisher Alexei passed in clanged against the side of the vent, sending an echo traveling along the air ducts. "That's it, announce I'm coming."

Alexei grinned. "It doesn't have ears."

"Perhaps not, but I felt the vibrations, so maybe it did also." After shooting a nervous glance along the vent where she expected the creature to appear, Svetlana dragged the extinguisher up her body and placed it in front.

"Do you want the broom yet?"

"No, I'll come back for it if it's needed. It's going to be awkward enough moving with the extinguisher." Fear spread across her face when she noticed something appear behind Alexei. As the black, greasy mass stretched into view, two eyes formed in the substance. Though nothing more than rips in the Black, they were full of menace and seemed to be studying her.

Though Alexei had played down the danger Svetlana faced, he was surprised she had agreed to enter the tight confines of the vent that offered little chance to defend against an attack. Svetlana had been correct when she said they had no idea of the creature's abilities, but how dangerous could a small black blob be? She would be fine.

At first, Alexei was confused by the terrified expression that appeared on Svetlana's face. When she raised an arm and pointed behind him, a bad feeling edged with fear washed over him. He spun and froze in terror when he came face-to-face with the black substance hanging from the ceiling like an oily bat with wings extended. Its eyes radiated a menace he had never experienced before. Piss dribbled down his wobbling legs when the Black moved its wings towards him. Instinctively he stuck out his hands to hold them back and screamed. It was like touching liquid fire. His vision was smothered with excruciating, burning pain when the creature released its grip on the ceiling and wrapped its black wings around him in an embrace of agony and death.

Svetlana had never known such fear. Though her senses screamed at her to flee, terror rooted her to the spot and forced her to witness the dreadful event framed in the vent opening. The greasy, viscous, flat snake-like head that grew from the creature and stretched towards the opening, wavered when it changed to mimic Alexei's features. When the black lips opened and screeched, Svetlana pushed herself away. When her shoulder knocked against the extinguisher, she reached back and dragged it onto her stomach. She aimed the nozzle at the creature and pressed the trigger. A whoosh of cold CO2 condensing in the air shot past her feet and sprayed Alexei's Black-mimicked face in white frost.

EV1L dodged back from the freezing blast and fell to the floor, taking the body of the human it was still absorbing with it. The frozen part of its body writhed to be free of the cold, white covering until the crystalized residue fell away. Eyes formed and stared at the vent it heard the human female escaping through. It had forgotten how devious these humans were. But the memories were returning with its strength; they had almost killed it once. It wouldn't let them do so again. It slithered off the partly digested human, stretched up and poured into the vent.

Pushing the extinguisher in front of her, Svetlana slithered through the duct. She should have listened to her senses and never entered the vent that might end up becoming her coffin if there was anything left of her after the creature had finished feeding. She shivered at the thought. Alexei's pain-wracked screams had indicated it would be an excruciating death. Though shocked and saddened by her friend's death, it wasn't the time to grieve. Her one thought was to escape the same fate.

Though her worries were many and she barely held panic at bay, her major concern was the duct would narrow, trapping her. She couldn't go back. When she reached an intersection that led left, right and straight on, she turned her head and shone the flashlight behind. Her worst fear was realized. The Black was in the vent and flowing towards her like an oil slick. Creepily, it made no sound. Even creepier was the single eye protruding from it on a thin stalk that looked at her. She needed to slow it down. Arriving at a crossroads of options, she slithered into the right turning she believed headed towards the storage rooms on this level and quickly squirmed backwards into the left tunnel. She had to hurry before the silent menace was upon her. With the nozzle aimed at the slithering monstrosity, she sprayed a twenty-second burst. As the cloud of freezing vapor whooshed along the duct, Svetlana shot along the right-hand passage.

Sensing the cold creeping through the metal, EV1L halted and abruptly backed up in a wave that tumbled back on itself until the frigid air had dissipated. Though the degree of coldness wasn't enough to cause its demise, it did bring unwelcome pain. It observed the white coating of frost on the vent sides until it had faded and then shot forward. The human female would not escape its wrath so easily.

Breathing heavily from the effort of moving through the constricted passage, Svetlana turned a corner. The surge of hope she experienced at the sight of the grill along the passage waned when something thumped into the side of the duct near the intersection behind her. The light she aimed at the sound picked out the Black mass filling the void. A long snouted face belonging to some alien beast she found difficult to comprehend, formed and spread jaws wide to reveal sharp ebony teeth. Moving too fast to waste time bringing the unwieldly extinguisher to bear, she rushed for the grill. It was her only hope. As soon as she arrived, she dropped the flashlight, gripped the grill and pushed. It didn't budge. A harder shove produced the same result. When she noticed the sharp tips of the four screws protruding through the corners of the frame, she realized escape wouldn't be so easy.

Her gaze shot back along the duct on hearing the slithering grow nearer. It seemed the creature had abandoned stealth in its rush to reach her. Caught in the flashlight's glow, the creature appeared out the turning she had recently vacated. It smashed into the side wall in its haste to reach her. The long snout forced into the mass on contact, appeared out the side facing her and snarled. It would be on her within seconds. She grabbed the extinguisher and smashed it into the grill; it buckled, freeing one corner. The second hit sent it clattering into the room. She dropped the extinguisher into the room, grabbed the flashlight and dived through the opening.

A tentacle stretched from the mass. The claw that formed grabbed at the human's leg but swiped only air. Without stopping, EV1L followed the human through the opening.

Svetlana rolled when her hands touched the cardboard boxes stacked against the wall and groaned when her back struck the floor hard. Using her momentum and ignoring the pain as best she could, she jumped to her feet. The flashlight picked out the maze formed of Stalinist-era document boxes, shelf units and cupboards. On hearing the creature crash into the boxes behind her, she dashed along the tight passage between the plethora of stored secrets detailing the cruel acts of Russia's long dead paranoid and power-mad dictator.

EV1L formed into a vicious four-legged beast it had absorbed long ago and bounded after its victim.

Confident her reward for negotiating the maze successfully would be the exit door she could rush through and slam shut behind her, trapping the creature in the room, Svetlana dodged left and right as she raced to escape it. Though puzzled by what was making them, she knew the Black was responsible for the pounding footsteps chasing her. If she survived, she would have gained some knowledge about the creature; it had the ability to change its form. The way it had mimicked Alexei's face was staggering.

The wall of boxes ahead of her exploded, toppling the shelf unit opposite. Svetlana glimpsed a movement of Black amongst the cardboard mountain, a claw searching for stability to pull its body free ripped cardboard and shredded secrets. With her way blocked and no wish to backtrack and re-enter the air duct, Svetlana rushed up the tilted shelf unit, scrambled over the top of a wide, wooden cupboard and dropped to the floor. Her flashlight picked out a door a short distance away. Praying it wasn't locked, she sprinted for it, grabbed the handle and turned. The door opened inwards, spilling light from the corridor into the gloomy room. A shriek behind spun her head. The Black-formed beast leapt from the top of the cupboard. Svetlana rushed through the doorway and slammed the door shut. It juddered when the creature struck it. The door held. She almost cried. She had done it. She was safe.

At the sound of scratching on the door, she turned to face the small glass panel set in the door. The creature's evil gaze stared at her. An evil grimace formed and faded when the Black changed, causing Svetlana to gasp at a copy of her own face staring back at her. Her eyes shot to the door handle when it moved. She staggered back when the door opened. An exact, but Black, copy of herself stepped into the doorway. It was like she was staring into an evil, malevolent mirror. She threw the flashlight at it, turned and ran.

EV1L caught the flashlight and glanced at it briefly before releasing it. Before it struck the floor, EV1L raced after the fleeing human. Finding two legs inadequate, it changed. As it dropped to its hands, it morphed into the four-legged beast again and bounded along the corridor.

*****

Stanislav halted his pacing across the room and looked at Krisztina sitting on the chair she had wheeled from an adjoining office. “What’s taking them so long?”

Krisztina inwardly sighed and glanced at her watch. Stanislav was the most impatient person she had met. “It’s only been twenty minutes.”

Stanislav raised his bushy unkempt eyebrows and glared at Krisztina like an owl would a mouse. “Are you certain?”

Krisztina nodded.

“Humph! I’d swear it was longer.”

“I’m sure they are going as quick as they can. It can’t be easy for Svetlana. I wouldn’t want to crawl through an air-duct with that *thing* in there.”

“It’s a defenseless black blob, not a tiger,” argued Stanislav. “All they have to do is chill it with the fire extinguisher, put it in the container and bring it here. How hard can it be?”

“You could always give them the benefit of your expertise and go help them.”

Stanislav glared at Krisztina for signs of insubordination. Recognizing none he could be certain of, he strode to the intercom and stabbed the button with a finger. “Alexei, what’s going on? Do you have it yet?” He released his finger and when the reply he expected didn’t materialize, he tried again. “Damn you, Alexei. I need an update, now!”

Krisztina stood and headed for the door. “I’ll go find out what’s happening.”

“No, stay here, they might be on their way down,” ordered Stanislav.

Krisztina returned to the chair.

After a few moments brooding silence, Stanislav spoke into the intercom again. “Luka! Stop whatever unimportant menial task you are doing, and go check on Alexei and Svetlana. Update me ASAP.”

After a few moments, Stanislav's finger heading angrily for the button was halted by Luka's reply. "*Yes, Herr Kommendant. Your orders are my only joy. Going there now.*"

Krisztina grinned.

"Less of the sarcasm, Luka, and do as you've been ordered. Be assured your attitude has been duly noted and will go in my report."

"*Sarcasm, sir? I don't understand. When you make your report, could you also mention it's only fair with all this extra work I am doing that an appropriate recompense should come my way?*"

Stanislav fumed. "Don't worry, I'll ensure you get an appropriate reward. Ten years hard labour in a Gulag. Now stop fucking about, or I'll have you taken outside and shot."

"*I think that's a bit harsh, Kommandant. Both the Gulag and the shooting bit. However, I am now going to carry out your orders as ordered with no hint of sarcasm or insubordination, sir.*"

Fuming, Stanislav turned to Krisztina. "The man's an idiot."

Inwardly smiling, Krisztina replied, "Yes, sir."

*****

Luka headed for the animal room. Though he knew it wasn't wise to goad Stanislav, it was an entertainment he found hard to resist. The man was a moron who only worried about advancing his own career without any remorse for those he trod on in the process. He glanced through the viewing panel set in the door before entering. Worried by the silence that greeted him, he glanced into the empty cages he passed. The damn creature had eaten them all. He halted at the gruesome sight that waited for him at the far end of the room. Though no features remained to identify the man, the brown shoes identified the mass of liquefied and half-eaten flesh as Alexei.

Fighting down the bile that threatened to spew forth, Luka gave the corpse a wide berth and pressed the Level 4 intercom button. “Alexei’s dead!”

Stanislav answered promptly. “*Dead! Are you certain?*”

“I’m staring at his partly devoured corpse, so yes, I’m damn well sure he’s dead.”

“*What about Svetlana?*”

Luka glanced around the area. “There’s no sign of her, dead or otherwise.”

“She went in the airduct.”

Luka gazed at the opening in the wall. “Why would she do that?”

“They thought the creature escaped from the room through the duct. Is she in there?”

Luka climbed onto the bench and peered along the dark passage. “Svetlana, are you in there?” After no reply, he called out again with the same result.

He jumped off the table and crossed to the intercom. “Negative, Svetlana is not in the vent.”

“Well, she must be somewhere, search the level,” ordered Stanislav.

Luka glanced at Alexei’s remains. “What about the creature that killed Alexei?”

“*Yes, find that, too, and bring it here.*”

“That’s not what I meant,” argued Luka.

“I know, but do it anyway. That’s an order.”

Sighing, Luka headed for the exit.

Luka stepped from the room and anxiously turned his head at the sound of footsteps running towards him.

“Run!” screamed Svetlana.

Luka was about to ask what was wrong when an unearthly black creature appeared at the end of the corridor. Fear gripped him as he took in the creature’s monstrous details. Four powerful limbs tipped with three claws propelled the bounding monster nearer. A deep rumbling growl came from jaws spread impossibly wide to reveal a long, pointed tongue and teeth designed for chewing flesh. Antler-like spikes protruded from around its thick neck bulging with sinews, reached past its jaws and would be first to impale any victim it felled. Its eyes—small, evil and piercing—locked with his own terror-filled ones. A second warning from Svetlana who was drawing level with him, snapped him from his terrified trance and prompted him into motion. He ran.

"What is that thing, and where did it come from?" he shouted to Svetlana close on his heels.

"A demon spawned from Hell!" was her reply.

Luka though it was a fitting description. Praying the elevator was still on this floor, he stabbed the button. The doors slid open. Svetlana followed him inside. He pressed the up button. The beast rushed for the doors' narrowing gap.

EV1L leapt for the closing doors and struck just as they met. Its form spread out like treacle thrown from a bucket and flowed to the floor. Rising into a pillar of Black, it formed Svetlana's effigy and stared at the doors while it contemplated its next move. Having expelled much-needed energy during the chase, it decided to return to the corpse it had abandoned to pursue the human female. After it had feasted, it would track down the rest of the humans. Svetlana's mimicked face and the front of her body melted through to its back, and it retraced it steps along the corridor.

*****

Trembling from the close encounter, Luka relaxed slightly when the elevator started moving, Luka turned to Svetlana. "What the hell just happened, and where did that thing come from?"

Shaking from the fading adrenalin rush brought on by her harrowing experience, Svetlana briefly explained what had taken place. "The thing, that black blob that attacked Waldemar, has grown, transformed. We were searching for it in the animal room when it killed Alexei and chased me through the vent. I managed to reach Store Room 7, but it followed me out and then I ran into you."

Luka scratched his head vigorously, a sign he was anxious. "But how could it have changed so drastically from a small blob to...that beast?"

"For the moment I can't see that matters. We need to warn the others and come up with an alternative plan to capture or kill it."

"Killing it gets my vote."

When the elevator halted they stepped out onto Level 1 and headed for the primary workshop.

CHAPTER 7

The New Plan

“What do you mean it’s changed?” uttered Stanislav in disbelief.

After informing Vadim and Pechka about Alexei’s death, Luka had appraised Stanislav of the situation, and they had all crowded into the security office to work out what they should do about the creature.

“I don’t know how to put it more clearly,” stated Luka, staring at the CCTV screens and lingering on the view from the camera in the animal room. Thankfully, Alexei’s corpse wasn’t in shot. “The creature that chased Svetlana, and later me, bore no resemblance to the small blob that attacked Waldemar. It’s bigger, faster and as vicious as a rabid wolf. Trust me, there’s no way you’ll be able to scoop it up into a bucket, though I’d like to see you try.”

Stanislav glared at Luka before speaking to Svetlana. “Is this true?”

Svetlana nodded. “Unfortunately. I don’t know how it does it, but it has the ability to change its form and mimic things—me, for instance. I tell you, it’s damn creepy looking at yourself replicated by that monster.”

Stanislav shook his head. "I can't understand how it has grown so rapidly. One minute it's a relatively harmless blob, then it's a ferocious murderous beast running amok on a killing spree."

"I imagine eating Luka's animals had something to do with its growth rate," offered Krisztina.

"It also ate Alexei—well, part of him," added Luka grimly. He found it hard to suppress the mental image of the poor man's gruesome corpse.

"From what you've described of its eating habits, it most likely absorbs its victims into its mass rather than eating and digesting them like an animal would," said Pechka. "So perhaps the more it eats, the bigger it grows."

"And now it's eaten all of Luka's pets, we are the only food remaining on the menu," stated Vadim ominously.

"Which doesn't bode well for our survival," added Svetlana. "It can open doors. It followed me from the storeroom."

Luka sighed. "It just keeps getting better and better."

"Although it didn't follow us up in the elevator, so maybe it hasn't worked out how to use buttons."

"Yet?" added Luka. "But the way our luck's going, it soon will. We should leave and call the army in to deal with it or blow up the facility with that nuclear bomb sitting below us."

"We'll be doing no such thing," stated Stanislav, glaring at Luka. "What we will do is capture this unique creature and then study it. We have all been presented with a fantastic once-in-a-lifetime opportunity. We will be the first scientists to examine an extraterrestrial species, and if we do it correctly, fame and fortune will follow."

"That might apply to you lot but not me. I'm basically a janitor and now my animals have been eaten, my job is done," argued Luka. "I'm leaving, and I strongly advise the rest of you to leave with me. If *Kommandant* Stanislav wants to risk his life capturing the vicious alien, let him."

Stanislav smirked. “That’s not strictly true, Luka. Your monkey is still on the loose, and there’s also a cow down below you are responsible for.”

It was Luka’s turn to glare at his superior. “It’s a chimp, not a monkey.”

Stanislav shrugged. “Whatever it is, it’s one of the reasons why you will remain here with the rest of us.”

“There’s a nuclear bomb in the facility?” asked Krisztina.

“It was a fail-safe if anything went wrong below when they were experimenting with certain dangerous substances here in the past,” explained Stanislav.

“Biological weapons?” questioned Svetlana.

“We need not concern ourselves with what went on here in the past. It’s the present and the future that we should focus on,” admonished Stanislav. “We need to put our heads together and come up with a plan to capture this thing that doesn’t involve any more of us being killed.”

“Good luck with that,” moaned Luka.

“Is this bomb safe?” asked Pechka.

Stanislav sighed. “Look, Comrades, don’t get sidetracked. Forget about the bomb. It’s probably been rendered inactive so it’s of no concern anyway, but this creature that might be hunting us as we speak *is*.” He gazed around at his subordinates. “Does anyone have any suggestions?”

“Obviously the scooping it into a container plan is off the table, but what about using the CO2 extinguishers?” Vadim looked at Svetlana. “You said you sprayed it with CO2. How effective was it?”

“It definitely didn’t like it and recoiled when I sprayed it, but it was occupied with killing Alexei at the time, not rushing towards me. How effective it will be against it while it’s attacking is anyone’s guess.”

“We should use fire,” stated Luka. “Rig up some flamethrowers and incinerate it before more of us are killed.”

"No flamethrowers will be used, Luka, by you or anyone else," stated Stanislav firmly.

"Maybe we could lure it down to Level 4 and trap it in one of the containment rooms," suggested Krisztina.

"Now there is an idea that might work," said Stanislav.

"What sort of lure would we use, though?" asked Svetlana.

"Ourselves," stated Vadim. "It chased Svetlana, so it will probably chase any of us."

"I'm not volunteering," stated Luka adamantly.

"We could use the cow," suggested Pechka. "Put it in the lower elevator, and when the thing enters, bring it down."

"I like it," said Krisztina. "We could leave the doors open leading to a containment room and hopefully it will make its way inside."

"Better still," added Vadim, gazing at Level 4 on the blueprint of the facility attached to the wall, "someone waits in one of the containment rooms"—he tapped Containment Room 6 on the blueprint—"this one seems ideal, it's in view of the elevator and has two ways in and out. If we manage to lure it down, and it takes the bait, when it enters the person baiting the room can escape through the other door. Someone in the adjoining control room then remotely shuts both doors, sealing it inside."

Stanislav was impressed. "Okay, everyone, that's the plan. Krisztina, Svetlana and Vadim will join me in the lower labs to set everything up. Luka and Pechka, you'll fetch the cow and put it in the elevator."

"What about Waldemar?" asked Krisztina.

"I gave him a sedative that will last for a couple of hours, so he should be okay," answered Pechka.

"That's not what I meant," corrected Krisztina. "That thing is on the loose and can open doors. Will he be safe in the infirmary?"

"I see your point," said Pechka. "I'll lock the door, and then it can't get to him."

"Now we all know what we're doing, let's move," ordered Stanislav, impatient to get the alien captured and his career heading in the right direction.

After Vadim shot a nervous glance along the corridor to check it was clear, the group filed from the room.

CHAPTER 8

EV1Ldoings

After EV1L had devoured Alexei's remains, it oozed from the bones, formed into a ball of smooth reflective Black and pondered its predicament. With no idea where it was on the human's planet, it thought finding a way above ground to get the lie of the land was essential. Though still not at peak strength, the humans nearby would rectify that. It could then think about reproducing before venturing farther across the planet it planned to colonize with the help of its brood.

EV1L morphed into an upright two-legged creature that would enable it to move through the facility in a manner similar to the humans it hunted. Slim and almost seven feet tall, its humanoid illusion sported claws for attack and defense and emphasized senses to track its prey. Its features held a hint of Svetlana's intermixed with an alien creature drawn from its extensive repertoire. Long smooth braids sprouted from the back of its head and wavered snakelike as it headed for the exit. On reaching the door, its claw turned the handle and EV1L exited the room.

*****

Luka finished tethering the bewildered cow to the elevator handrail, shoved its large smelly rump inside, and stepped into the corridor. Pechka removed his hand preventing the doors from shutting and watched them automatically close against the short length of wood he had placed in the entrance. The doors came to a stop against the obstruction and slid open again. The process would repeat until the wood was removed. The cow mooed in protest at its strange surroundings and the sounds of the sliding doors.

Luka stared at the length of string Pechka held, its other end tied to the wooden batten blocking the doors. "I expected something a bit more technical than a piece of wood and string."

Pechka shrugged. "I could have rigged up a remote device, but I neither had the time or the inclination to do so with that form-changing alien on the loose. It could turn up at any moment."

"Good thinking," agreed Luka. The sooner this was done and dusted, the better he would feel.

"One good thing with keeping it simple is there's nothing to go wrong," added Pechka confidently.

"The string could snap," said Luka, helping Pechka lay the mat over the string so the creature didn't notice it, or get it tangled around its feet, if the form it arrived in even had feet.

"How do we know it will come?" asked Pechka, glancing nervously along the corridor.

"If the noise of the doors doesn't bring it to investigate, then hopefully the large mooing hunk of steak will."

Satisfied everything was in place, they entered the room opposite and closed and locked the door. While Pechka knelt on the floor and checked the string leading under the door moved freely, Luka grabbed a fire extinguisher from its wall bracket.

Pechka glanced at him. "You won't need it."

"I'd rather have it handy and not need it than need it and not have it."

Pechka rolled his eyes. "Let me know when it's in the elevator."

Placing the CO2 extinguisher beside him, Luka placed an eye to the small hole he had made in the sheet of paper he had used to cover the small glass viewing window in the door. He had a perfect view of the elevator entrance.

Now all they had to do was wait.

*****

Worried the alien might be able to escape in its liquid form, Svetlana and Krisztina checked the seals on the two doors leading from the containment chamber were still in good condition after their years of abandonment. If they could hold back gases and bacteria, they should hold back liquid. Satisfied they would still form an airtight seal, Svetlana turned to Stanislav in the control room and gave a thumbs-up sign.

Stanislav pressed buttons to swish the doors open and closed a few times. They worked perfectly. His voice came over the room-to-room communicator. "Krisztina, take up your position by the elevator control, and as soon as we've been informed the creature's inside, bring it down."

Krisztina nodded and headed for the corridor exit.

"Krisztina."

She turned to see Vadim returning from the lavatory; his nerves were playing havoc with his bowels.

"Don't hang about. Press the call button and run as fast as your lovely legs can carry you to the control room."

"Don't worry, I won't be hanging about. Make sure you do the same with your less shapely legs."

Vadim smiled. "I will."

Krisztina headed across the hall to the elevator.

Worried the man might panic and freeze when the creature appeared, Vadim went to speak to Stanislav. "Don't be too hasty closing the doors. Make certain it's fully inside first, but more importantly, ensure I'm out."

"You worry about your part, and leave me to worry about mine. I can press a couple of buttons."

"I hope so," Vadim mumbled, heading for the corridor.

When he passed Svetlana heading for the control room, she whispered, "Don't worry, I've got your back."

Reassured by her words, Vadim took up his position a short distance from the confinement chamber. The creature would see him when it arrived and hopefully chase him inside. He briefly wondered how appetizing he looked to a vicious hungry alien but quickly pushed the gruesome thought aside. He put a hand to his churning gut; he wasn't used to all this stress. Hoping everything went according to plan, he stared at the elevator doors and waited.

*****

On the level above, Pechka scrunched forward and placed an ear to the door. "I think I hear footsteps," he said softly. "They're moving fast."

Luka altered his viewpoint to try and see farther along the corridor, but the small hole limited his vision. "I can't see anything, but get ready," he whispered.

Pechka moved back into position and held the string ready to yank free the piece of wood obstructing the elevator doors.

When something moved past outside, Luka nudged Pechka with his foot and placed a finger to his lips to warn the man to keep silent.

Luka pressed his eye to the hole in the paper. Whatever had arrived, it had stopped directly in front of the door but was too short for him to see more than a dark shadow. He pictured it looking at the cow. Urging it to take the bait, he waited. When the shadow moved nearer the elevator, Luka saw it wasn't the creature but Boris.

He grabbed Pechka's shoulder. "Relax, it's Boris."

"What's he doing?" whispered Pechka.

"Nothing, just staring at the cow." Luka reached for the handle to call Boris to him but froze. "Oh, oh!"

Pechka tilted his head at Luka. "What?"

"I think Boris has sensed something. He just jerked his head along the corridor."

"It has to be the alien." Pechka stared at the gap beneath the door worriedly as he imagined the alien oozing into the room. Trapped, they would be at its mercy, something which he was certain it lacked.

Luka stared at Boris, willing him to flee.

Suddenly Boris turned and loped out of view.

Luka sighed with relief and tensed when something dark entered his view. He tapped Pechka's head and mouthed, *it's here*, when he looked up.

Returning his eye to the viewing hole, Luka watched the alien horror move away.

Sensing the evil creature, the cow mooed fearfully. It strained against its tether and kicked out a rear hoof that shook the elevator when it struck the side.

EV1L observed the large creature for a few moments, noticing its lack of claws, spikes, sharp teeth or armor. It had rarely encountered such a defenseless beast. Even the weak humans had weapons, this had nothing. Taking in its generous size that would provide abundant nourishment, EV1L moved in to feed. Though the wide-eyed cow panicked, shook its head and kicked out, it was no match for its attacker.

Luka observed the attack with emotions a mixture of fear, fascination and disbelief. The upright alien creature approached the cow and then seemed to melt from the head down, becoming a tower of liquid that bent forward and flowed over the unfortunate beast until it was completely covered.

The cow's death screams sent a fearful shiver through both men in the room.

Pechka tugged Luka's trouser leg and whispered, "What's happening?"

Brought back to his senses, Luka looked down at Pechka. "It's inside, do it!"

Pechka yanked the string.

Luka watched the wood slide from the door, curling up the edge of the rug. A face, little more than slits for eyes and a mouth, morphed into existence in the black devouring the cow. It looked at the wood, the rug and then straight at the hole in the paper. Luka gasped in fear from the malicious stare.

A tentacle shot out and wrapped around the wood, holding it in place.

Feeling the strain on the string, Pechka looked at Luka. "It's stuck."

Luka watched the doors close against the wood and slide open. "Keep pulling, the alien's grabbed the wood."

Worried the string would snap, Pechka tugged but failed to pull the wood from the alien's strong grip. "It's not working."

Keeping his eye to the spyhole, Luka unlocked the door and gripped the handle. "Move over so I can open the door but keep the string taut."

Pechka shuffled to the side. "You're going out there?"

"I have an idea."

When Pechka had shuffled to the side and the elevator doors were sliding closed, Luka turned the handle and opened the door. "Pull hard."

Pechka strained against the string. The alien pulled back hard enough that the string wrapped around his hand bit into his flesh.

Luka rushed out, took the lighter from his pocket and flicking it to flame held it under the taut string. The twine snapped. Pechka fell back. The alien's grip slid the wood into the elevator and stopped with an inch protruding through the doors about to close on it and open again. Luka threw the lighter hard. It bounced off the end of the batten and clattered to the floor. The force shoved the prop clear of the doors. Luka glimpsed an alien tentacle reaching for the gap a second before it closed. He collapsed to the floor, his heart pounding against his chest.

Pechka unwrapped the string from his hand and rubbed the bright red welt as he climbed to his feet. He stepped into the corridor, looked at the doors and then at Luka. "Like I said, keep it simple and nothing can go wrong."

Luka rolled his eyes. "It's our comrades' problem now." Suddenly realizing he still had more to do, Luka jumped to his feet, barged past Pechka into the room and rushed to the intercom. He pressed the talk button and shouted, "It's inside! Bring it down! I repeat, the creature is in the elevator."

He relaxed when he heard the winch motor start up, and the elevator beginning its descent.

*****

Boris was frightened, confused and missing the companionship of his human friend he couldn't find. Though he had no idea what the strange, black animal was, he had seen how dangerous it was and knew it was to be avoided at all costs. Its scent was wrong—like no other animal he had encountered before. It smelt bad, evil, something to be feared. Boris glanced back along the corridor to check the strange creature wasn't in pursuit. Pleased to see no sign of it, he carried on. If he couldn't find his human friend soon, he would find a place to hide until the creature had gone.

*****

Krisztina pressed the elevator call button before Luka's warning had ended. As soon as she heard it descending she sprinted for the safety of the control room and called out a warning to alert the others. "It's coming."

Vadim nodded nervously at Krisztina rushing past. It was his turn now. He shot a longing glance towards the toilet before fixing his gaze back on the elevator doors. It would all be over soon.

*****

EV1L halted its reach for the corridor when the doors closed. Though it had no idea what the humans were up to, it assumed its demise was part of their plan. They had tried before and failed. This time would be no different. When it felt the metal box it was trapped in move, it returned to devouring the large beast.

*****

When Vadim noticed his legs were trembling, he took a deep breath and held his fear in check. He glanced behind at the room he would have to rush through; a short sprint and he would be safe. It wasn't a problem. He could do it. He shifted his gaze to the control room where Stanislav, Krisztina and Svetlana focused their gazes across the hall. On hearing the elevator arrive, he refocused on its doors.

The doors slid open. The short length of timber propped against the join fell into the elevator. It would stop the doors from automatically closing and returning to the upper level if the creature lingered inside. Prepared to flee as soon as the creature had spotted him, Vadim stared anxiously at the opening and waited for it to emerge.

*****

With senses alert for danger, EV1L reached out a black tendril from its feasting form and stretched it into the corridor. The eye that formed on its tip looked around before focusing on the human watching it. After a few moments deliberation, the black tendril pulled free from the main mass and slithered snake-like along the corridor.

Unable to see inside the elevator from his position, Vadim was surprised by how small the creature was; he had expected something much larger from the description his comrades had given. Emboldened by the arm-length size of the evil black serpent slithering towards him, Vadim's anxiousness waned slightly. This would be easier than expected.

In the laboratory control room, Stanislav dragged his gaze away from the approaching creature and shot Svetlana a condescending stare. "I thought you said it had grown?"

Perplexed, Svetlana stared worriedly at the black snake. "It had. A lot bigger."

Stanislav humphed. "You must have been so scared you imagined something that didn't exist. That worm is hardly dangerous."

"I might have been scared, but I imagined nothing," Svetlana defended. "Luka saw it also."

Stanislav snorted his derision of the man. "Luka's an idiot."

"Maybe it needs to keep eating to retain its size," suggested Krisztina.

"It just had a whole cow to feast on," argued Svetlana. "No, something's wrong."

"Yes, yours and Luka's overactive imaginations and proneness to exaggerate," scoffed Stanislav.

Svetlana ignored the man and crossed to the intercom. "Luka, how large was the creature that entered the elevator?"

Out in the corridor, Vadim was about to retreat when the serpent grew near but held his ground when the snake stopped and lifted its front half into the air. He watched in fascination when a triangle head lacking any features formed at the tip. It looked around before staring straight at him. Though Vadim noticed no eyes on the menacing head unnervingly pointed at him, he had no doubts it could see him and probably smell the fear he radiated. It was damn creepy. Sensing danger when its head bulged four times its size, he took a step back. When a small rigid tube grew out from the front and aimed at him like a gun barrel, he turned and fled.

Observing the creature with interest from the safety of the control room, Stanislav had no doubts that it came from the alien spaceship in Antarctica. Though how it got here to the facility was still a mystery, it wasn't something that concerned him. His thoughts were occupied by how he could advance his career from this fortunate event fate had seen fit to present him with. His name would go down in history. The first man to capture, study and prove the existence of extraterrestrial life. However dangerous it proved to be he had to ensure the others didn't destroy it. As long as he wasn't one of them, a few deaths were acceptable losses and might even prove interesting. Information on how it hunted and killed would be invaluable for his research on the alien.

"Big enough to cover the cow, why?" replied Luka over the intercom. *"Have you caught it?"*

"Not yet," answered Svetlana. "It was bigger than a snake about half a meter long, then?"

"Hell, yes! A lot bigger. It covered the cow."

Svetlana crossed to the glass wall, glanced at the snake and then the elevator doors sliding back and forth against the timber prop. The elevator was set in the side wall, making it impossible to see into the interior. She turned to Stanislav. "It's tricking us."

Stanislav scoffed. "I doubt it's that intelligent."

"Oh, my God!" Krisztina pointed through the glass wall at the snake creature.

The tube and front of the snake's expanded head sucked into itself and then shot out, stretching forward. When small missiles of Black shot from the tube, the snake's tail began to shrink, providing fodder for the missiles it spat out.

Unaware of what was happening behind him, Vadim's only thought was to reach the chamber and exit from the far door safely. His first inkling that something was amiss was when he felt a tap on his shoulder. A turn of his head revealed a small black splat. Taps across his back signaled more hits. Buttons pinged to the floor when he ripped his white coat open. As he scrambled to remove it, the splat on his shoulder formed into a small worm and leapt at his head. Vadim screamed in fear when it slithered across his cheek and crawled up a nostril. The other splats became worms and leapt for his head. Vadim threw the coat on the floor and rushed for the far door. It closed before he reached it. He jerked his head at Stanislav in the control room.

"Stanislav, you bastard! Open this..."

Observing the worms crawling over Vadim's face, Stanislav pressed a button on the console. "Sorry, Vadim, you are contaminated. We'll do all we can to help you, but..."

Seeking out orifices, the worms crawled into Vadim's ears, nose, mouth and eyes. Vadim screamed when Black ooze seeped from the pores in his face a moment later. The hands he put to his face to claw at the burning pain sunk into his melting flesh, covering them in blood and scorching Black. Stricken with agony, he rushed erratically around the room, crashing into walls.

The snake, reduced in size now, slithered into the room and observed the human that collapsed to the floor. It turned its tip at the door closing behind it and then crossed to the writhing human. It crawled up the man's trouser leg and started feasting.

Coming to his senses, Stanislav screamed, "The cameras, the cameras, switch them on!"

Stricken by shock at their colleague suffering an agonizing death, the two women ignored his request.

Cursing their unprofessionalism, Stanislav switched on the two cameras attached to the ceiling above the console. Aimed into the containment room they would record every stage of Vadim's demise. The Black's method of killing and devouring its victims was something his superiors would want to see. After checking the red recording lights were on, he resumed watching the Black consume his colleague. History was being made. He sighed and rolled his eyes when one of the woman behind him screamed. He turned to order them to silence and froze. A Black column rose from the floor and spread out over the glass wall. It seemed Svetlana may have been correct after all. While the snake had distracted them, the bigger creature had crept up on them. *It can separate.* More information to add to his research. He could almost taste his fame and promotion.

"It can't get in, can it?" fretted Krisztina, stepping back from the wall.

"I doubt it, but neither can we get out," said Svetlana. "It's turned the table on us. We're the ones trapped." She looked at Stanislav. "Still doubting its intelligence, Director?"

Though concerned by the unexpected turn of events, Stanislav was confident the creature couldn't reach them. What went on down here, back then, depended on airtight seals in every room to stop contaminants spreading. No, they might be momentarily trapped, but they were safe.

Stanislav turned to Svetlana. "However intelligent it is, we have the greater intellect. We need to put our brains together and come up with a plan to defeat it. As I'm sure we will."

Svetlana huffed. "Our first two plans didn't work out so well, did they?"

Stanislav found it difficult to argue with that. His mouth dropped open when three faces appeared in the Black spread across the glass. He shifted his gaze to each in turn. The faces were perfect facsimiles of Krisztina, Svetlana and himself. He reached for one of the camera controls and turned it to face the creature. His superiors would never believe him if he didn't back up his report with hard evidence.

"How is that even possible?" uttered Krisztina, staring into her greasy black face looking back at her. Her human face reflected in the alien facsimile was a creepy effect that was also fascinating.

"It's alien and for the moment beyond our comprehension," stated Stanislav, enthralled by the creature's abilities.

Svetlana approached the wall and laid a hand against the glass. All of them watched in fascination when an identical hand formed in the Black. She pulled it back and made a fist. The black hand copied her. She flexed her fingers. The black fist didn't change but instead pulled back and shot at the glass. The transparent wall shook with the force. Svetlana staggered back. Though she had witnessed it forming into different shapes, creatures, *them*, she had assumed its form was still soft, malleable.

Svetlana looked at the others. "It can make itself solid."

"It's remarkable," uttered Stanislav.

"How's it going down there?"

Stanislav crossed to the intercom. "Luka, though I'm reluctant to say it, we need your help."

"Damn, you must be desperate. What's the problem?"

"We underestimated the creature. It killed Vadim and has us trapped in Control Room 2."

"Vadim's dead?"

"Yes, but let's not dwell on those beyond your help. You need to come up with some way of rescuing us." To avoid holding down the talk button, Stanislav switched the intercom to conference mode.

"Are Krisztina and Svetlana okay?"

"We are fine but also trapped in the control room," answered Krisztina.

A slight pause, then, *"I'm not sure how I can help? Do any of you have a plan?"*

"Maybe you can distract the creature and lure it away," Stanislav suggested.

"Sounds dangerous to me," replied Luka. *"Wasn't that Vadim's job, to distract and lure? Look how that turned out."*

"He was careless," lied Stanislav.

"Anyway, how can I help stuck up here? The elevator's the only way down."

"There's another way," explained Stanislav. "An emergency ladder located in Storeroom 9 at the end of the hall leading past the elevator. Open the floor hatch and climb down. It leads to the main generator room down here."

"Let's get this straight, you want me and Pechka to..."

"Um, he didn't mention me, only you," interrupted Pechka.

"If I'm going, so are you," argued Luka. *"You still there, Kommandant?"*

Stanislav ignored the slur. There would be time for repercussions later. "I have nowhere else to go."

"Let me get this straight—you want us to come down there and what? Wave and yell at the creature to get it to chase us so you can escape?"

"You," argued Pechka.

"A less grandiose plan than I envisioned, but it might work," replied Stanislav.

"I was being sarcastic," stated Luka.

"I know, Comrade, but unless you have something else..."

"There might be another way," offered Krisztina.

Stanislav looked at her expectantly.

"Let's open the containment room door and see if the creature enters." She looked at the pulsating mass of Black smothering some parts of Vadim. "There's part of it in there, so it might enter to be reunited or feed. If it does, we close the door, trapping it."

"I like that plan a lot better," enthused Luka over the intercom.

"As do I," added Pechka.

"And if it fails to take the bait, what then?" questioned Stanislav.

"We let it in here," said Svetlana.

Stanislav raised his eyebrows cynically. "And just how will that save us?"

"Assuming it will chase us as soon as the door is open, we flee through the attached laboratory, through Containment Room 6 and into the corridor. We close the far door as we exit and one of us nips back in here and shuts off its retreat, trapping it like we originally planned."

Stanislav considered the merits of Krisztina's and Svetlana's variations of their original plan. "Though your plans lack the simplicity of Luka's moronic proposal, I believe both have a far higher rate of success."

"I agree," said Luka. *"Their plans are much better. Go with them."*

"We'll try Krisztina's less-hazardous-to-our-health idea first." Stanislav reached for a button on the console and pressed it. The corridor containment door swished open.

On hearing the noise, EV1L focused its senses along the corridor. It peeled its form from the glass and flowed over to the door.

"It's working," whispered Krisztina, practically holding her breath.

EV1L peered through the opening and studied the room before focusing on the part of it that feasted on the human. Its energy would be added to its form when they were reunited. Sensing the humans were trying to trap it again, it formed into the two-legged beast and walked back to observe the humans.

Backing farther away from the terrifying monster peering in at them through the glass wall, Krisztina groaned with disappointment. "Why didn't it enter?"

"It sensed a trap," replied Stanislav, admiring the creature's intellect. "Time for plan B." He hovered his hand over the door control buttons and looked at the women. “Get ready.”

Krisztina and Svetlana moved to the far laboratory door, opened it and waited.

Stanislav opened the containment room’s second door and then pressed the control room door button. As soon as it began to open, the three of them rushed into the adjoining laboratory. They halted when the creature remained in the corridor.

“It’s not following,” said Svetlana, fearing their plan would fail.

Krisztina shot a glance at the Black in the attached containment room and was relieved to see it seemed unaware of them and continued feasting.

“It’s thinking,” said Stanislav.

Deciding on its course of action, EV1L shed a small pool of Black and entered the control room.

Svetlana led Krisztina and Stanislav into Containment Room 6. Taking a wide berth around the feeding Black, they headed for the far exit. While Svetlana and Stanislav continued along the corridor, Krisztina halted by the door with her hand near the exterior door control, ready to close it.

EV1L halted at the far entrance and stared at her.

What’s it waiting for? Wondered Krisztina. *Come on, just a few more steps.*

Along the corridor, Svetlana stopped so abruptly, Stanislav stumbled into her.

“Don’t stop,” he urged, glancing back through the transparent walls at the creature.

“We can’t go on. Look!” said Svetlana.

Stanislav peered past her at the black mesh stretched across the corridor. “Damn, that thing’s clever and too devious for my liking.”

“Hey, you two, we have a problem,” called out Krisztina.

Svetlana and Stanislav glanced back and saw the part of the Black that had killed Vadim rise from the partially digested corpse while the main bulk of the creature turned away from the far door and headed back through the laboratory towards the control room.

"It's tricked us, again," stated Svetlana fearfully. "We can't go back, and we can't go forward."

Stanislav, desperate to survive, only had seconds to act before the main beast creature cut off their escape route. He glanced back at Krisztina when she closed the containment room door, her attention focused on the Black inside approaching her. He shoved Svetlana forcefully into the mesh. She screamed when the Black net touched her skin. Stretching like elastic when she fell against it, the mesh was pulled from the walls. Ignoring the woman's screams, Stanislav leapt over her writhing form. A tendril shot out and grabbed his foot. Stanislav crashed to the floor, smashing his nose hard. When he spotted the tendril wrapped around his foot, he pushed off the shoe with his other foot and scrambled away. He climbed to his feet and sprinted for the elevator.

Gripped by fear from Svetlana's terrible screams, Krisztina rushed to help her. She gasped at the small Black puddle seeping into Svetlana's eyes, ears, nostrils and mouth, gagging her pain-wracked screams. She was beyond help. Krisztina glanced fearfully at the creature moving unhurriedly, it seemed, through the control room as she ran to catch up with Stanislav.

Stanislav entered the elevator, kicked the timber aside and pressed the Level 1 button.

Seeing the prop sliding across the floor and the closing elevator doors, Krisztina screamed, "Stanislav, wait! I'm coming!"

Stanislav ignored her plea as he silently urged the doors to close quicker.

The doors closed. The elevator jerked when it began its upward journey.

Stanislav sighed with relief. He was safe. He smeared blood across his face when he wiped the drip oozing from his smashed nose. Puzzled by the sound he heard behind him, he turned to look at the partly digested cow. Its hide moved, as if something was inside. Fear spread across his face when a tendril of Black wriggled from beneath the cow's flesh. He staggered back against the door as more appeared and stretched into the air with their tips pointed at him.

"Please, God, no! Not this!"

Stanislav turned away when the tendrils stretched towards him. His hand thumped the up button in the hope it would make the elevator rise faster. Fearing what he would see but unable to resist, he turned his head slowly. The tendrils wavered menacingly in front of his face. As one, they shot forward. They liquefied on contact with his skin and spread out, forming a tight Black mask around his head. Stanislav's muffled, agonized screams filtered through the elevator shaft.

Though she knew her efforts were wasted, Krisztina pressed the call button and cursed Stanislav while she thumped on the elevator doors. She stopped when Stanislav's tortured scream reached her. Gleaning a little comfort from the man's suffering, she sobbed when she looked back at the black beast skulking menacingly nearer. It knew she had nowhere to go. Krisztina turned and fled along the corridor.

*****

"I wonder what's happening down there?" pondered Luka aloud, after failing to contact those below over the intercom. Already worried by the woman's scream he'd heard a few moments ago on the open intercom, his unanswered calls had increased his anxiety.

"They are probably heading for the elevator," said Pechka. "If I was being chased by that thing, I wouldn't stop running for anything. They'll be fine."

Luka wasn't as confident. He had a feeling something bad had happened.

Pechka cocked an ear to the doorway. "It's the elevator. I told you they would be okay."

They went into the corridor and waited by the elevator.

They looked at each other when a man's terrified scream filtered from the lift shaft.

"That was Stanislav," stated Luka.

Both men looked at the doors fearfully and backed away when the elevator arrived. The doors slid opened. Something fell out and thudded to the floor. It was Stanislav. Both men focused on what was left of Stanislav's head being consumed by the Black smothering it. A glance inside revealed the remains of the cow but no sign of Katrina or Svetlana. The two men backed away from the feasting Black and ran.

"Do you think the girls are dead?" asked Pechka, glancing behind fearfully and pleased to see the Black wasn't following.

Remembering the woman's scream, which could have come from Krisztina or Svetlana, Luka nodded sadly. "I doubt anyone could have a survived an attack from that thing before it separated. Now there's more than one…"

"Shit!" cursed Pechka. "What do we do now?"

"We save ourselves," replied Luka. "We'll call in the troops like they should have been as soon as that thing was first discovered and then get out of here before we become its next victims."

"What about Waldemar? He's still in the infirmary."

"Damn, I'd forgotten all about him." Pondering their options, Luka slowed his pace. "While I head to the security office to explain what's happened and call for reinforcements, you fetch Waldemar and meet me at the main exit elevator. The guard post down the road is nearest. They'll get to us the quickest and have weapons to shoot that thing."

The two men headed up to Level 1 and split up to carry out their allotted tasks.

CHAPTER 9

Checkpoint Siberia 3

Ice-chilled wind blasted Sven when he stepped from the warmth of the Checkpoint Siberia 3 shelter into the Siberian wilderness. His windblown comrades gathered around the coal burner playing cards shouted and cursed at him to shut the damn door. Ignoring them, Sven zipped up his fleece-lined coat tight to his neck. Sheltered against the draft as much as he was able, he closed the door and headed for the small shack twenty yards distant.

At twenty years old, Sven was the youngest member of the five-man team stationed at the remote outpost. Having joined them when the abandoned facility they protected was hastily brought back into service, he was still going through the jibing, new boy on the team phase. It wasn't anything he couldn't handle. They were a good bunch really.

He entered the small hut, balked at the stench rising from the latrine pit and tugged the sagging door shut. His glance into the toilet hole revealed, as he suspected, a pyramid of turds resting on the crust of ice formed on the water. Cursing his lazy comrades, Sven grabbed the pole leaning in the corner and hacked at the ice until it broke, releasing a fresh stench of stale urine and feces to assault his nostrils as the turds slid beneath the foul surface like sinking ships. He replaced the pole in the corner, pulled down his trousers and shivered when his bum cheeks touched the cold wooden seat.

While he waited for nature to run its course, he flicked through the pile of dog-eared porn mags on the floor and pulled out an old edition of *Chobix*. After dreamily imagining losing his virginity to the large breasted Russian beauty on the cover for a few moments, he flicked through the well-thumbed pages.

*****

Inside the main hut warmed by the coal fire in one corner, the other four guards of Checkpoint Siberia 3 had settled into their usual routine of card playing. Zacharov halted his hand reaching to pick up a playing card from the table as, in unison with his three comrades, he turned his head to stare at the ringing phone fixed to the wall across the room. Their surprised expressions were an indication it rarely rung.

"Are we expecting anyone?" asked Verez, trying to sneak a peek at Jaroslav's cards while his comrade was distracted.

"We are not," stated Zacharov, screeching his chair back noisily when he stood.

As he crossed the room, Zacharov wondered who was calling. They had already had their monthly delivery of stores when Sven arrived a week ago, which included food, bottled water and coal, so that couldn't be it. He glanced at the calendar when he passed, its picture a striking woman dressed in a lowcut camouflage patterned top straining against her ample, braless breasts. Ringed in black was tomorrows date, and above it scrawled in his handwriting, *Diesel delivery*. It was the delivery of fuel for the facility's diesel generators; there were no power lines this far out in the tundra. If the diesel hadn't arrived a day early, which was possible, it had to be a surprise visit connected to the sudden re-opening of the secret base.

Zacharov reached for the phone and noticed the green light wasn't glowing. Whoever was calling, it wasn't one of the other outposts positioned along the road ringing with advance warning of a visitor. He wiped the soot thrown up by the coal fire from the other two lights with a finger. The yellow light glowed weakly. This is a first. Someone from the facility was ringing. He lifted the old receiver and placed it to his ear. "Comrade Zacharov, commander of Checkpoint Siberia 3 speaking."

As he listened to the caller, his features formed a cynical frown. "We are on our way." He hung up. Wearing a puzzled expression he turned to his comrades. "There's some sort of disturbance at the facility. People have died."

"I knew it!" stated Makar. "They've been experimenting with germ warfare, and some highly infectious disease has leaked out and killed some of them."

"I'm not going in if the plague or something worse is floating around inside," said Verez, throwing in his hand he now knew Jaroslav could easily beat. "No way am I setting foot in there."

"It's nothing like that," said Zacharov, stroking his beard worriedly. "Apparently there's an alien creature running amok and killing off the scientists."

"Phew," uttered Verez, standing up and grabbing his rifle. "Alien monsters I can handle."

As the men dressed in warm clothing and gathered their weapons, Jaroslav approached Zacharov. "Is this on the up, sir? There really is an alien in the facility?"

Zacharov shrugged as he slipped a folded plan of the facility into his pocket. "That's what the man on the phone indicated. He was obviously distraught, so I believe something's happened. Whether an alien is involved, I doubt it, but I guess we'll soon find out." He glanced around at his men to check they were ready. "Let's go."

As they filed out the door, Verez asked Zacharov, "Did he say what this alien looked like?"

"Only that it was black and deadly."

"I bet it's some sort of black lizardy thing, reptilian looking," said Verez. "Snake eyes, fangs and long, sharp teeth."

"Just get on the damn truck," ordered Zacharov, closing the door behind them.

*****

With his toilet business finished, Sven stood and pulled up his trousers. He cocked an ear to the sound of a truck starting. Thinking the mechanic, Maker, was carrying out another check of the vehicle, he paid it no heed; the man started it a couple of times every day to check nothing was frozen. However, when its doors slammed and it roared off along the road, he kicked the door open and ran out buckling his trousers. "Hey, wait for me," he shouted, waving an arm.

Maker glanced in the side mirror and smiled. "It seems we've caught Sven with his trousers down again." He glanced at Zacharov. "Shall I stop and pick him up?"

Zacharov shook his head. "He's so green, whatever the crisis he'll be a hindrance. He can remain here and man the guard post."

Maker double-clutched and shifted into higher gear, spurting the lumbering truck along the rough road with a burst of dark exhaust fumes.

Resigned that they weren't going to stop, Sven stared after the vehicle. They had to be going to the facility, there was nowhere else. Wondering what had happened to stir the men from the comfort of their cozy lethargy, he headed for the hut. It was probably another of their silly games to rile him. Leave the new kid all alone in the middle of nowhere so he gets scared.

Sven glanced at Makar's motorbike covered by a thermal blanket in the garage area and briefly considered using it to catch up with the others. He dismissed the idea. Leave them to their childish games. It will make a welcome change to have a little alone time. He entered the warm hut, hung up his coat and crossed to the bookcase and shelf unit along one wall. His gaze wandered over the stack of Russian and English titles he had brought to help pass away the long bouts of inactivity this remote posting offered. He pulled out an English book, *Horror Island* by Ben Hammott, which looked like an exciting read. Though Sven's English wasn't perfect, he could hold a conversation and found reading English books helped improve his vocabulary. He stretched out on the sofa and started reading in the warm glow of the fire.

CHAPTER 10

Welcome to Russia

The lone passenger of the helicopter glanced through the side window at the grassy tundra that stretched out in all directions for as far as the eye could see. It did nothing to offset his beliefs that Siberia was little more than a frozen wasteland of hardship and gulags, though so far, he had glimpsed no evidence of either. In fact, he had seen very little of Russia during his long, tiring journey from England as it had been dark when he arrived at *Irkutsk Airport.* A long uncomfortable car ride in a vehicle lacking any decent suspension and a noisy heater that blasted out air barely warmer than the outside temperature had then brought him to a small airfield as dawn approached. After two hours wait, the helicopter pilot arrived, and they had set off for a remote area of the Siberian tundra.

The passenger turned his gaze ahead. Peering through the cockpit's bubble, he noticed a road drawing nearer. He followed the anomaly's straight line into the distance and glimpsed the small cluster of buildings it led to. Though their purpose seemed agricultural in nature, he couldn't imagine what sort of farming would have been carried out in the middle of nowhere. With his interest piqued, he pulled the mic on the headset he wore nearer his mouth and pointed out the building to the pilot. “What’s that?”

The pilot briefly turned his head at the distant buildings. “If I was telling you, I would have to kill you and then myself.”

The passenger rolled his eyes. “I’m not that interested.”

The pilot laughed. “Welcome to Russia.”

“I thought the cold war had ended.”

The pilot shrugged. “Maybe, maybe not. Perhaps it has different name now. I warn you this. It not advisable to be asking questions about such things.” He nodded his head at the distant building. “Better you nothing see.”

As they flew over the road, the passenger noticed a small group of simple wooden buildings. Smoke curled from the chimney of one, and beneath a roof that jutted from the largest hut, he saw what seemed to be a Russian transport truck. The barrier stretched across the road leading to the mysterious building designated it as a security checkpoint. Suddenly, men slipping on coats and gripping rifles in hand rushed from the hut with the smoking chimney. A few glanced up at the helicopter as they rushed for the truck and clambered aboard. Two soldiers pulled the thick insulation blankets wrapped around the vehicle to protect the engine and the fuel tank from the cold before climbing into the cab. Thick black smoke belched out from the exhaust when the engine roared to life. The truck eased forward, turned onto the road and sped for the distant buildings.

Wondering what had happened to prompt the soldiers into action, the passenger gazed after the speeding truck.

“I remember to you, it’s better you nothing see,” warned the pilot.

Hoping the pilot’s grasp of the helicopters controls was considerably more proficient than his grasp of English, the passenger sighed and returned to staring out at the landscape that was as desolate as his life had become. *Where had it all gone wrong?*

CHAPTER 11

bedEV1Led

After finishing off the human, the fragment of Black that had killed Stanislav, now strengthened and larger, changed into a segmented two-meter-long centipede-like creature and scurried along the corridor after more human prey.

When it failed to find them, it returned to the bones it had found in the room of cages. Though they offered little nourishment, it was something. It was about to melt over the bones to absorb their limited sustenance when its head shifted to faint human voices drifting out of a hole in the wall. Eager to consume more human flesh, it slithered up to the air duct, crawled inside and headed for the voices.

*****

Having failed to find the human female, EV1L returned to the Level 4 elevator. It would seek her out after it had disposed of the humans above before they called in other humans who might prove to be more of a threat. It reformed into the image of Stanislav and waited for the Black heading along the corridor to re-join it. EV1L rippled in delight as the burst of energy flowed through it. When the two had become one again, it copied what it had seen the human do earlier. It reached out a hand and pressed the call button. When the elevator arrived, it stepped in, cast a glance over the remains of the large beast it would devour later, and rode the elevator up.

*****

Waldemar was too heavy for Pechka to lift on his own, so desperate to leave the underground complex, he revived Waldemar with an injection. When his patient had recovered from his abrupt awakening, Pechka rapidly explained a condensed version of what had happened. After what he had witnessed, Waldemar had no trouble believing the horrific events that had unfolded during his sleep.

Still a little groggy from the sedative, Waldemar let Pechka help him to his feet. After the wave of dizziness from being upright subsided, Waldemar assured his comrade he was able to move without support. Pechka anxiously poked his head out the door, and after checking the corridor was clear, he led Waldemar from the infirmary and along the corridor.

They halted on hearing a slithering around the corner ahead. Pechka placed a finger to his lips to bade Waldemar to silence and crept to the corner. Already stressed and anxious, he almost gasped in fright when he peeked around the corner. Black poured through the grill of an air vent and turned into a huge insect that seemed to have leapt from prehistoric times. It rose on its back segment of legs and turned to look down each corridor of the intersection it had arrived at. Its mouth opened and shut, emitting chattering clicks, as if testing each route. Pechka dodged back when its grotesque prehistoric head turned in his direction.

"What is it?" whispered Waldemar, uncertain he really wanted to know.

"A giant alien centipede thing," mouthed Pechka, his voice barely a whisper.

When he turned to check if it was gone, the centipede's terrifying head appeared around the corner level with his own. It hissed foul, corpse-tainted breath in his face. Pechka screamed and dodged back. He stumbled into Waldemar, and both tripped to the floor. The creature scurried around the corner, down the wall and split into two. The back half grew a head, and each headed for their chosen victim.

Pechka's attacker opened its mouth to an impossible degree and dived at one of the legs the human kicked at it. To accommodate the limb, it spread its jaws wide and swallowed it up to the knee. Its body bloated like a Halloween horror balloon designed by Lovecraft before dissolving into Black glutinousness tar that oozed over his body. The evil puddle of creeping pain slowly dissolved clothing and flesh.

The centipede after Waldemar grew two long back legs that propelled it through the air. Waldemar pushed his screaming comrade off him with his good arm and crab-walked backwards, away from the approaching monstrosity launching its attack. It landed on his chest and melted. Terrified and trembling, Waldemar watched horrified as the Black he couldn't stop flowed over him. His screams joined Pechka's echoing though the corridors.

*****

Luka halted his sprint to the exit elevator and stared fearfully back along the corridor as the painfilled screams of his comrades drifted through. He had lingered too long. It was time to leave and let the soldiers already on their way deal with it. At least he wasn't completely defenseless. He glanced at the alien weapon he had grabbed from Stanislav's office. He had turned the dials until a tiny light came on, which he hoped indicated it was ready to fire. Eager to reach the exit elevator and get above ground, he was about to turn and run when he noticed movement at the far end of the corridor. It looked like someone was turning the lights off one by one. He then realized the darkness drawing nearer was a wall of Black the width and height of the corridor flowing towards him. Fighting back the fear that threatened to turn him into a trembling wreck, he raised the weapon and fired.

The green ball of light that shot from the barrel grew and gave Luka hope he might survive the encounter. His hope rapidly diminished when a hole formed in the Black just before the light ball struck, allowing the deadly missile to pass harmlessly through and strike the far wall in a shower of sparks that sent lumps of concrete skidding across the floor. Luka fired off another shot before he fled.

EV1L easily avoided the second shot and spurted forward.

Luka shot a glance behind and saw his fear reflected in the greasy Black almost upon him. His agonized screams echoed along the corridor when it latched onto his back and folded around him. He forced the gun to his head and pulled the trigger.

*****

As soon as the truck pulled to a halt inside the compound, Verez and Jaroslav jumped out the back and roamed their weapons over the building and around the compound.

Zacharov rolled his eyes and climbed out of the cab at a more leisurely pace. On touching firm ground, he stretched and grabbed at his aching back. He was too old for this energetic excitement. In his younger days he had seen his fair share of action, kill or be killed and do as ordered however crazy and suicidal the command. It was a wonder any of them had survived. But that was far behind him, which was why he liked the Siberian guard post detail. Cushy and boring, just what he needed in his twilight years. He gazed out at the surrounding tundra. Desolate and miles from civilization, it wasn't for everyone, but he liked it. It gave a man time to think, to reflect on life. He had even pondered writing a book. He had a few ideas, but, as yet, the notebook he had bought remained absent of words.

"We going in or staying here admiring the view?" asked Verez impatiently.

Zacharov sighed at the impatience and lack of respect shown by today's youth as he headed for the entrance. When staring at the camera failed to release the electronic lock, he pulled a key card from his pocket and slipped it into the reader fixed to the frame. When the door buzzed, he pushed it open and stepped inside. The men followed him through.

Though Luka had informed him he and two others, one wounded, would be waiting here for them, Zacharov wasn't unduly concerned by their absence.

Makar crossed to the elevator and pressed the call button. The doors slid open, and they piled inside.

As the doors closed, Zacharov glanced around at his men. "Though I'm not expecting us to be greeted by anything alien, something has happened to cause some fatalities. We have no idea what these scientists have been doing down here, but it's a secret facility, so it's likely to be nothing good. They have animals here that I assume were used for testing their experiments, which included primates, so maybe it's one of these that was infected in some way and went crazy."

"Zombified DNA-altered apes, cool!" said Verez, smiling. "It'll be like playing a PlayStation shooter game taking them out."

Zacharov shook his head in dismay. "I very much doubt they have any apes here and definitely none that have been zombified. Just stay sharp and don't fire at anything until you're certain it isn't human. There are still, or was a short while ago, people alive down here."

They focused on the doors with weapons raised when the elevator juddered to a halt and the doors slid open.

Verez and Jaroslav stepped out. Standing back-to-back, they aimed their weapons along the empty passageways.

Zacharov glanced along the corridor as he pulled out the map of the facility. He unfolded it and found their position.

Looking over his shoulder, Makar tapped a finger on the plan. “There’s the security office. As there’s no sign of those three scientists we were meant to meet up with, we could head there and look at the CCTV feeds to find out who or *what* is about and if anyone needs our help.”

Zacharov nodded. “Let’s do it, but we move slow and controlled.” He tapped Verez on the shoulder. “No shooting at shadows. Identify, appraise and shoot if required. That goes for the rest of you. If anyone shoots a scientist, they’ll suffer the consequences. Understood?”

“Yes, sir,” They replied sharply in unison.

“Makar, you lead. Verez, you’re at the rear. I don’t want anything creeping up on us.”

“You can rely on me, sir.”

They moved along the corridor in an alert, tight group that almost looked professional and nearly made Zacharov proud. Checking each room as they went, they moved stealthily towards the security office.

Makar raised an arm. “Scientist, dead.”

Zacharov pushed through his men gawping at the corpse and knelt to examine it. Stripped of flesh, he could see some of the bones showed evidence of melting. His gaze scanned the area around the corpse for signs of scorching, but there were none.

Makar voiced his thoughts. “What could melt bone but leave no evidence of fire?”

"Acid!" stated Verez. "Maybe the creature responsible spits acid or something like that thing in the American Alien movie."

"That alien didn't spit acid, its *blood* was acid," corrected Jaroslav. "And there's no acid damage to the floor.

"Quiet, you lot," ordered Zacharov, now convinced someone or something was in here killing people. "Stay alert."

He nodded at Makar to lead. They stepped around the skeleton and headed along the corridor.

*****

Makar turned a corner and stared along the dark corridor stretching out before him. At its end the light from a junction still with light revealed nothing obstructing the square of yellow tinted light between them and it. When Makar edged forward to let the others enter the dark passage, something crunched beneath his feet.

Taking a small flashlight from his pocket, Zacharov pushed forward and aimed it at the floor. The beam reflected off broken lightbulb shards.

"Someone, or *something*, broke them deliberately," whispered Makar.

Frowning, Zacharov aimed the light along the passage. It was creepy as hell but seemed absent any menace. He glanced at Makar. "Move slow and cautious." He turned to the others. "Heads on a swivel."

His men nodded.

Each glass-crunching step amplified their unease as Makar led them forward.

About halfway along, Zacharov aimed his light at a section of the ceiling he had noticed was different from the rest. It was black. At first he thought a fire might have been responsible, but the straight edges at either end indicated otherwise. It was as if someone had fixed a long board as wide as the corridor to the ceiling. As he directed the light away, he thought he detected movement within the black and shifted it back. He gasped when the ceiling rippled. The warning he shouted when it dropped was quickly muffled by the rubbery black blanket that smothered them.

Men yelled in surprise and pushed hands at the Black to free themselves, but it stretched like tar and then flowed over them like treacle. They screamed when the burning started. Panicked gunfire erupted. Bullets punched holes in the Black and peppered the ceiling and walls. A line of bullets fired from Jaroslav's weapon crept up Makar's back, shattering his back bone and cutting short his pain and life when the bullets reached his head. The Black held Makar's corpse upright as it enveloped him.

Zacharov had never felt such pain. His whole body burned. Lit by the flashlight now stuck in the oozing substance, he watched his Black-gloved hands melt. He closed his eyes when the ooze flowed over his face and screaming, prayed death came swiftly.

Jaroslav stumbled back firing when something fell on him and wrapped around his head. It burnt like acid. He screamed as his melting skin slithered from his skull. Forcing his finger from the trigger, he dragged the weapon through the clinging substance and turned it on himself. As he pulled the trigger, he said goodbye to his wife and son he would never see again.

Knocked away when Jaroslav barged into him, Verez stumbled clear of the black and tripped to the floor. Screams and weapon fire rolled him onto his back with his rifle ready to fire. His mouth dropped open when he saw the sheet of rubbery Black covering his comrades, their forms and stretching hands pushing at the pliable mass visible in the elastic cloak that liquified before his eyes and began flowing over them. Reluctant to fire for fear of hitting his comrades, he jumped to his feet and shouldered the rifle. When he rushed forward to pull his nearest comrade free, an arm of one of his comrades shot through the mass. He froze and watched in horror as the flesh slipped from the man's fingers and hand and rolled back on itself when it travelled down the raised arm. The black flowed up the arm and pulled it back into its mass.

Verez, sickened and horrified, stepped back when a gooey piece of Black stretched towards him and formed into a sharp spike. Reaching for the rifle as he stumbled backwards, he screamed when the spike entered his stomach and continued though until it erupted in a spray of blood out his back. It rose up behind him and yanking him off his feet it curled around his face and pulled him into its mass.

When the screams and movements of its latest victims ended, EV1L began the absorption process, drawing in the humans' nourishment like water to a dry sponge.

CHAPTER 12

Gateway to the Underworld

The helicopter pilot's voice over the headset opened his tired passenger's eyes that had drooped closed. "We're here." The pilot pointed at the large gash in the tundra they sped towards. "Hell's Mouth."

The passenger wiped the spittle of sleep-induced drool from his cheek as he stared at the cancerous growth that blighted the landscape, a vast area of permafrost. It was Mother Nature's version of a flesh-eating disease whose cliff faces expanded ten meters or more each year farther into the surrounding tundra. The pilot flew around the tadpole-shaped gouge in the frozen earth, currently almost 0.6 miles (1km) long and 282ft (86m) across, and up to 328 (100m) feet deep. Some had labeled the deep pit the Gateway to the Underworld, others called it Hell's Mouth. However, its actual and less ominous name was Batagaika crater.

Though some who misunderstood the phenomenon assigned its existence to otherworldly events, Batagaika crater was known as a megaslump, the largest of its kind and still growing. The trigger that led to the crater's creation started in the 1960s when rapid deforestation caused the ground to be no longer shaded by trees in the warmer summer months. The sunlight then warmed the ground it hadn't shone on for eons, melting the permafrost and turning it to mud that slumped to form the ever-expanding crater.

What may prove to be fatal for the current Siberian landscape was good news for scientists and paleontologists. Some parts of the exposed ground reached back two hundred thousand years to the time of long extinct creatures. Trapped in the steadily thawing permafrost were the fossilized remains of ancient forests, mammoths, woolly rhinoceroses, cave lions and other ice age giants that once roamed the area.

The passenger took in the inhospitable features of the crater's floor and the steep hills and gullies that dropped away from precarious cliffs forming the sides. People working around the site looked up when the helicopter swooped overhead. He turned his gaze to movement on the cliff that filled the left-side window. A huge chunk of frozen tundra loosened by the thawing process slipped from the steep side and tumbled to the bottom, exposing another section of the past for the scientists and paleontologists to examine.

As the helicopter decreased its revs, the passenger directed his gaze upon the small group of brightly colored tents pitched on a flattish, raised peak of earth far from the treacherous sides of the pit. When the helicopter turned, hovered and then began its descent onto a flat ridge of ground, a man exited the largest of the tents whipped frantically by the rotor wash and approached the makeshift landing pad. After the helicopter had touched down and the pilot had killed the engine, the passenger slipped off his headset and climbed out.

The man approaching the helicopter smiled warmly at the disembarking passenger and held out a hand to the man ducking far lower than necessary to clear the slowing rotors. "Hello, Richard. You made it then?"

Richard grasped the man's hand and shook. "Hello, brother." He glanced around at the area encased on all sides by sheer, precarious cliffs that looked too unstable and dangerous to climb. "What arse-end of hell have you brought me to, David?"

David laughed. "It might not look like much, but we are making some amazing discoveries—treasures of the ice age. We've discovered remains of an ancient forest, frozen remains of a musk ox, mammoth, and a 4,400-year-old horse inside the crater, and there is much more down here waiting for us to find. The preservation of some of the frozen specimens is remarkable. Skin, muscle and perhaps even blood and viable DNA have been preserved."

Richard had read about the fervour around a new buzzword that was a hot topic in some areas of the scientific community—*de-extinction*. "That might be of interest to someone keen to bring an extinct beast into the modern world, but I'm not one of them. I've faced enough monsters to last a lifetime."

"Still the grumpy old sod you always were, Richard. I thought recent events might have mellowed the old you."

"Nope, the opposite in fact. I'm more bitter and pissed off with the world than I ever was before."

"That's a shame," said David sadly. He placed a hand on Richard's shoulder. "Whatever your mood, it's good to see you again." He glanced at the pilot stepping down from the helicopter. "Hi, Lev, did you bring the supplies we requested?"

The pilot lit a cigarette and aimed a thumb at the helicopter. "All in the back."

"Give us a hand to unload, Richard. All the others are out working the ground."

After the supplies had been unloaded and stored in one of the tents, the helicopter lifted into the air and flew away.

Rubbing the base of his aching back, Richard glanced around the site. "Where's this rock you think might be a meteorite you want me to examine?"

David pointed towards a section of crumbling cliff. "Over by the edge. It's too large to move. Follow me. On the way I have something special to show you."

Richard followed his brother along a path formed by the passing of many boot-clad feet. After scrambling over a large section of rough ground, they climbed a mound of hard-packed earth dotted with tufts of coarse grass. Richard gazed over at a group of people gathered under a canopy stretched across metal poles. David descended the mound and strode towards them with Richard following.

After David had introduced his brother to his team, he led Richard to the wide pit they were currently excavating and waited for him to gaze at the spectacular find.

Impressed more than he had imagined he would be, Richard wrinkled his nose at the stench rising from the pit—like wet dog times a hundred on the reek-meter—and roamed his eyes over what the team were busy exposing. The large hairy beast was amazingly well-preserved. He stared into the face of the woolly mammoth looking up at him, as if it was asleep and could wake at any moment. He altered his gaze to something a man and a woman were working on beside the enormous beast. He took in the animal's large size, a little over a meter high at the shoulder and two meters long, its large paws tipped with long claws. A formidable beast.

"Impressive, isn't it," commented David. "It's a cave lion, and there's two of them." He shuffled Richard around the side of the pit and pointed out a claw protruding from beneath the mammoth's back. "They were attacking it when the mammoth fell on it. We believe a flash-freeze event froze them in their attack, preserving them to this day. It's now a race to free them from the permafrost and preserve them before the rotting process held at bay for thousands of years claims them."

"It's a spectacular find, David, and you and your team are to be congratulated," complimented Richard, genuinely impressed. "Pity is, it makes my rock from the sky rather boring in comparison."

There were a few good-natured chuckles from the gathered group.

David placed a hand on Richard's shoulder. "Let's go look at your meteorite. I think you will be surprised when you see it and will find it as exciting to you as our mammoth and lions are to us."

Richard followed his brother farther across the site and nearer the edge of the crater. Rising high above, the cliff revealed thousands of layers of sediment marked out by strips of various shades of brown. It was like looking at a cross section of tree rings made of soil. In a few areas close to the top was what seemed to be roots or rotted vegetation hanging out from the side of the cliff.

"It's just over there."

Richard turned his attention on his brother and followed him along a rough gully and over two mounds of muddy thawing tundra. After passing around a pile of what looked to be recently excavated earth, he saw it. Immediately he realized if it was a meteorite it was something very special. He moved to the green rock and ran a hand over its rough surface. It was beautiful. He examined each side until he found what he was looking for. He ran excited fingers over the wrinkled glassy coating on one face of the rock that was obviously a fusion crust, a kind of glaze formed when the rock was heated during its passage through Earth's atmosphere.

Noticing Richard's smile and his hard-to-miss excitement, David said, "It seems it's not such a boring rock after all."

Richard smiled at his brother. "Far from it. There will have to be tests to confirm it one way or the other, but from what I can tell from my initial examination is that this" —he slapped the rock with a hand— "is special and might surprise us all."

David was genuinely astounded. "I had an inkling it might be something extraordinary and not a typical meteorite, which is why I called you. Is it rare?"

Richard nodded. "I have a good feeling it is, but I'll need some of my tools and equipment to carry out a few tests. We also need to work out how it can be moved and transported to England."

David glanced up at the approaching grey clouds and the dimming light. "All that might have to wait until tomorrow as it looks like we might be in for some bad weather, strong winds and perhaps snow. Also night is drawing in."

"Though I'm keen to get working on it, it's waited a few thousand years to be discovered, so I can wait a few hours."

"I also expect you're hungry after your long journey."

"I am. What's for dinner?"

David grinned. "Your favorite, humble pie."

Richard laughed. "Perfect. I think I need a huge plateful."

Pleased his brother's mood had changed to a more cheery and positive outlook, David led him back to camp.

CHAPTER 13

EV1Lution

Sven dragged his eyes away from the exciting story in Horror Island and glanced through the window at the early evening gloom descending on the desolate landscape. His watch revealed his comrades had been gone for three hours. Wondering what they were doing, he placed the book aside, climbed off the sofa and walked to the coal fire highlighting the room in its cozy red glow. After adding more coal, he slipped on his warm coat, grabbed the binoculars hanging on a nail beside the door, and went outside. He crossed to the road and peered through the binoculars at the distant buildings and focused on the cab of the truck parked by the entrance. It was empty. A sweep of the compound revealed it to be just as vacant.

Surmising that something must have happened at the facility to hold the men there for so long, he turned his head at Makar's covered motorcycle. Deciding on his path of action, he nipped inside the hut, slipped on Makar's driving goggles, slung over his shoulder the rifle he had thus far only fired at inanimate targets, slipped a flashlight into his pocket and went outside. He dragged off the motorcycle's thermal cover, sat astride the seat and kickstarted it into life. The engine roared like a powerful beast waking from a long slumber. He clicked it into first gear with his foot and pulled away, spraying a jet of soil in his wake when he throttled the powerful machine along the track.

Slowing down when he reached the compound, Sven steered the bike through the gates and circled the truck before stopping beside the building's entrance. He switched off the engine, raised the googles and looked at the key card protruding from the electronic lock. Kicking the stand out, he climbed off the bike and approached the door. He slipped the key card out and reinserted it. When the door buzzed, Sven pushed it open. Leaning in, he cast an anxious glance into the empty room.

Though he had no idea what had brought the men here so hastily or caused them to remain for so long, he no longer felt they were playing a game on him. He slipped his rifle from his shoulder, checked it was ready to fire and walked to the elevator. The doors swished open with a press of the call button. He entered and rode it down to Level 1.

The old elevator jerked to a halt. The doors opened. Lit by the elevator's dim light spilling into the corridor, Sven stepped out and nervously peered at the darkness stretching deeper into the facility. He fished the flashlight from his pocket, switched it on and aimed it along the corridor. The beam glinted off glass shards littering the floor. He frowned worriedly at the discovery that someone had broken the lightbulbs. He knew that was something his comrades wouldn't have been responsible for. Pushing back the anxiety that urged him to leave, he raised his weapon and careful to avoid treading on the broken bulbs that would warn anything down here of his approach, he moved along the corridor.

When his light picked out the skeleton, he cautiously approached. He picked out scraps of clothing and partially melted shoes that identified it wasn't one of his comrades. Assuming it was one of the scientists who worked here and wondering what had killed the man, he pushed away the images of monsters that invaded his thoughts and warily pressed on.

After a few turns, Sven's light fell on something ahead. He approached with caution. Saddened by what he saw, he halted by the four skeletons strewn across the floor. Though he couldn't identify them by their fleshless bones, the scraps of clothing and four discarded weapons, identical to the one held in his trembling hands, labelled them as his comrades. Horrified that someone could have done such a thing, Sven contemplated his next move. He should leave and contact someone in authority to let them know what had happened. If the four men with vastly more experience than him had fallen at the hands of whatever killer was down here, human or otherwise, he wouldn't stand a chance.

Sven was about to retreat when he halted and cocked an ear to the noise drifting along the corridor from around the turn in the passage a short distance ahead. Careful to avoid shining the light towards the noise to give away his presence, Sven stared at the turning. Whatever was making the noise, it didn't seem to be moving. Curiosity, stupidity, and the chance of becoming a hero—the man who took down a savage cold-hearted killer—moved him towards the corner.

Halting at the end of the corridor, Sven stood tight against the wall and contemplated the squelching, sucking sounds that were now much louder. They reminded him of walking in boots sodden with water while trudging through thick, sloshy mud that sucked at your feet; both were discomforts he had experienced during his army training. Pushing away the imagined visions of possible horrors that might be creating the sounds, Sven steeled himself for what he was about to encounter and peered nervously around the corner.

Because darkness concealed whatever produced the unnerving sounds, Sven risked using his flashlight. He froze in fear at the terrible thing caught in the flashlight's beam.

The squelching sounds came from within a bulbous, black, pulsating cocoon suspended from the ceiling. As his frightened gaze took in the monstrosity he had difficulty comprehending, a tube sprouted from the base and bulged when something slithered through its length and dropped onto the floor with a squishy thud.

Rooted to the spot by his fear, Sven stared at the ejected, misshapen glossy black ball. After a few moments of inactivity, it slowly unfurled into a worm which then changed shape, shrinking to form a fatter mass. Four tendrils stretched out into legs with clawed feet. A tail, short and stubby grew out from its rear as a short neck pushed from the front and grew a head. After it had struggled onto its newly formed legs, it yawned its teeth-lined jaws and screeched a high-pitched squeal. Panic motivated Sven's sprinting retreat for the exit.

As EV1L dropped from the ceiling, it changed into its previous bipedal creature form and stared after the retreating sounds of glass-crunching footsteps. It looked at its new born offspring and hissed a command. EV1L 2.0 sprang into action and bounded around the corner after the fleeing footsteps.

Panting from fear and panic, Sven careened around a corner and sprinted along the corridor. He aimed the flashlight behind when sounds of pursuit reached him. The small, monstrous...*thing* was chasing him. A new influx of adrenalin spurred him forwards. He punched the elevator button and heard the winch start up. He cursed the elevator that had returned to the upper level. He spun when crunching glass announced the creature's approach. With the rifle on full auto, he sprayed the creature with bullets.

The creature screeched and stumbled when bullets tore through it and peppered the floor and walls behind. Sven released his finger from the trigger, his ears ringing from the gunfire echoing through the constricting corridors and stared at the creature full of holes lying still. He had killed it. He sobbed in dismay when the holes closed, and the creature unsteadily regained its footing.

Sven threw his flashlight at the creature and rushed into the elevator as soon as the doors were open wide enough. After frantically stabbing the upper level button, he aimed his weapon at the narrowing door gap and fired when the creature appeared. When the force of the bullets slammed it against the wall, the creature splattered into a dark stain. The doors closed. The elevator vibrated into motion. Trembling, Sven collapsed against the side. *What in hell's name was that thing?*

Whatever it was, Sven was certain it wasn't something Mother Nature had created. He believed either the scientists had created it in their laboratory or it came from another world. Sven was inclined to believe the latter. He had just battled with something from outer space, an alien.

Sven rushed from the building, slipped the strap of his weapon over his shoulder and leapt onto the motorbike. He kicked it into life and spinning a rooster tail of earth into the air behind him, he roared through the gates.

CHAPTER 14

Plea for Help

The Communications Security Establishment Canada (CSEC), now located in the architecturally spectacular new Ottawa headquarters, had cost Canadian taxpayers almost $1.2 billion. Linked to covert spying posts around the world that relayed information back to central command, the data it gathered variously was reviewed and filed away or disseminated to the relevant organization to be acted upon.

One of CSECs almost two thousand employees housed in the technologically advanced listening post sipped her lukewarm coffee as she listened to the boring chatter between two German politicians conversing on mobile phones in Berlin. As her eyes flicked to the silent flashing red alert on her screen, a finger automatically moved and tapped the icon to send the reason for the notification to her headphones. After listening to the live Russian conversation between a frantic soldier informing his superior of the event that had just taken place, which she found hard to believe, she copied the recorded message onto a secure thumb drive, switched her listening station to *Unattended* and headed for her supervisor's office.

*****

When the select few invited to the secret meeting in the White House's Oval Office were ready, President Conner nodded to his Chief of Staff, Samuel Hopkins. Hopkins pressed play on the portable recorder on the President's desk and stood back. All eyes focused on the player when a man, his voice tinged with obvious fear, began talking frantically in Russian. Interspersed into the conversation was the calmer, male voice of the person in authority the other man had contacted.

When the conversation ended, Hopkins pressed pause. "What follows is the less agitated English transcript of the call." He restarted the player.

"This is comrade Sven Kulikov stationed at Checkpoint Siberia 5. There is an urgent situation here. Deaths have occurred. I need to speak to someone from command."

(A woman's voice.) "Hold the line, Comrade Kulikov."

(Unknown voice of authority. Male.) "Comrade Kulikov, what is your situation?"

"Something's happened at the Kamera, sir. My comrades have been killed. Slaughtered."

"Explain how this happened and by whom."

"Yes, sir. While my four comrades entered the facility, I remained at my post..."

"Why did they enter the facility?"

"Reason unknown, sir. When I hadn't heard from them after three hours, I went to investigate. I entered the facility and found the bodies of a scientist and my comrades stripped of flesh. Only their bones remained. On hearing a noise along the corridor, I approached and came across a... I have no idea what it was."

"Describe it, Comrade."

"It was a large black bag, a cocoon I think, that hung from the ceiling. Something was moving inside, then a black worm dropped out."

"A worm, Comrade? Have you been drinking?"

"No, sir. I'm one of the few Russians that don't like vodka. It was definitely wormlike—as long as my arm and as thick as my wrist. But it didn't remain a worm for long. It changed into a creature like I've never seen before. It was alien, sir. Not of this Earth."

"Alien? Really, Comrade?"

"Yes, sir, I'm certain of that. It was small, cat size, though looked nothing like a cat. It had big teeth and looked like a devil. Scaly, no fur."

"Then what happened?"

"It chased me. I shot it, but the bullets went straight through it without killing it. I barely managed to escape."

"This...thing, this creature, is it still in the facility?"

"Yes, sir."

("Translator: A 42-second pause.")

"Comrade Kulikov, you are to remain by the phone and await further instructions. Contact no one, understand?"

"Yes, sir."

The line went dead.

("Translator: After eleven minutes and fourteen seconds the conversation continues.")

"Comrade Kulikov."

"Yes, sir."

"When you were in the facility did you notice any strange pistol-sized weapons?"

"Er, no, sir. Because of the alien I didn't venture inside very far. Sorry, sir."

"We have tried contacting the facility to no avail. From what you witnessed inside and finding one dead scientist, do you believe all who were working there have perished?"

"I'm not sure, sir. As I said, I didn't go very far, and I only came across the remains of one scientist and my four comrades."

"No matter, Comrade. Your orders are to remain at your post and keep the facility under observation. If this creature you encountered tries to leave you must do everything in your power to stop it, but don't harm or kill it. Under no circumstances are you to re-enter the facility. A team of specialists will arrive within twenty-four hours to take command and capture it for research. You are to inform no one else about this incident, understood?"

"Yes, sir. I understand."

(The line goes dead.)

General Nathanial Colt raised his eyes skeptically. "Is this on the up?"

Hopkins shrugged. "As far as we can tell, yes. The facility where this took place was called Laboratory 12 before becoming known simply as *'The Kamera,'* or as we would say, *The Chamber,* under Stalin. Located in the remote Siberian tundra, we believe it was decommissioned sometime in the seventies and later used to store confidential documents from the Stalinist era. It has obviously now been brought back into service for another purpose."

"What was The Kamera's original purpose?" asked Colt.

"It was once used for the creation and testing of chemical and biological warfare agents, and later, under the administration of the Soviet secret police, it was where the Russians created exotic poisons used to kill dissidents in hideous and mostly untraceable ways."

"That though is not the reason for its reopening," said the President. "We believe the *strange weapons* mentioned in the conversation we just heard are the alien weapons the Russian salvage team collected from the spaceship in Antarctica. We believe The Kamera is where the Russians planned to reverse engineer them."

"That doesn't explain this...*thing* that killed the Russian soldiers and scientist and maybe everyone who worked there," said Colt.

"Based on the conversation, we also believe," said Hopkins, "that along with two light-blaster pistols the Russians have, they also have in their possession a species of alien from the spaceship."

"It was this creature, this alien, that must have escaped from whatever confinement the Russians caged it in and killed some or all of the facilities' personnel," added the President.

"Our concern," continued Hopkins, "is that we have no idea what threat this creature poses humanity if it escapes from the Russian facility and reaches civilization. We've all read the reports on the types of alien creatures the scientists and salvage team encountered in the spaceship. None of them are the type that should be loose to feed upon humanity."

Everyone in the room agreed.

Colt faced the President. "Have you contacted the Russians about this, Mr. President? Or is it something you are considering?"

"That is one of the reasons for this meeting. Whoever the man at the command post spoke to, by his reaction, it was obvious he had no knowledge of the alien at the secret facility. This might indicate only the higher echelons of the Russian government are aware of its existence and why they selected such a remote outpost to study it. What I need to hear from you, Colonel, are our options because I am unwilling to believe the Russians have the situation under control."

Colt pondered the dilemma for a few moments before answering. "If contacting the Russians doesn't give you confidence, Mr. President, that they can reliably contain the alien creature and thus prevent it from perhaps signaling the end of humanity, then I foresee only two options open to us.

One, we destroy the facility with a targeted airstrike, which will obviously upset the current diplomatic relationship, such as it is, you have with the Russians, and two—my favored option—we send in a covert strike force to kill the creature, which may involve destroying the facility to ensure the alien threat is neutralized."

It seemed by President Conner's speedy reply that he had already considered the options presented by Colonel Colt. "I also favor the covert strike force option. A small team goes in, neutralizes the threat as best they see fit when they are on the scene, and gets out before the Russians are any the wiser. They may suspect we are involved, but without any evidence, it will be speculation I can comfortably deny."

"Then I have your permission to proceed with the mission, Mr. President?" confirmed Colt.

Conner nodded. "Proceed with all haste, Colonel. As the Russian team is expected to arrive at the Kamera facility within twenty-four hours, I suggest the team of your choosing completes the mission within twelve—preferably sooner."

Though with the flight time to Russia Colt knew it would be tight, he nodded his understanding and strode from the Oval office.

"You are aware there's going to be fallout from this," said Hopkins.

President Conner nodded. "I am, but I can handle a bit of Russian flack—the end of humanity because I failed to act, not so much."

CHAPTER 15
Abduction

Bright and early the following morning, Richard returned to the meteorite to examine it more thoroughly. Aware silicate mineral laced with chromium colored the meteorite its peculiar green, Richard gazed at the impressive rock that could hopefully repair in part his ruined reputation. Most meteorites were stony, almost all, around ninety percent, are termed *ordinary chondrites,* small, un-melted asteroids that are uniform in composition throughout. Richard examined all the faces of the rock David's team had cleared of soil. It was without doubt a type of meteorite called an *achondrite*, which made it an exceptional discovery. Achondrites are pieces of large asteroids or planets at least 200 kilometers in diameter and make up only five percent of the meteorites that have been found.

Richard couldn't wait to have the rock tested with a scanning electron microscope energy-dispersive spectrometer to accurately identify the chemical composition of the rock. From that and other tests, its origin should be able to be determined. However, there were a few tests he could do in the field that weren't as precise that would give him a sense of its composition.

He spent the next hour setting up his equipment, drilling a hole and collecting the dust, which he placed in a test tube and added chemicals that would break it down. While the chemicals went to work, Richard switched on the laptop and plugged in the probe that would read the chemical makeup of the sample and transfer the information to the computer software to reveal some of its secrets.

After the allotted time, Richard placed the thin probe into the meteorite slurry and clicked the software's analyze sample icon. Almost immediately, the data appeared on the graph displayed on the screen. Richard read through it twice. The meteorite's chemistry was highly unusual. High in magnesium and low in iron, the readings seemed familiar. He switched to another window, opened his documents folder and opened a report from NASA's Messenger probe, which had recently surveyed the surface of Mercury from orbit to determine its chemistry. He scrolled to the chemical graph down the page and glanced at the readings. Though his sample had *plagioclase*, an aluminum-containing mineral, and plotted strange in oxygen isotope space, both results were suspiciously similar.

Richard looked at the meteorite with fresh eyes and excitement. “Have you travelled all the way from Mercury?” If it had, it was spectacular discovery and more than he could have hoped for.

A deep thrumming cast his eyes to the sky. In the distance a helicopter headed towards the crater. After watching it for a few moments, Richard returned his attention back to something far more interesting, his possible Mercury meteorite.

*****

Gathered around the excavation of the mammoth and cave lions under the makeshift tent, the team's conversations fell to silence at the sound of an approaching thrumming.

“That's a helicopter,” stated Crookshank.

Gilmore looked at David. "I didn't know we were expecting visitors or supplies?"

David shook his head as he stood. "We're not."

The thrumming increased as the helicopter drew nearer. The plastic tent cover protecting the dig site flapped so violently from the rotors downwash, they feared it might be yanked from its moorings. David and a couple of his colleagues stepped from beneath the cover and observed the large unmarked helicopter swoop in a low circle and hover. A man leaning out the rear door roamed binoculars over them and then at the few team members working a short distance away. Another man tapped the one with the binoculars on the shoulder and pointed towards the cliff. After refocusing his gaze at the indicated position, the helicopter headed for whatever had caught their attention. It hovered across the crater, and three men slid down on ropes.

"Wait here," ordered David. "I'm going to see what this is all about." He strode away towards the helicopter.

*****

Richard closed the lid of his laptop and clasped it to his chest when the helicopter swooped nearer and hovered a short distance away. Wondering what the damn fools were doing, he shielded his eyes from the downdraft kicking up swirling dust and ice particles and gazed up at the man staring down from the open door. When three ropes were dropped, and three men slid down them, he knew something bad was about to happen. Thinking they had come for his meteorite, he glanced at the rock he believed was about to stolen from him. As the helicopter turned away and hovered above a raised piece of ground, Richard scrutinized the man leading the other two towards him. Recognizing his face, he groaned. It was worse than he had thought.

"Hello, Richard."

"What the hell are you doing here, Colbert?"

“We came for you.”

“Me? Not my meteorite.”

Colbert’s eyes flicked to the green rock and back at Richard. “You can keep your pretty rock, but you’re coming with us,” ordered Seal Team Commander Colbert.

Richard looked past Colbert at the other two SEALs, armed and menacing. “And why would I do that?”

“You don’t have a choice,” replied Colbert curtly. “You either come willingly or by force.”

“Hang on a damn minute,” argued David, barging past the two SEALs.

One of the armed soldiers thrust a hand at David’s chest, halting him. “That’s near enough.”

David pushed the arm away and focused on Colbert. “Who are you and what gives you the right to barge in here and harass a member of my team?”

Keen to hear the answers, Richard looked at Colbert expectantly.

“That is none of your business,” said Colbert. “Richard, get on the helicopter.”

“He will do no such thing,” argued David, stepping closer to Colbert.

The nearest armed SEAL held his weapon menacingly.

Richard held up a hand, calming the man. “It’s okay, David, I don’t believe I have a choice.” He looked at Colbert. “I assume this has something to do with the alien spaceship our governments categorially deny exists.”

“Just get on the damn helicopter, Richard, before I drag you onboard.”

“Stay where you are, Richard,” ordered David, stepping forward to block Colbert’s path. “I demand you leave immediately.”

Colbert smiled. “Happy to oblige.” He looked at Richard. “Move!”

David went to protest but found himself restrained by one of the SEALs.

Richard walked over to David and handed him his laptop. “Don’t worry, brother, it’s not the first time I’ve been kidnapped. I’ll be fine.” He glanced back at the rock. “Can you gather up my equipment and I’ll finish off when I return.” He glanced at Colbert. “I will be returning, won’t I?”

“As soon as you’ve completed what we want you to do, you will be brought back here.”

“How long will that take,” asked David, reluctantly accepting the situation.

Colbert shrugged. “A few hours at most.”

“Let’s get this over with then,” said Richard. He headed for the hovering helicopter, climbed onboard and glanced around at the serious stares the men gave him. He smiled at Ramirez and Sullivan. “Did you miss me?”

Ramirez scowled. “Not for as long as I hoped.”

Richard was pushed along the seat when Colbert climbed in and sat beside him. As soon as everyone was back onboard, the helicopter lifted into the air and flew away.

Richard looked down at the worried and confused expression his brother wore. He obviously wondered what the hell was happening. Richard smirked. Welcome to my world, brother.

After putting on his own headset, Colbert grabbed another hanging from the ceiling and thrust it at Richard.

Richard slipped on the headset and adjusted the mic until it was near his mouth. “So, Colbert, who’s responsible for my abduction this time?”

Colbert smiled at him. “Me.”

Richard’s eyebrows rose in surprise. “I didn’t think you liked me?”

“I don’t, but you have this uncanny knack of surviving against the alien creatures we encountered in Antarctica and the mission I am currently in command of might need all the help it can get. Like me, you have also faced this type of creature before and survived.”

"So, it is to do with the spacecraft. Has it been salvaged from the ocean floor?"

"No, it's still there, though I believe a feasibility study is being carried out to determine if salvaging it is even possible."

"It's not Little Lucifer you took from me is it? Has it grown into a hideous, vicious monster you want me to calm with my loving personality?"

Colbert scoffed. "It's to do with that black alien we encountered on the boat."

Richard's thoughts briefly relived the moment. "I thought we destroyed it."

Colbert nodded. "We did, but it seems there was another one the Russian salvage team captured and brought back to Russia with them. It also might be a completely different but similar type of alien. Details are sketchy, and we'll only find out when we meet it."

The penny partly dropped for Richard. An alien creature was in Russia. Of all the places he had chosen to come to, it was the one where an alien creature resided. Though he supposed the SEALs could abduct him from anywhere. "What exactly is the mission you so desperately want my help with?"

"The alien was taken to a secret underground facility about two hundred kilometers from here. All we know is what we've gleaned from an intercepted call for help from the only survivor of the five-man team of Russian soldiers that went inside. It isn't much. It seems that a black creature able to reform into different species is running loose and has probably killed everyone that worked there. Our mission is to enter, seek out the creature and destroy it. Failing that, we will destroy the facility to prevent it from escaping."

"And you need me, why?" asked Richard. "You know I'm not a team player and will do anything to ensure I survive, even if that means sacrificing some of you. Yet you still want me on your team. It makes no sense."

"I guess it's a case of better the devil you know," answered Colbert. "You have encountered more of these alien creatures and survived than anyone else on the planet, which makes you an expert. I and some of my men were chosen for this mission based on our experiences with the alien creatures, and I believe your unique brand of self-preservation strategy may enable us all to successfully complete the mission with minimum loss of life."

It was Richard's turn to snort. "Good luck with that." He glanced around at the men staring at him. "From my experiences with alien creatures, you are all dead men walking. You should blow it up with one of your big bombs instead of all this foolhardy nonsense, which I assure you will not end well."

"Remember, Richard, it's only one creature," said Colbert. "You, and some of us, faced much worse."

Richard wasn't convinced. "Do I get a weapon this time?"

Colbert grinned. "What do you think?"

Richard shrugged.

"In case you need to scream for help, I'll introduce you my team," said Colbert.

Richard rolled his eyes.

"You, Ramirez and Sullivan are old buddies, so no intro needed. At the end there is Mason, then Buckner and opposite you, Dalton."

Richard looked at each man in turn. There wasn't a smile amongst them. However the mission turned out, it wasn't going to be fun. He gazed out at the tundra passing below while he wondered if he would survive his third encounter with the spaceship's alien monstrosities.

CHAPTER 16

Ingress

Peering through binoculars, Mason scanned Checkpoint Siberia 3's compound and swept them up to the top of the lookout tower. He focused on the man training his gaze upon the secret facility half a kilometer away. The Russian lookout had to be Sven Kulikov, the soldier who had called for help earlier. After he had scanned the area a second time and spotted no evidence of anyone else present, Mason headed closer.

Though Mason was confident from Sven's intercepted conversation with his superior that the Russian was alone, his comrades killed when they entered the underground base, it had taken SEAL Team 5 a little over eleven hours to get here. Aware of the other checkpoints stretched along the road that may have sent soldiers to reinforce Sven's soldier-depleted post, Mason switched his gaze back and forth from the door of the hut that light shone from and the sentry in the tower.

Mason moved past the simple road barrier and took position in the covered garage. He glanced at the twin set of tyre tracks that led out and stretched along the road, evidence the truck that had taken Sven's comrades to their deaths was once stored here. He lifted the edge of the thermal cover to discover a motorbike beneath. It looked old but well maintained. He moved to the edge of the building to observe the sentry. Climbing the tower without being detected by the Russian wasn't possible. Though he could easily pick off Sven with his rifle from here, their orders were clear; unless it was unavoidable, they were to avoid killing any Russians.

His eyes flicked to the latrine and back to Sven. However, the clock was ticking away the limited time they had to complete the mission before reinforcements arrived. If Sven didn't come down for a piss or visit the hut to get warm or eat soon, he'd have no option but to take him out.

*****

Sven shivered against the cold that somehow found its way under his layers of clothing to crawl across his skin and suck the warmth from his body. He paced around the small exposed platform in an attempt to reinstate some warmth into his body, but again it failed to chase away the chill that seemed to have seeped into his bones. He glanced down at the inviting light seeping from the windows of the hut and then at the smoke the icy breeze whipped away as soon as it drifted from the confines of the flue. Sven pictured the coal fire at its base and the promise of warmth it offered.

Sven placed the binoculars to his eyes and again focused on the facility's entrance. It hadn't changed. No activity and no evidence to tell anything had passed through it. He had retired to his bed when darkness fell, bringing with it a drastic drop in temperature, but thoughts of the creature attacking him while he slept had caused him a restless night. He glanced at the moody sky. Gray clouds blocking the sunlight would make for another typical day on the Siberian tundra, cold and gloomy, matching his mood.

Convinced whatever the thing was that had killed his comrades wasn't about to venture forth into the cold, Sven decided to wait a few more minutes before he climbed down the tower to get warm and fix himself something to eat.

*****

Mason glanced at his watch. Their twelve-hour deadline to complete the mission was ticking away. He couldn't wait any longer. He raised his rifle and aimed at the sentry's head. As his finger pressured the trigger, the Russian moved to the ladder and began climbing down. Mason lowered the weapon, moved back a few steps so he wouldn't be seen, and waited.

When Sven reached for the hut's door handle, he gasped at something cold pressed against his neck.

"Remain calm, do as I say, and you will live," ordered Mason firmly but quietly in Russian. "Try anything, or disobey me, and you will die. Understand?"

Sven nodded.

"Is anyone else inside?"

Sven shook his head.

"Open it."

Sven turned the handle and pushed the door open.

Keeping his Sig Sauer P226 pistol pressed against the man's skin and using Sven's body as a shield, Mason peered into the gloomy interior as he disarmed the Russian. He prodded the man inside and swept his gaze around the room. Keeping Sven between himself and anyone who might suddenly appear, Mason crossed to the only other door and searched the bunkroom. Satisfied they were alone, he shut the bunkroom door, and herded Sven over to the table, the evidence of an interrupted card game spread across its top. "Sit."

Wondering why the American soldier was here and if he was about to die, Sven sat and anxiously watched the

American move to the other side of the table, the weapon aimed at him never moving from his chest.

Mason sat across from the Russian and stared into the man's eyes when he spoke to him in Russian. "Now, Sven, I am going to ask you a few questions. Some I already know the answer to, so don't lie or I will cause you pain."

Surprised the man knew his name and worried he might be tortured if he resisted, Sven nodded anxiously. "I will tell you truth."

"Good. Are there any soldiers in the facility?"

Sven shook his head. "Nyet. All dead."

"What about the people that work there?"

Sven shrugged and answered in English. "I think also all dead."

"Good, you speak English. We know reinforcements are coming, but do you know when they will arrive?"

"Last night I was told they come in next twenty-four hours, but this Russia. Anything possible. Might arrive in ten minutes or one week."

Mason touched his radio mic. "Mother Goose, you are clear to proceed. Facility is clear of soldiers. Civilian presence unknown but believed dead. Likelihood of reinforcements arriving early high. Suggest you proceed with all haste. Will advise with updated details on the creature when I have them."

"Understood, Eagle 4, proceeding to facility," affirmed Colbert.

Mason refocused on his prisoner. "Now, Sven, tell me everything you know about this creature that killed your comrades."

*****

The helicopter, as nondescript as the camouflage clothing the SEAL team wore, passed over Checkpoint Siberia 3 and turned towards the distant structure bathed in gloomy daylight. To bring light to the shadows, the pilot, Ethan Kelly, switched on the forward spotlight when he circled the compound. Windblown dust passed through the bright beam that swept over the unassuming cluster of agricultural buildings. The only hint that they might be used for a purpose other than some type of farming was the security fencing around the perimeter.

Colbert focused on the truck parked by the entrance. The soldiers who arrived in it yesterday were now dead. Though concerned he might soon face another of the alien creatures he had battled with on the ship, Colbert focused on the mission and ordered the pilot to land. As soon as the helicopter touched ground, the doors slid open and SEALs piled out with weapons ready to fire.

Sullivan and Kessler split off from the pack and moved to the smaller building attached to the side of the larger structure. Inside they found a diesel generator and a large diesel storage tank raised on a metal platform. One of the fuel feed pipes leading from the tank was attached to the generator while a slightly thicker one disappeared into the concrete floor.

Sullivan crossed to the silent generator, laid a hand on it and glanced at Kessler. “Cold.”

“Might be a backup for a main generator located in the facility,” offered Kessler, looking at the fuel pipe that went through the floor.

The two men returned to the group outside.

While Kelly, the pilot, remained with the powered down helicopter, Commander Colbert, Richard and the other four members of the SEAL team headed for the entrance.

While Ramirez examined the key card lock, Richard seized his last chance to try and convince Colbert to change his mind. “I really don’t see the point of including me on your reckless mission. Let me wait here with your pilot, and if you need my advice, contact me over the radio.”

Colbert glared at Richard. "You're coming with us. If you plan on surviving, I suggest you help us defeat what we find down there." He nodded at Kelly standing by the helicopter. "Because if we don't and you return above ground on your own, you won't be leaving."

Richard looked at the pilot, who shot him a knowing smirk and tapped his rifle. "That's hardly fair with the dangerous nature of this suicide mission. I can hardly be held responsible if the alien kills you all, can I?"

"That, Richard, is why you are here. To help ensure that doesn't happen."

Richard shrugged. "Don't say I didn't warn you when the shit hits the fan and slaps you in the face." He glanced around at the powerful assault rifles the soldiers held. "I really think it would be better if I had a weapon."

"You're not getting one because I don't trust you not to shoot us all in the back."

Richard smiled at Colbert. "Good, you're learning. There might be hope for you yet."

"They've left the key card in the lock," uttered Ramirez in surprise, pulling out the card and turning it in his hand. "You'd think a secret underground base would be better protected."

"I suppose when you're fleeing from an alien monster, pausing to lock the door isn't a consideration," offered Buckner.

Ramirez reinserted the key card. The door buzzed, and Sullivan pushed it open. With weapon raised, he cautiously entered, and the others followed him inside. After a sweep of the room revealed it to be empty, they focused on the elevator at the far end of the room.

With weapons trained on the doors, Sullivan pressed the call button.

The doors slid open, revealing the empty elevator.

"Buckner, Sullivan, head below," ordered Colbert. "If the exit's clear, send the elevator back up."

"And if it ain't?" questioned Buckner.

"Follow Sullivan's lead," replied Colbert.

The two men entered the lift and rode it down. Sullivan stepped out onto Level 1 before the doors were fully open. The tactical flashlight attached to his MP7 swept both directions of the corridor. It was clear. He poked a lightbulb shard with the toe of his boot and frowned worriedly as he shone the light along the floor. He recognized the broken bulbs twofold purpose; they brought darkness and crunching underfoot would warn anything skulking nearby of their approach. Wondering if the alien creature was responsible, he turned to Buckner and whispered. "Hold the lift while I see what's around the corner."

Buckner nodded, and keeping a foot against the door recessed into the jamb to prevent it from closing, he positioned himself so he could cover both directions with his eyes and weapon.

Sullivan avoided treading on the broken glass when he moved to the corner and peered around the edge into darkness. Moving his weapon forward, he aimed its light along the passage. Apart from broken lightbulbs littering the floor the corridor was empty. He returned to Buckner. "It's clear for as far as I can see. Send it up."

Buckner removed his foot. The doors closed and the elevator automatically returned to the upper level. The others arrived on Level 1 a few moments later.

After Sullivan had made his report, Kessler said, "It's a little worrying that the alien is intelligent enough to smash the lightbulbs. Even if was only to make it dark down here and not warn it someone was coming."

"We could always leave," suggested Richard.

Colbert ignored the remark. "We move slow, steady and cautious and avoid treading on the broken glass as much as possible. Sullivan takes point and we'll follow in his footsteps. If we come across the creature, we'll assess the situation and respond appropriately." Colbert glanced at Ramirez. "Cover our backs and keep an eye on Richard."

Sullivan led them along the corridor and around the corner, checking each room as they went. The skeletal remains of the scientist Sven had mentioned were missing, only scraps of his clothing remained.

Noticing something protruding from a scrap of ragged shirt, Richard knelt and picked up a piece of clothing while palming the object he had spied in his other hand. He sniffed the rag. "Acrid—it's the creature from the spaceship, all right. I remember the smell." Standing, he thrust the rag into Ramirez's face as he slipped the alien pistol into a pocket. "Smell it."

Ramirez pushed Richard's hand away. "Get a move on."

Pleased with the alien treasure he had found that he could sell to a foreign power for an extremely high price—the Chinese for one would surely pay millions for the alien technology—he began to think that being forced to come here might not be so bad after all. He just had to make sure he survived to take full advantage of it.

A little farther through the complex they came to where the bones of Sven's four comrades had lain. Now only scraps of their clothing and weapons remained. Richard reached for one of the Russian rifles, but Ramirez's rifle poking Richard's back prompted him to leave it where it lay.

Continuing on, Sullivan poked his head into another room, scanned it until he was satisfied it was clear, and glanced back at Colbert. "It's the security station."

Colbert entered and glanced at the screens positioned above an antiquated Cold War era console sparsely covered in large buttons. None of the views from the CCTV cameras presently on the nine screens revealed any presence of the scientists or the creature. He focused on one of the two clunky twelve-button keyboards before turning to the door.

"Buckner, swop places with Ramirez, I need him in here."

Ramirez appeared at the door and glanced at the console.

"See if you can flick through different camera views so we can see what we're facing," ordered Colbert.

Unphased by the Cyrillic writing and numbers indicating the controls functions he couldn't read, Ramirez sat in one of the two chairs and began punching buttons.

Colbert crossed to the door. "Everyone except Buckner and Kessler inside."

As the others began filing into the room, Colbert examined the facility's blueprint fixed to a wall. Realizing its usefulness in helping them navigate through the levels, he took a tablet from Ramirez's rucksack and took a photograph. Turning to Richard, he thrust the tablet into the man's hands. "You can be our navigator."

Richard glanced at the small screen. "Gee, thanks."

Colbert crossed to the CCTV console and looked over Ramirez's shoulder as different grainy greyscale views from the low-quality cameras distributed throughout the subterranean complex flickered onto the screens. Colbert's gaze studied each in turn but detected no movement or signs of life, be it human or alien, in any of them.

Ramirez's fingers pressed buttons on the chunky keyboard to show views from other cameras. Movement, nothing more than a fleeting shadow, focused Colbert's gaze on one of the screens.

Colbert pointed at the monitor. "Can you pan that camera? I thought I saw something."

Ramirez glanced at the Russian text in the bottom right corner of the screen that indicated the camera providing the view, pressed the corresponding number indicated on the row of buttons positioned above the keyboard and began moving the joystick.

Everyone in the room stared at screen three when the camera moved. It panned past glass-walled rooms that seemed to be laboratories, and then an empty corridor came into view.

"Nothing there, Commander," said Ramirez.

"Pan down," instructed Colbert.

Slowly something dark and indistinct came into view on the floor. It was difficult to tell if it was formed of shadow or substance. When Ramirez zoomed in, the dark shape sprung at the camera. The view briefly went black before dissolving into static.

"Whatever that thing was, it destroyed the camera," said Ramirez.

Though it was difficult to tell from the low-quality camera feed, Colbert was certain the black thing he had glimpsed was a smaller type of the creature he had encountered from the spaceship in Antarctica. The damn fool Russians had brought it here. "It seems we've found our alien."

"And it now knows we are here and were looking at it," said Richard ominously.

"My Russian isn't that good," said Ramirez, studying the information in the corner of the dark screen, "but I think the camera the alien put out of action is on Level 4, the lowest level."

"Then that's where we'll head," said Colbert. "Ramirez, you remain here and keep us informed of the creature's movements. We'll search each level room by room to check for survivors and make our way down until we find it."

Colbert headed into the corridor.

Before Richard reluctantly followed the others out, he glanced at one of the screens and focused on the small dark creature moving through one of the rooms. At first angry, then resigned to his current predicament, the proof that an alien species was here turned his thoughts to how he could gain a second stream of profit from his forced involvement. If he could collect irrefutable evidence of the existence of an alien entity and reveal it to the world, everyone would know he had been telling the truth about the spaceship in Antarctica. With his reputation repaired and the recognition of being the first person to prove the existence of extraterrestrial life, the fame so cruelly snatched from him before would surely follow.

"Richard, you're with me," ordered Colbert.

As the alien creature moved from the camera's view range, Richard turned away and joined the others heading deeper into the facility and closer to the alien creature that would, along with the sale of the alien weapon, bring him everything he wanted from life: fame, fortune, beautiful women and all the luxuries he could ever need. He ignored the suspicious glare Colbert gave him and moved to the middle of the pack to ensure he was protected on all sides. For the moment he needed their help, but later, maybe not so much. As soon as he had what he required, and it was safe to do so, he would leave this place, even if he had to sacrifice his escort to achieve that. He would also need one of their weapons to persuade the pilot to fly him away from here.

CHAPTER 17

Krisztina

Hoping she had remained hidden long enough for the creature to give up its hunt, Krisztina anxiously cracked open the door of the cramped cupboard where she had taken refuge and peered into the gloomy room lit by two bulkhead wall lights. She gradually opened it wider until she could see most of the storeroom. It was littered with abandoned pieces of equipment and trollies adorned with dangling restraint straps her fear imagined to be tentacles. Calming her anxiety, she scrutinized the patches of shadows for signs of a darker form hidden within. Believing the room to be free of the Black menace stalking her, she plucked up the courage to climb out and headed for the exit.

*****

EV1L 2.0 had been tasked with seeking out the human female that was hiding somewhere on this level. Its reward when it found her was the feast she would provide. Soon its queen would produce more offspring and the rivalry between siblings would soon follow. The human's substance would enable it to grow stronger and increase its mass, giving it an edge over its younger, weaker brethren.

*****

Pressing her face against the small viewing window set in the door, Krisztina's gaze searched her limited outlook of the corridor. She dodged to the side when something small, dark and evil padded into view. Praying the creature would pass on by, she pressed her trembling body against the wall. Her fear shot up a notch when a tar-like liquid oozed beneath the door. Her heart pounded against her chest as panic swept over her. Knowing she would die if she let her panic take control and prompt reckless actions, she calmed her nerves and fearfully watched the menacing puddle flow into the room. When a crude, stretched skeletal face formed in the oozing mass and bulging golf-ball-size eyes, glossy black and malevolent, looked at her, she screamed and grabbed the door handle. The yanked open door bunched up the glutinous Black when it was dragged along with it. Krisztina rushed into the corridor and fled.

EV1L 2.0 shot out a tentacle at its fleeing prey, but lacking the mass required, its reach fell short. It pulled its bunched-up bulk from beneath the door, morphed into its previous creature form and set off in pursuit.

Aware of the Black's ability to separate into different sentient lifeforms, Krisztina thought it likely there were more roaming this level she couldn't risk encountering. Desperate to escape the lower level and notify her superiors of the alien entity—if any of her surviving comrades hadn't already done so—so they could send reinforcements equipped to deal with it, she pondered her options. Due to the alien creature inside that had killed Stanislav, the elevator was no longer a viable means of escape. There remained only one other route open to her. She just had to reach it.

She glanced back fearfully on hearing the padding of small feet on the floor. Drawing nearer with every bound of its small powerful limbs, the swiftly moving creature snarled at her. Krisztina turned away before her trembling legs failed her and glanced at the labels attached to the doors she passed. Relief that she might still survive swept over her when she read the label of the room she sought. Skidding to a halt, she grabbed the handle and urging it not to be locked turned it. The door opened. The repetitive throbbing chug, chug and faint scent of diesel from the generator that provided the facility's power welcomed her. She rushed in and slammed the door shut. Though she doubted it would prevent the creature from gaining entry, it should buy her the few precious seconds she desperately needed.

Krisztina hurriedly crossed to the only other door in the room, which would look more at home in the U-boat it seemed to have been plucked from. She spun the metal wheel that was almost as wide as the door. The rods holding the airtight door in place slowly retreated from their internal docks with protesting squeals.

Krisztina glanced fearfully behind at the Black oozing beneath the door, a single protruding eye watching her. In a few seconds it would be upon her. A hiss of positive pressure air escaping from around the frame signaled the locks were free. She pulled open the door, its hinges stiff from inactivity, and slipped inside. As she pulled the door closed, she glimpsed the Black stretching towards her. The satisfying clang of the door against the frame echoed through the chamber as she spun the wheel, redocking the locking rods.

Hoping the airtight seal would hold the creature at bay, she glanced around the small round chamber as air was pumped into the tall tube to increase the pressure to higher than that outside, a precaution against contaminants filtering throughout the upper levels. The escape chute was warmed by the generator's exhaust fumes being sucked up the hand-width tube running up the side of the shaft. She focused on the metal ladder that would lead her to safety and stared up its towering length lit by dim lights set at intervals.

It stretched so high she couldn't see its end. Though not particularly good with heights, her fear of the Black and the gruesome, painful death it brought outweighed her fear of slipping from the ladder and plummeting to her death. Resolved to the task ahead, Krisztina began her long climb.

Reforming its stretched mass into its preferred creature for its current size, EV1L 2.0 padded over to the door its prey had escaped through. After a few moments studying the door mechanism it had observed the human operate, its head extended from its body on a glutinous tarry thread and formed into a hook it latched onto the wheel. Its paws formed suckers to anchor it to the floor as it pulled. The wheel turned. It shifted the hook to the top spoke of the wheel and repeated the process.

Krisztina glanced below at the metallic squeaks and gazed at the door wheel turning. "You have got to be kidding me."

Fear of what was coming increased the speed of her climb up the towering ladder.

CHAPTER 18

Level by Level

The team of alert Navy SEALs and an anxious Richard out of his depth moved cautiously through the facility's upper level. Pausing at each door, Dalton and Buckner ventured inside each room to check it was clear. The constant halting to search made for slow progress.

Mindful their window of opportunity was ticking away with every second they spent in the secret base, Colbert changed tactics when they reached the elevator that provided access to Level 2 and 3 and the elevator to Level 4.

Colbert informed his team of his decision. "We're running out of time, and as we've seen no sign of the scientists, I think it's safe to assume they've all fallen foul of the alien creature, which for the moment seems to be confined to level 4. We'll head to the laboratories on the lowest level, plant the explosives to kill or trap the creature below ground and leave before Russian reinforcements arrive."

After receiving nods of acknowledgment from his men, he tapped the button on his radio mic. "Eagle 2, we're moving straight to Level 4 to plant the explosives. Any movement on the monitors?"

"Copy that. Nothing on the top levels and no sign of the Russians yet, but that creature we glimpsed has put all of Level 4's cameras out of action. Whether that's because it doesn't like being spied upon or it's up to something it doesn't want us to see, I can't say. I recommend you keep on your guard and expect the unexpected. It might be a trap."

"Understood. Keep me appraised if you spot anything we should be concerned about."

"I have your backs," assured Ramirez.

Colbert glanced around at his men. "Let's do this."

Kessler punched the call button, and they piled inside the elevator.

When they arrived on Level 3, the men roamed their weapons around the corridor as they cautiously stepped out.

Colbert glanced at Richard. "Which way to the Level 4 elevator?"

Richard scrolled the blueprint on the tablet. "Head left, then first right and it's about halfway along the corridor.

Without having to be ordered to do so, Sullivan led them left. He slowed his approach at the right-hand turning and peered cautiously around the corner. His gaze wandered past the elevator doors as he searched the corridor. "It's clear."

The others followed Sullivan along the corridor. They halted at the elevator doors that would take them to the facility's lowest level and stared at the ripped bloodstains clothes dotted with pieces of melted bone.

Sullivan lifted the remains of a long white coat with the tip of his rifle. "Looks like we've found one of the scientists."

Colbert glanced at the charred end of a piece of string and followed its route beneath a bunched-up rug and beneath a cracked open door. He pondered the viewing window obscured with paper and the spyhole in its middle. It seemed the scientists had set a trap for the alien creature.

Pondering their success or failure, he turned to Kessler and pointed at the door.

Kessler nodded his understanding.

Colbert pushed the door open. The two men stepped inside smartly and scanned the room. Finding it was empty of any threat, they returned to the corridor.

When his men had formed a semicircle of firepower around the doors, Colbert pressed the call button. The scent of death and blood wafted out from the parting doors.

*****

Krisztina's body and limbs ached from the climb. Though she wanted to pause for a moment's rest, the thought of the Black below catching her kept her moving. She gripped the cold metal ladder tightly when a strong current of air whooshed over her with a hissing roar, loud within the confines of the chute. The Black had opened the hatch. She shot a fearful gaze below and watched the evil creature enter and look up at her. Its shriek sent an icy chill along her spine. When it leapt onto the curved chute wall, it morphed into an articulated insect-like monstrosity. To Krisztina, it looked like an amalgamation of ant, centipede and scorpion sculptured in an alien design. It clicked the curved pincers jutting from its jaws menacingly, as if informing her they would soon be sinking into her flesh. It was all the encouragement Krisztina needed to snap her out of her terrified frozen state. She climbed.

Without pausing in her frantic climb, Krisztina shot glances down at the creature scuttling up the chute in a circular direction around the wall. It had already covered half the distance separating it from her. She directed her gaze at the hatch still high above. She almost sobbed in despair. The creature would be upon her before she reached it. Fear induced adrenaline drove her on.

The numerous feet of the Black insect clicking on the concrete wall was as unnerving as the clash of the pincers it continually clapped together. Both sounds grew nearer, louder, far too quickly. Breathing heavily from the exertion of pulling her body up the ladder with limbs now leaden and weakening with every rung she climbed, Krisztina faced the fact that if she didn't do something she would die, excruciatingly sliced into strips by the gnashing pincers or melted when the Black seeped over and inside her. Unarmed and lacking the weaponlike appendages of her pursuer, she was at a loss as to what she could do to survive.

She pondered letting go of the ladder and hoping the fall would break her neck, offering a less painful end. She pushed the defeatist thought away. She wasn't ready to give up yet.

When a faint distant shriek drifted up the chute, the clacking of the creature's footfalls suddenly ceased. Krisztina glanced down. The insect had stopped with its vicious head turned below. Sensing the creature's halt was connected to the call she assumed was from the original Black alien, she wasn't going to waste the slim chance it presented and continued climbing.

EV1L 2.0 halted at the call for assistance from its queen and pondered its dilemma. Go to its queen or disobey and continue its pursuit of the human? It looked up at the fleeing female. Desperate for the nourishment she would supply, it ignored its queen's second call and scuttled after her.

The restarted click-clacking signaled the creature's continued pursuit. Moving her tired limbs from rung to rung as fast as she was able, Krisztina looked up at the hatch set in the roof of the chute now barely ten meters away. *Not far now. I can do this. Get to the hatch. Turn the wheel to open it. Climb out, slam it shut and lock it. Then find something to jam the wheel to stop the cleverly adaptive creature from following.*

Her hand grabbed at the wheel as soon as she was within reach. Her arm, tired from the climb, failed to turn the stiff mechanism. Ignoring the scuttling clacks that seemed to have increased in speed, she climbed one rung higher, grabbed one of the wheel's spokes and pulled with all her remaining strength. The extra leverage worked, rewarding her with the metal screech from parts long dormant forced into motion. As she readjusted her grip and turned the wheel again, she looked down at the creature now almost upon her. When it grew level with her feet, it pulled back its head in preparation to strike. Its head darted forward with pincers opened wide to receive her ankle.

Krisztina yanked her feet away. The creature's hard-shelled head clanged on the ladder. With one hand gripping a rung and the other the wheel, Krisztina dangled above the long drop. Hoping her foot would find something solid and not sink into the Black, she kicked out at the creature, striking a hard blow to its—for now—solid head.

Unprepared for the surprise attack, EV1L 2.0's many footed grip slipped from the wall. As it fell, its legs became tentacles that grabbed at the ladder. With its plummet halted, the tentacles pulled it up the ladder.

Aware she only had seconds before the creature was upon her and doubting kicking it again would prove successful now it had tentacles, Krisztina was on the verge of panicking. Sobbing fearfully, she spun the wheel. The slithering of the creature's latest limbs grew ever nearer. Her legs began trembling violently, almost slipping her feet from their tenuous perch. Her bladder threatened to empty its contents when it began clicking its sharp mandibles together, now too close to be of comfort. *Don't panic! Don't panic! Don't panic!* she urged herself, not daring to look down for fear she would freeze in terror.

When the multiple locking pins clunked open, she heaved the door open. Escaping air rushed past her as she scrambled out. As soon as she was clear, she gripped the top of the open hatch and slammed it shut. She heard the creature's frustrated screech and glimpsed the tentacle it stretched towards her, a last desperate attempt to seize its escaping prey. The satisfying clash of the hatch landing in its frame echoed around the room as Krisztina spun the wheel. Aware of the creature's incredible ability to split apart and form separate creatures, she examined the edges of the hatch for the slightest sign that part of the Black had made it through.

Thankfully there was none. Her glance around the room revealed it to be a janitorial and maintenance storage closet. Cleaning chemicals and materials, brooms, mops, a floor polishing machine, boxes of spare lightbulbs, a large box of tools on castors for easy maneuverability, and tins of paints of the few basic colors used throughout the facility, most with drips running down the edges, lay on the shelving racks covering three of the four walls forming the small room.

Krisztina's gaze shot at the hatch when the wheel began to turn. She grabbed a mop, knelt beside the hatch and tugged the wheel closed again. Holding it with one hand to prevent the creature from turning it, she slid the mop handle between two spokes and jammed it against the leg of a shelf unit. She released her grip on the wheel and observed it juddering as the creature below tried to turn it. To double ensure the wheel couldn't be turned and remained locked, Krisztina enforced the first prop with a broom handle jammed through the wheel in a similar fashion. Satisfied the creature couldn't follow her, she let relief sweep over her.

Though she would have liked to lay on the floor and rest, she needed to warn her superiors of what had happened and leave the complex before the Black creatures made their way to the upper levels. She crossed to the door and exited the room.

*****

Failing in its attempts to open the hatch the human had fled through, EV1L 2.0 unwrapped its tentacles from around the wheel, withdrew them into its form and scuttled down the chute to find out what its queen required of it.

*****

Aware more humans had entered the complex and fearing they would again attempt to kill it by using the loud explosive weapons that had nearly brought about its demise previously, EV1L initiated its birthing phase and became female, a queen. Normally she would produce a few offspring as guardians to protect her during the pregnancy cycle, but with the humans making their way down through the levels, she didn't have the time.

She raised her head and let out a long piercing scream to call her single offspring to her. It would guard her until the process was complete. Then her small formidable army would hunt down the humans and absorb their nutrition.

As her mass began making the changes required for the process, she walked through the chamber she had selected to bear her brood and smashed the lights that aided the humans' weak sight. She reached for the iron girder stretching the width of the room and hoisted her bulging body off the floor. As her form morphed into a cocoon, tentacles shot out and anchored her to the ceiling.

When EV1L 2.0 arrived at the dark chamber, it stared at the bulging, pulsating cocoon hanging from the ceiling. Instincts it couldn't disobey now guided its actions. It took sentry by the end of the corridor leading to the birthing chamber, and ready to give up its life in defense of its vulnerable queen, it waited for the younglings to be born.

CHAPTER 19

Early Delivery

Two Russian soldiers at Checkpoint Siberia 2 stepped from their warm hut into the cold air. Moving to the barrier across the track, they aimed their rifles at the approaching headlights. Dazzled by the glare, they followed protocol and waited for the arrival of the vehicle Siberia Check point 1 had informed them was coming.

The driver peered out through the windborne snow splattering his windscreen and studied the armed soldiers. He slowed the truck with a loud hissing of air brakes and halted a short distance from the barrier. He wound down the window when one of the soldiers approached and handed him his official documents.

The soldier took the papers and lazily flicked through them. Though the tanker truck was a day early, it was on their official list, a diesel delivery to the facility at the end of the road. Even out here in the middle of nowhere procedure had to be observed, especially with all the recent activity. He handed the papers back, and hoisting himself up onto the step, he glanced around the cab. Scrunching his nose at the foul stench of body odor wafting over him, he stepped down.

Unaware of the alien infestation in the facility the man was headed for, he waved the driver on.

He nodded at his comrade and the barrier was raised.

The driver wound up his window to keep out the chill, steered the truck through the barrier and roared down the road.

Keen to be out of the cold, the two soldiers returned to their comrades in the warm hut. After removing their coats, one of them crossed to the telephone to let Checkpoint 3 know the tanker was on its way.

*****

After Sven had answered Checkpoint 2's call and returned to his seat, Mason radioed his commander to inform him of the situation.

CHAPTER 20

Birthing Chamber

"Is that a cow?" uttered Buckner, staring at the bones stripped of flesh. Sinews, muscles and viscera lay amidst the large dry bloodstain that covered the elevator floor.

"What's left of one." Sullivan stepped into the elevator and crouched to examine the hole in the top of the large skull. He pointed at the edges. "Whatever devoured it seems to have melted bone to get at the brain."

"What the hell is a cow doing in an elevator?" asked Dalton, his eyes constantly scanning the corridor.

Colbert suspected it was part of the trap the Russian scientists seemed to have set for the alien. "Let's not lose focus, people. We have a mission to complete."

"Mother Goose, be advised a diesel tanker is heading our way. ETA, approximately 35 minutes."

After pondering the news briefly, Colbert replied. "Received Eagle 4. Delay driver at checkpoint until mission completed."

"Understood," confirmed Mason.

Stepping around the scientist's scant remains, the team crowded into the elevator and rode it down. Their attention and weapons focused on the widening gap of the elevator doors sliding open. When nothing attacked, they stepped out into the glare of light shed by the elevator's internal lighting, the only brightness in the dark hall. Eyes and weapons scanned both directions for signs of the creature they knew was down here.

"Seems clear," said Sullivan, lacking the conviction it was. A creature as black as the darkness that might be concealing it would be difficult to spot.

All had been briefed with the available information they had on the alien creature. It was intelligent, dangerous, and had the amazing ability not only to change its form but also to split apart to become separate versions of itself that not only shared the characteristics of its main mass but was just as formidable. In short, it was vicious, adaptable and extremely dangerous—a real badass.

Sullivan glanced at Colbert. "Flashlights or night vision?"

Colbert briefly pondered the merits of each given their situation. Though their NVGs were fitted with the latest high-resolution intensifiers and Pulse IR that bathed the surroundings in infrared to enable them to see in pitch black situations like this, Pulse IR was only effective for a short distance. They wouldn't see the Black coming until it was upon them. "Flashlights."

Multiple beams of light from tactical flashlights attached to assault rifles pierced the darkness.

Colbert moved to Richard and looked at the tablet screen. "Where's the main labs?"

Richard nodded his head along the corridor. "That way."

Colbert touched the screen and zoomed out to view the whole level. To their right was a cluster of laboratories. Opposite and to their left was a series of what looked like cells, storerooms and the main generator. In a hushed voice he called Sullivan over and pointed at the tablet screen. "Take Dalton and distribute the explosive charges this side of the elevator. I'll take the rest of the men, and Richard, and plant the charges this side." He glanced at his watch. "Sixty minutes should be enough time for us to complete the mission and leave, so set the timer for seventeen hundred hours."

Though Sullivan suspected the commander's sixty minutes assessment might be cutting it fine with the alien creature they might have to deal with somewhere down here, he kept his doubts to himself. "Dalton, you're with me."

The two soldiers split from the pack and headed along the corridor.

Richard stared after them. *And it begins*. The splitting of forces made them easier to pick off. Certain men were about to die. His sense of self-preservation went on full alert to ensure he didn't become a casualty of this foolhardy mission.

Commander Colbert led them towards the laboratories.

*****

EV1L 2.o intently observed the humans who had just arrived. It took in their numbers, their weapons and the threat they presented to its queen. It glanced behind into the birthing chamber where its queen was giving birth to the first batch of her hoard that would overrun the humans' world. Its gaze switched to the egg sacs littering the floor. The younglings inside were forming quickly. Ever-changing limbs, bodies and heads pressed against the thin rubbery walls as memories of creatures they had never met were passed on from their queen, implanted into their subconsciousness to be recalled at a moment's notice. Sensing they would soon hatch, EV1L 2.0 turned back to the approaching humans it needed to delay and kill. Avoiding the light beams they swept before them, it slithered up the wall and along the ceiling.

*****

Richard glanced behind at Buckner covering their rear. Since it was imperative that he keep the alien weapon concealed from the others if he hoped to sell it, his gaze fell on the holstered pistol he coveted. He preferred the smaller weapon to the larger rifles he found difficult to control. His experience with the alien menagerie on the spaceship had taught him that even though human weapons hadn't always proved effective against some of the alien species, it did slow most of them down. Though he thought he could snatch the pistol from the quick release holster, Buckner would only take it back. He would have to wait until one of them was killed before he claimed a weapon, something he didn't think would be long in coming.

Richard refocused his attention ahead at the glass walls the SEALs' light beams swept over. They had arrived at the laboratories. God knows what foul deeds the Russians had carried out down here. The remoteness of the underground subterranean complex indicated it would have been something obviously clandestine and likely extremely hazardous. The laboratories screamed bioweapons and germ warfare to Richard, which caused him to worry about any traces of toxins that might still be down here. They could be breathing contaminants in with every breath. They, or at least he, a civilian forced to accompany them, should be wearing HazMat suits.

Colbert raised a fist to halt his team and aimed his flashlight through the layers of glass walls encasing the cluster of hexagonal laboratories, control rooms and preparation chambers. His cautious surveillance halted on a dark object that seemed to be moving slightly, expanding and contracting, alive. It was difficult to discern exactly what it was in the darkness through multiple layers of glass that distorted both the beam and the object his light was focused upon. It would need checking out.

Colbert glanced at Buckner and Kessler as he quietly issued his orders. “Place the charges around the laboratories with the timer set for seventeen hundred hours. That gives us fifty-six minutes to complete the mission and leave. If anything moves that isn’t human, shoot it.”

The two men headed for the nearest laboratory.

Colbert took the tablet from Richard and stowed it. He then unholstered his pistol and handed it to Richard, who eagerly took it. “It’s time to put your expertise to use.” He nodded to Richard to go first. “Because I still don’t trust you enough not to panic, shoot me in the back and flee, I’ll be watching you.”

Richard, surprised he was now armed, smiled at Colbert as he walked past. *You kidnapped me and brought me here by force. You shouldn’t trust me at all.*

*****

Pressed flat on the ceiling, the eyes in the puddle of Black hungrily watched the humans below when they separated, increasing its chances of success. Picking out its first victims, EV1L 2.0 waited until the two groups had put some distance between each other before releasing its grip on the ceiling. As it dropped, it morphed into a creature with the semblance of a spider monkey minus the cuteness of the species. Talons grew from its paws and six-inch porcupine-like spikes grew from the back of its head. Its elongated snout sprouted teeth a rat would envy. By the time its claw-tipped paws landed softly on the ground, its mutation was complete. With the lumbering gait of a monkey, EV1L 2.0 rushed at the unsuspecting humans that had entered one of the rooms.

*****

Buckner set the timer on the first charge and switched it on. The red light, which would flash slowly at five minutes to detonation and increase in speed as the minutes ticked down, lit up. He pulled the protective cover from the strip of industrial pressure sensitive adhesive on the back and pressed it against one of the metal I-beam supports. Satisfied it was stuck fast and operational, he fished another charge from the bag and moved to the support column on the opposite side of the room.

On full alert against the alien menace, Kessler constantly turned as he kept guard, his weapon steady and ready to fire. He glimpsed his commander's flashlight beam through the walls of glass across the far side of the laboratories. He would be thankful when the charges were set and they could leave. The thought of the alien somewhere close by creeped him out. This was like no combat mission he had been on before. He lowered his weapon when his turn carried him past Buckner and raised it again when the man was clear. His rifle light jerked to the corridor. He thought he had glimpsed movement. He stepped to the glass wall and lowered the angle of the weapon. Caught in the beam, the Black monkey-like atrocity bared its teeth at him. Kessler fired through the glass.

EV1L 2.0 looked at the bright light and snarled at the human that had spotted it. Flinching from the loud retorts reverberating throughout the level, it leapt onto the far wall, narrowly escaping the bullets peppering the floor. It sprung from the wall, crashed through the cracked glass and landed on the human's chest. It savagely raked claws down the man's face, shredding flesh until the panicked firing ceased. As he rode the screaming man to the ground, it focused on the human across the room.

Buckner spun at the sound of gunfire and glimpsed a small vicious creature crash through the glass. He dropped the charge he was preparing when Kessler screamed, and snatched the weapon from his shoulder when the creature ripped at his friend's face. As he brought the rifle to bear on the creature, it leapt from Buckner's chest and rushed at him. His years of experience counted for nothing against the alien being. Fear gripped him. He frantically pulled the trigger before he had the creature in his sights. Bullets racked gouges in the floor, sending the creature leaping to the side. The creature moved so damn quick it was impossible to hit. He released his finger on the trigger when he lost sight of it. His eyes, weapon and light jerked around the room. His hands trembled. As black as the surrounding darkness, the alien could come at him from any direction. He glimpsed a light moving towards his position through the transparent walls. Colbert was coming to help.

Buckner's eyes raised to the ceiling. His weapon light quickly followed. Caught in the beam, the creature shrieked and dropped. Bullets passed harmlessly through the gaps that opened in the creature and struck the ceiling. Buckner screamed and grabbed a hand at the creature that landed on his head. His fingers found nothing solid, only a stretchy, glutinous mass that wrapped around his hand. He screamed again when his flesh melted and dropped his weapon when he collapsed to the floor.

In agony from the burning pain dissolving his flesh, the last thing Buckner saw before the Black flowed over his eyes, was the red light of the explosive charge he had dropped. His remaining hand grabbed it and brought it to his chest. Fighting the pain and unconsciousness creeping up fast, he advanced the timer. His screams ended when merciful oblivion claimed him.

*****

Richard halted in the corridor and stared through the glass wall at the dark pulsating shape suspended from the ceiling.

Richard jumped when Colbert touched his shoulder. "Is that a cocoon?"

Recalling the slug monster he had encountered in the bowels of the spaceship, Richard scrutinized the hanging mass as a fearful shiver flowed through him. "We had better hope that's all it is." He turned to Colbert. "We should leave."

"We'll leave when the charges are set, not before." He nudged Richard into the laboratory. "We'll plant the bulk of the explosives in here. It should be close enough to destroy whatever that thing is."

Colbert followed Richard through. He roamed his flashlight and weapon over the foul wriggling things trapped within rubbery pods on the floor in the adjoining laboratory before concentrating on the bulbous mass in the middle of room. Both men watched a slippery sack slurp from a tube attached to the cocoon. After a few seconds of inactivity, whatever monstrosity was encased within began to move, pressing its ever-changing form against its pliable prison.

Richard took in the many eggs littering the room, all of which seemed about to hatch, and the glass barrier separating them. It seemed far too flimsy to hold back what he pictured would shortly erupt from the alien egg sacs. He looked at Colbert. "Again, we should leave."

Colbert ignored Richard's request and slipped his weapon strap over a shoulder. "Hand me three charges."

Sighing, Richard pulled three explosive charges from the rucksack and handed them to Colbert. "Hurry, as I think some of those eggs are about to hatch."

"Trust me, I don't plan on lingering." Colbert made his way around the room planting the charges. He spun to face the weapon fire erupting from the far side of the laboratories. Bursts of rifle fire strobed Kessler's silhouetted form and briefly highlighted the creature attacking him.

When Richard heard the gunfire, he knew it signaled the slaughter had begun. He grabbed Colbert's arm to halt him when the man moved to the exit. The damn fool was going to try and help them. "I wouldn't do that if I were you. Buckner and Kessler are as good as dead."

Kessler's horrified scream cut short reinforced Richard's conclusion.

Colbert shrugged away Richard's grip. "Stay here if you want, but I'm going to help my men."

"What's the point of going to the trouble of getting me here when you ignore my advice?"

"Maybe I just like seeing you suffer." Colbert rushed from the room.

Richard had no flashlight. Unless he wanted to wait in the pitch black with the egg laying monstrosity and its soon-to-hatch brood close by, he had no choice other than to run after Colbert.

As they sprinted towards a second burst of gunfire, Richard briefly thought of shooting Colbert in the back, grabbing his weapon equipped with a flashlight and leaving, but he decided it might be beneficial to his health to hold off until he'd first determined the level of the threat they foolishly rushed towards.

Colbert entered the laboratory, cast his gaze over Kessler's corpse, his ripped face and the pooled blood around his head, then across the room at Buckner. Black substance covered the man's head and slowly oozed down his chest. His eyes focused on the red rapidly blinking light by Kessler's hand and the bag of explosives too close to escape the blast when the charge erupted. He spun, almost stumbling over Richard snatching up Kessler's rifle.

Colbert shoved Richard towards the exit. "Run!"

Glimpsing the prophetic flashing red LED, Richard was more than willing to obey the command. The damn SEALs were almost as dangerous as the aliens.

They dashed from the room and sprinted along the corridor. When they reached the hall, a loud explosion rang out. An even louder, more violent blast followed in its wake. Glass, metal and pieces of unrecognizable scientific equipment broke into thousands of fragments to become deadly shrapnel spraying in all directions. Blown off their feet by the confined blast funneled through the level, Colbert slammed into Richard and both were thrown to the floor.

Carried by the blast, shards fashioned from multiple material, all with edges as lethal as any blade or claw, shot over them. Debris rained down around the men, clanged down the corridor, became embedded in the walls, floor and ceiling. A few pieces pierced flesh.

When the explosion subsided, Richard raised his head at the chaos around him and the smoke drifting down the corridor. Feeling the weight pressing him to the floor, he at first thought part of the ceiling had collapsed on him. When groans close to his ear indicated what trapped him, he squirmed and pushed Colbert off. As soon as he was free of the man's weight, Richard sat up and examined his body for wounds. Miraculously, he had received none.

Groans nearby brought his gaze to Colbert, who hadn't been so lucky. A jagged twist of metal protruding from the man's left shoulder and two long slivers of glass in his side and right leg were highlighted in Colbert's weapon light, which had landed a short distance away. Colbert had shielded Richard when he fell atop him and took the full brunt of the shrapnel. Richard grinned. Lady Luck was still with him.

With his ears ringing, Richard slipped the pistol Colbert had given him earlier into a pocket and retrieved the rifle he had taken from Kessler's corpse. He climbed to his feet and aimed the weapon at Colbert, bathing the prone man in the tactical flashlight.

Colbert opened his dazed eyes, painfully sat up and ran his gaze over Richard's uninjured form and then at the three large fragments sticking from his flesh. "How in hell's name did you remain unscathed?"

Richard shrugged. "You fell on top of me, which I now assume wasn't an intentional act to save me from harm."

"No, it damn well wasn't! Geesh, you lead a charmed life."

"Not really." Richard put a hand to his leg. "I didn't escape completely unharmed. I banged my knee when you knocked me to the floor."

"Quick, call a medic. Richard has a bruise on his knee," quipped Colbert.

"Oh, I don't think I hit it hard enough to bruise."

When Richard noticed Colbert's weapon a short distance away and out of reach of its owner, he sensed an opportunity he might not get again. His plan to head for the elevator and flee was thwarted by running footsteps heading nearer. Cursing inwardly, he noticed Colbert grinning at him, as if the man guessed what he had been about to do.

Richard shrugged and looked at Sullivan and Dalton. "Colbert's wounded."

"What the hell happened?" asked Sullivan, taking in the wreckage. "We heard the explosion."

The man's accusing gaze wasn't lost on Richard. "It was nothing I did. Buckner and Kessler were attacked and killed by the alien."

"That doesn't explain the explosion," argued Dalton. His weapon jerked along the corridor when an iron girder from the weakened structure crashed to the floor.

Wincing from the pain radiating out from his wounds, Colbert glanced at the destroyed labs. Though the right-side labs had been destroyed and every pain of glass around the epicenter of the explosion had blown out or cracked, the left-side group of labs remained more or less intact.

Colbert turned to Dalton. "As Richard said, Buckner and Kessler were attacked, and both were dead by the time we reached them. Buckner was responsible for the explosion. He must have advanced the timer on a charge before he died, probably an attempt to kill the creature that attacked them."

Sullivan gripped the twisted seven-inch piece of metal in Colbert's shoulder. "You ready? It's gonna hurt."

Colbert gritted his teeth and nodded. He grimaced when it was pulled free.

"Did it work?" asked Dalton, staring at the wreckage for signs of movement. "Is the creature dead?"

Richard shrugged and waved an arm at the destroyed laboratories. "You're welcome to go find out, but an explosion killed one a lot larger in Antarctica, so hopefully Buckner's death wasn't a complete waste."

"I wouldn't go down that route," warned Dalton, stepping threateningly close to Richard.

Richard stepped back. "You can cut out the macho bullshit, your friends are dead, end of story. We aren't and have more important things to worry about." He pointed back at the laboratories that remained relatively intact. "There's a huge, alien, egg-laying monster back there and a roomful of eggs about to hatch. If you don't want to suffer the same horrendous fate as your buddies, I strongly urge we take that elevator out of here ASAP."

"Great! The alien's breeding," moaned Dalton. "Can this mission get more fucked up?"

"We're not leaving until the mission's completed," stated Colbert, flinching when Sullivan removed the two shards of glass from his side and leg. "We still have the remaining charges to set and the egg-laying alien to destroy."

Sullivan helped Colbert to his feet. Though none of his wounds were overly serious, they seeped blood and needed attention.

Aware the soldiers wouldn't let him leave, and their chances of survival were slim if the alien eggs hatched, Richard knew he'd have to take matters into his own hands if he was going to survive. The longer he remained in the secret facility the more chance he had of being killed. Also, the Russians were on their way and could arrive at any moment. If they were discovered violating one of their secret bases he couldn't see them letting them walk away. They'd be killed or interrogated and imprisoned in a gulag, events he wished to avoid at all costs. He picked up his dropped bag of explosive charges, set one of the timers for seventeen hundred hours and dropped it back into the bag with the others.

Richard turned to the soldiers watching him. "Dalton, you're with me. Sullivan, you help Colbert to the elevator and wait for our return."

"What are you up to, Richard?" enquired Colbert, suspecting bringing Richard along was about to pay off.

"I'm going to complete your damn suicide mission for you. There's a roomful of those aliens about to be born, and I can't see how we can fight them all if one managed to take out your two buddies." Richard nodded at the bag slung over Dalton's shoulder. "How many charges you got left?"

Dalton looked to his commander for guidance. When Colbert nodded, he glanced in the bag. "Nine."

"This is what we'll do," stated Richard with an authority that surprised the SEALs. "Because Colbert needs medical attention, whatever we're going to do we need to do fast. Dalton and I will head to the alien birthing chamber, throw the explosives inside and return to the elevator. We'll then head for Level 1, planting the remaining charges on the way, get Colbert patched up in the first aid station we passed earlier and leave this hell hole. The explosives will destroy the creature, its unhatched offspring and the facility, job done."

Expecting an argument, Richard was surprised by the commander's reply.

Colbert shrugged. "Well, Richard, as you said a short while ago, what's the point of bringing you here if I'm going to ignore your advice."

Dalton glared at Richard and looked at Colbert. "We're taking orders from a civilian now?"

"Believe me, Richard's not doing this solely for our benefit. He wants to survive and we're just tagalongs, but if he survives, so should we. Also, his plan has merit."

Though Richard was far from enthusiastic for any plan that would take him nearer to the alien creature when he favored heading in the opposite direction, the foolhardy SEALs would only leave when they had completed their mission. If helping them increased his chances of survival, then so be it.

"Okay, Richard," said Dalton. "let's get this done. You lead."

Richard slung the bag of explosives over his shoulder and headed for the laboratories and the alien birthing chamber.

As Sullivan aided his limping commander to the elevator, Ramirez made contact.

CHAPTER 21

Hostage

Fearing the nuclear bomb had exploded when what could only be an explosion set off on a lower level shook the complex, Krisztina halted in the corridor to await her annihilation. When all fell still, silent, and she remained alive and the building around her intact, she knew the atomic bomb hadn't been the cause. Distracted by voices, she cocked an ear at the security office a short distance ahead.

*****

Ramirez was alerted to the explosion erupting from below by the muffled boom and the shockwave that rippled through the complex, vibrating the floor, the cameras feeding the screens and the CCTV monitors. After a few minutes of no contact, concern for his team creased his brow as he pressed a hand to his radio. "Is everything okay down there?"

It was a few anxious moments before he received a no-nonsense reply from Sullivan. *"Buckner and Kessler are down, killed by the alien. Explosion seems to have killed one creature, but there's more. Commander and Dalton wounded. Heading for the elevator. I'll update you when we reach the first aid station. What's the situation up there?"*

"No activity yet," replied Ramirez. "Shall I rendezvous with you at the first aid station?"

"No, stay on watch for now. We'll join you shortly."

Ramirez's gaze flicked to one of the screens when he thought he glimpsed movement. It was a view of the corridor outside the security room. Though the corridor was empty, Sullivan had just informed him there were more than one of the aliens roaming the facility. Worried one might be creeping up on him, he grabbed his rifle and moved to the door. Cautiously he peered out. Surprise barely had time to register on his face before the female lunged at him. The fire extinguisher she wielded smashed into the side of his head. Dazed by the hard blow, his knees buckled.

The extinguisher clanged to the floor when Krisztina dropped it and snatched the assault rifle from the dazed American soldier's hands.

As the bright pricks of lights dancing before his eyes began to fade, Ramirez turned his throbbing head to his attacker. He groaned at seeing his own weapon aimed at him by the female, who he assumed was one of the Russian scientists working in the facility. When the other SEALs heard of this, they would rib him about it for years to come.

"My Russian not good. Do English speak you?" asked Ramirez in terrible Russian.

Surprised the American spoke any Russian, however badly—in her experience the Americans, like the English, were language lazy and expected everyone else to learn their *universal language*—Krisztina nodded. "What you Americans soldiers doing here and where my comrades are?"

"We received a report that you had an alien creature running loose killing those who worked here, which I expect explains the fate of your co-workers. My superiors feared that if it escaped into the outside world, it would pose a serious threat to humanity. They sent us here to ensure that didn't happen. And we're Navy SEALs, not soldiers."

Krisztina shrugged. "Soldiers, Marines, is all same."

Ramirez reluctantly let her comment slide.

Suspicion clouded Krisztina's next question, "Are you here to kill alien, or capture it and take back to America?"

"Destroy it. Most definitely destroy it!" stated Ramirez firmly. "Unlike your Russian superiors who brought it here from Antarctica to study, we can see the danger the alien threatens to mankind and want to see it annihilated."

"You can cast your accusations elsewhere because, as far as I aware, we not responsible for bringing alien here. How it got into facility from Antarctica is much a mystery to us as is you."

"Well, I don't suppose that really matters now. Can I stand?"

Krisztina nodded and taking a step back watched him climb groggily to his feet.

Ramirez gently probed the painful swelling on his head and glanced at the discarded extinguisher. "You sure packed a wallop with that thing. I'm surprised you didn't crack my skull, and I'm not entirely sure you haven't."

"I not think tickling you under chin with it would have same effect," quipped Krisztina, "and you trespasser here. I defend Russian territory."

"And very well you did, too." Ramirez pondered grabbing his weapon back, but she was a few steps too far away for it to succeed, especially with her finger resting on the trigger. If she wasn't experienced with weapons, she gave a healthy impression she might be. "What happens now?"

"How many you are, where are they and what was cause of explosion a moment ago?"

Ramirez saw no reason to hold back. "We were nine until the alien killed two. They tracked the creature to Level 4 and were planting explosives when it attacked. Cause of explosion is as yet unknown, but I think it might have been an attempt to kill the creature. I don't know how it happened, but there seems to be a few of them now."

"They can split apart to be separate creatures. I've seen it. One chased me up escape ladder."

"That doesn't bode well for our survival."

Krisztina pondered her next move. "I must contact my superiors to let them know what has happened."

"They already know," revealed Ramirez. "A team is on its way to capture the alien for study. It's one of the reasons why we rushed here. It's suspected they might try to fashion it into a weapon to use against America or other nations."

It was as Krisztina feared. She agreed with the Americans that the alien menace should be destroyed. God knows what destruction the creature could cause if unleashed into the population. "You believe your explosives will kill every part of all alien creatures?"

Ramirez shrugged. "That's the plan. Even if the explosions fail to kill it all, it will be trapped below so it won't present a threat."

Krisztina shook her head. "No, that won't work. It can become liquid and seep through smallest gap to find way above ground. I have better way to ensure its demise, a permanent solution."

"I'm sure the commander will be open to suggestions when he gets here, which shouldn't be long now."

Doubtful she would be able to fend off all of the armed Americans heading her way and hesitant to leave until she was certain the alien had been dealt with, Krisztina made a decision that could possibly backfire on her.

"As far as I see, we all want same thing, no? To see the alien creatures dead. To do that, there needs to be trust between us."

After a few moments of indecision about what she was about to do, she lowered the rifle aimed at Ramirez's chest and held it out.

Surprised by the action, Ramirez gratefully reclaimed his weapon and held it loosely by his side.

"Thank you. Now what's this permanent solution of yours to destroy the aliens?"

CHAPTER 22

dEV1Lkin

Cracks splintering across glass walls, glass smashing to the floor, debris falling from the ceilings and the creaking of weakened metal supports and stressed concrete had Dalton's nerves on edge. Richard glanced back at the nervous soldier jerking his weapon to every sound. It was Dalton's first experience battling aliens. He would either learn quickly or suffer the consequences.

"Keep it together, Dalton. I've faced worst and lived to tell the tale."

"Yeah, unlike most who accompanied you, so I've heard. Just do your job and I'll do mine."

"Not to be pedantic, but I'm actually doing your job. You abducted me from mine."

Concentrating on his surroundings, Dalton ignored him.

When they reached the end of the corridor, Richard glanced through a cracked glass wall into the birthing chamber. The oversized Black cocoon hanging from the ceiling had stopped pulsating, and no eggs were presently being ejected from the tube. Wondering if the explosion had killed it, he stared at the unmoving mass for signs of life. His speculation ceased when the egg tube retracted into its form; it was still alive. He pressed forward, and then jumped back, careening into Dalton when something slammed against the glass, increasing the number of cracks spreading over its surface with a splintering that was both ominous and nerve-wracking. Fortunately, the glass held.

Dalton shoved Richard away and raised his rifle at the Black sludge sending out thin tentacles searching for weaknesses in the barrier preventing it from getting at its prey. As Dalton's finger applied pressure to the trigger, Richard pushed the barrel down.

"Shoot, and you break the only thing stopping them from getting at us." Richard released his hold on the weapon and pointed out other Black forms moving within the gloom-filled room.

Dalton shuddered as he watched a small alien creature claw its way from an egg sac, the flashlight beam glistening off the glutinous albumen covering its evil form. The new-born monstrosity puffed up like a bladder fish and sprouted short, sharp spikes along the ridge forming along its back. A long tail snaked out from its rear and grew a small spiked club on the tip. Legs and a head with stumpy flat teeth and tiny, piercing eyes quickly followed. Spying the two humans and recognizing them as something to be eaten, it bounded forward and leapt at the glass. The cracked and weakened pane vibrated alarmingly from the blow. The spiderweb of splintering cracks increased and slithered to the edges of the frame. The other birthed hatchlings turned their vicious heads at the sound and stared hungrily at the humans all wanted to devour.

Dalton glanced at Richard. "Let's get this done and get gone. I doubt the glass can stand much more punishment."

In total agreement, Richard rushed through the short corridor, turned the bend and halted at the birthing room door. His fearful gaze picked out the cocoon dropping from the ceiling and landing on the floor with a wet smack. It immediately started changing, morphing into some species of alien monstrosity he didn't want to dwell on. As he slipped the bag from his shoulder, his gaze shot to the sounds of padded paws and clicking claws coming closer. The hatchlings rushed at the door.

Though his fear screamed for him not to, Richard pushed open the door and lobbed the bag of explosives inside. He pulled the door shut and watched two creatures leap onto the bag sliding across the room and then fight for dominance over the prize they believed was edible.

The remaining creatures continued their dash for the humans. Richard and Dalton made a hasty retreat as the dark creatures slammed against the door and walls. When glass smashed to the floor behind them, Dalton shot a fearful gaze at the creatures diving through the breaches in the wall.

One veered away from those heading for the already crowded hole and dashed for the humans running past outside. It leapt and reformed its head, shoulders and front limbs into a rigid pointed tusk.

"Worry about what's in front," Richard advised Dalton. "You don't want to see what's coming when there's nothing you can do to stop them."

Dalton heeded the advice and turned away. Glass exploded beside him. He glimpsed something dark pass before his face and yelped painfully when a large shard slid along the back of his hand deep enough to scrape across bone. The weapon slipped from his injured hand and clattered to the floor. He clasped his still functioning hand over the deep gash to try and stem the blood.

Richard halted when the wall ahead sprayed out, showering Dalton with glass. His eyes followed the evil form responsible. Turning pliable, it concertinaed into itself when it struck the opposite wall and sprung off. Reforming into a creature of viciousness it stretched claws at Dalton. Wondering what the SEALs would do without his assistance,

Richard raised the rifle and fired a short burst. Though one of the bullets clipped Dalton's ear, removing a small chunk, Richard managed to focus the unfamiliar weapon and the remainder of the bullets on the creature. Carried by the force of the bullets slamming into its body, the creature shot along the corridor. On striking the wall it liquefied into a dark, oily sludge.

Aware of the creatures rushing at them from behind, Richard shoved Dalton forward. "Move!"

Dalton moved, taking a wide berth around the reforming Black.

Richard scooped up the man's dropped weapon as he rushed after him.

Aware only the first to reach the prey would feast on the much-needed sustenance offered by the humans, EV1L's offspring set off after them in rapid pursuit.

CHAPTER 23

Rendezvous

Spying the elevator doors held open by Sullivan, who had his troubled gaze focused on something behind the two men sprinting towards him, Richard shot a fearful glance behind. The shrieking and snarling creatures were drawing close far too speedily to inspire any confidence they wouldn't be upon him before he reached the relative safety of the elevator. Through the walls, he saw the previously pregnant cocoon had evolved into a beast just as terrifying as any he had encountered back on the spaceship in Antarctica. With all thoughts of collecting a sample of the alien Black now firmly banished, Richard focused on his survival. He briefly considered tripping Dalton. Feeding on him might slow the creatures down and give him the precious few seconds he needed to escape, but with Sullivan observing from the elevator it wouldn't be a wise move. The man would probably shoot him in retaliation.

Richard decided on a different tactic. He spun as he skidded to a halt, gracelessly pointed both rifles along the corridor and pulled the triggers. Though the powerful weapons hardly had any recoil, they lurched erratically in his inexperienced hands, spitting bullets in the general direction of the creatures.

Bullets struck the walls, floor and some of the creatures as Richard roamed the weapons around the corridor. The painful shrieks emitted by those hit had the desired effect of slowing the creatures as they came to terms with the onslaught. Adapting quickly, they also changed tactics. Splitting from their previous huddled mass, creatures scampered up the walls and some chose the ceiling to continue their pursuit.

Dropping one of the weapons when it clicked on empty, Richard grabbed the still firing one with both hands and adjusted his aim, sweeping an erratic swath of bullets over the fragmented monstrosities. The creatures reacted quickly and leapt out of the bullets' path. It was like watching some bizarre acrobatic circus act. Creatures constantly leapt from wall to wall and wall to ceiling and floor in all directions, passing each other's foul forms in majestic flight. Though none were killed, their avoidance techniques did slow their progress. The gunfire reverberating around the level faded when the bullets ran out. Richard glanced at the large beast that smashed through the glass wall back along the corridor. Mother was coming. The large maternal creature wasn't something he was eager to meet face-to-face.

"Richard, we need to leave now!" shouted Sullivan.

Richard, who excelled in retreat, was in full concurrence. He turned away from the oncoming mass of evil intentions and sprinted for the elevator as Dalton slipped inside. When he was few steps away, Sullivan removed his hand from the frame that had prevented the doors from closing. Fretting that he wouldn't make it before the doors shut him out, consigning him to a painful and imminent death from the ravenous hoard, Richard focused on the narrowing gap. Sucking in his chest, he sidled through with barely enough room to accommodate him. As soon as the doors met, Sullivan punched the up button a few times. The old elevator lurched into movement and began to rise. Loud thumps from the frustrated creatures slamming against the door echoed up the shaft.

They had done it.

"Did you plant the charges?" asked Colbert, leaning against the wall for support.

A little breathless, Dalton glanced at the blood seeping from his hand and the commander's wounds; both needed medical attention. "Richard threw the bag into the room where the alien egg layer was, but as you know, some have hatched and are no longer in the room."

Richard sighed. He had risked his life for nothing. He could have left the explosives in the hall.

"No matter, they'll still destroy the level and hopefully everything on it," added Sullivan, sticking an explosive charge to the elevator ceiling. "At the very least those creatures will be trapped down there."

Colbert glanced at his watch. "Forty-three minutes before the big bang. Plenty of time for us to move to a safe distance and watch the fireworks."

Sullivan nodded at Dalton's hand. "What's the damage?"

"Serious, but I'll live. Though I don't think I'll be firing a weapon any time soon."

"Hopefully you won't need to," reassured Colbert. "As soon as we're patched up good enough to prevent blood loss, we're leaving."

Sullivan leaned closer to the side of Dalton's head. "You've also lost part of your ear."

"I have?"

Keen to draw the attention away from Dalton's ear and who might be responsible, Richard turned to Colbert. "Now I've completed your mission for you, can we please get out of this damn Russian hellhole?"

"That's the plan," replied Colbert. "We'll head to the helicopter, move to a safe distance and wait for the charges to go off to make certain the facility's destroyed."

"Good, then what happens to me?"

Colbert shrugged. "You can come with us, or we'll return you to the dig site we picked you up from."

"Abducted," corrected Richard.

Colbert grinned.

"Take me back to the crater. I have work to do, and I'm sure my brother's worried about what's happened to me."

"Probably the only one that is," uttered Dalton, looking at his damaged ear in the reflective wall of the elevator.

When the elevator arrived on Level 3, Sullivan and Colbert stepped out and covered the corridor with their weapons. Uncertain how intelligent the creatures were, and if they could operate an elevator, Dalton kicked the short length of timber between the doors to prevent them from closing and sending the elevator down for the aliens to ride up. Sullivan led them along the corridor that would take them to the secondary elevator, which they would ride to Level 1 and the first aid station.

They paused when a loud crash of tortured metal rose up the elevator shaft and travelled along the corridor.

"That didn't sound good," Dalton said, as he and the others gazed worriedly back the way they had come.

*****

Sensing her hatchlings were in danger, EV1L dropped from the ceiling, sucked in her bulbous reproductive mass and formed a creature selected from its extensive repertoire. Four-legged, armored and vicious, Ev1L turned her large head to the men fleeing along the corridor with her offspring in pursuit. A glance around the birthing chamber revealed most of her eggs had hatched. When gunfire rang out, she observed her younglings dodging the bullets; they had inherited her experiences with the human weapons and were quick to react. Those that were hit suffered, but they would survive. She sent out her senses to search for her first produced. Failing to detect its presence, she assumed the humans had killed it.

Ev1L growled menacingly as she padded lazily to the cracked wall, lowered her head and pushed through. Ignoring the glass showering to the floor around and over her, she headed along the corridor and watched the fleeing humans escape into the chamber that could move up and down. She headed for the doors her offspring sprung frustratingly against. Some turned to liquid and tried to seep through the joints but protective seals that could hold back gases and contaminants foiled them.

EV1L growled an order, stilling her younglings. They looked at their parent and subserviently backed away when she approached. EV1L pressed her head against the doors and felt them give a little. She moved away, turned until she faced the doors and rushed at them.

The impact of beast against metal echoed up the shaft. The doors screeched in protest as they buckled under the force. EV1L enlarged the hole when she poked her head through, turned it 180 degrees and gazed up the dark shaft. It was vital for her minions to feed to become stronger, and the only food source available was the fleeing humans. She growled a series of drawn out deep growls before stretching her body through the doors. As her elongated mass touched the concrete side of the shaft, it formed into a large archaic alien centipede and climbed the wall. Her hatchlings poured through the gap and formed smaller facsimiles of their mother. The clicks of a thousand claws filled the shaft as the wriggling mass of Black horrors continued the hunt for human prey.

*****

Armed with Colbert's rifle and on guard outside the first aid station while Sullivan was inside patching up Colbert's and Dalton's wounds, Richard cocked an ear nervously along the corridor and raised the weapon at the sound of approaching footsteps. He turned his head to the doorway and whispered, "Someone or something's coming."

Sullivan thrust the roll of bandage he was binding around Dalton's hand into his commander's hands. "Can you finish this off."

Already patched up, Colbert nodded.

Sullivan grabbed his weapon and joined Richard in the corridor."

"It might be the Russians," offered Richard anxiously, thoughts of interrogation and gulags flitting through his head.

The possibility of a firefight creased Sullivan's brow. Though all of them were battle-hardened veterans, except for Richard who he doubted would be of much use, he was the only one not wounded. A small force could easily pin them down and block their only escape route. In addition to that, if the Russians had grenades they might be forced to retreat nearer to the creatures that seemed to be making their way up through the levels. They would be caught between two evils. The lack of any warning from Ramirez was also worrying. If it was the Russians approaching, he must have been overpowered or worse, killed.

As Sullivan's hand moved to his radio mic to contact Ramirez to hopefully shed some light on the situation, the man appeared around the corner. Sullivan's gaze flicked to the woman accompanying him. Ramirez's relaxed manner inspired confidence there was no imminent threat from the Russians or the woman he assumed was one of the surviving scientists who worked here.

"How's the commander and Dalton?" inquired Ramirez on reaching the group.

"They'll survive." Noticing the angry swelling on the side of Ramirez head, Sullivan indicted the woman with a slight nod. "Who is she?"

"*She* is Comrade Krisztina Evgeny," replied Krisztina. "And *she* speaks English."

"Good to hear," said Colbert.

"Krisztina is concerned the explosives won't kill the alien creatures or prevent them from escaping. Apparently, they can liquify their bodies and ooze through small cracks."

Frowning worriedly, Sullivan refocused on Krisztina. "Is this true?"

"It is. Even if you turn The Kamera into rubble pile, I fear creatures still find way to surface."

"That's not good," stated Sullivan. They had lost two good men on a fruitless exercise.

"However, not all is lost," continued Ramirez. "Krisztina has come up with a viable plan that I believe will work and guarantee nothing in the facility survives."

Sullivan turned back to Krisztina for her to explain further.

"Because of dangerous substances worked on before here, which I won't elaborate on, a failsafe against anything escaping into outside atmosphere was installed. A nuclear device planted beneath lowest level."

"An atomic bomb!" uttered Richard.

Krisztina ignored the man's reaction. "Yes. I assume it's connected to a self-destruct control located in facility somewhere."

"Not much help if you don't know where it is, but I'll inform the commander of your plan and he'll make the decision." Sullivan turned to the infirmary door.

"I don't need your commander's decision to do anything," argued Krisztina. "You all trespassing on Russian territory, something my superiors won't look kindly upon if they find out. No, this is what we will do. We locate self-destruct control, set it off and leave. I assume you have transport to return you to wherever you come from?"

Sullivan nodded.

"Good, you take me along road safe distance, and I wait for my comrades to arrive."

"Correct me if I'm wrong," said Ramirez, "but Russian superiors don't seem to have forgiving natures. Won't you get into trouble for destroying their secret facility and the alien they wanted captured alive?"

"Why would I get in trouble when I tell my superiors it was Stanislav, head of facility, who now dead, blew it up? Sacrificing his life to stop alien from reaching outside world."

Ramirez smiled. "Sneaky."

"Do you know how to operate this self-destruct system if we find it?" enquired Colbert, buttoning up his jacket as he stepped from the infirmary. "I suspect it's not like in some movies where a conveniently placed large red button is typically pressed to set it off."

Dalton stepped from the infirmary and eyed up the pretty Russian.

"You heard her plan, then?" asked Sullivan.

Colbert nodded. "And I agree with her. The only way to be certain every part of the creature is obliterated and ensure our mission isn't a total bust is to nuke it." He looked at Krisztina while he waited for her to answer.

"Nyet, not exactly. I unaware of bomb until short while before," explained Krisztina. "Though large red button would be preferable, I imagine it be a little more complicated. I'm assuming there is instruction manual in Stanislav's office that provide information to activate it and where it is located."

"Then that's where we'll head next," stated Colbert.

After Krisztina had given directions to Stanislav's office, Sullivan led them along the corridor.

*****

Mason glanced at the antiquated radio gathering dust in the corner when it crackled into life and spat out a tinny voice speaking Russian.

"Colonel Grigori of strike force Kremlin to Siberia checkpoint 3. Be advised, we will arrive at The Kamera in sixty-three minutes. Request an update on the situation?"

The unmistakable thrump-thrump of spinning rotors barely discernible in the background above a noisy engine, indicated they travelled by helicopter. It wasn't good news. Mason directed his gaze upon his Russian captive when the man spoke.

"Is best I reply, no?" suggested Sven, concerned he'd be accused of abandoning his post if he didn't.

As Mason pondered whether he could trust the Russian not to warn the approaching force of the American presence at their secret base, the Russian colonel spoke again.

"Checkpoint Siberia 3, respond," demanded the colonel.

Mason nodded at Sven and stood. Keeping the man covered with the rifle, he followed him to the antiquated radio.

"I'm surprised it still works," joked Sven, picking up the bulky handset.

Mason pressed the tip of the rifle barrel against the side of Sven's head. "You warn them we're here and it will be the last words you speak. We hope to be gone before your comrades arrive, so except for you, no other Russian will be the wiser. As far as anyone will know, you followed protocol and did everything expected of you. If you force me to kill you, we will take your body with us and drop it in the tundra never to be found. Your comrades will believe you deserted your post, and the shame will fall on your family. Understand?"

Sven nodded enthusiastically. The barrel against his head would have been sufficient to ensure he complied.

"Comrade Sven Kazimir at Checkpoint Siberia 3 to Colonel Grigori, I understand you will arrive shortly. All has remained quiet here since my departure from the facility, and there's been no activity above ground."

"Received, Comrade Kazimir. Remain at your post and advise if the situation changes."

"Da, Colonel." Sven replaced the handset in its cradle.

"Return to your seat," ordered Mason.

As Sven crossed to the table, Mason touched a hand to his radio mic. "Eagle 4 to Mother Goose, be advised, hornets ETA one hour. Repeat, hornets will arrive in approximately sixty minutes."

*****

Outside the facility, Kelly continually scanned the horizon. With no idea if the Russians would arrive by road or air, his gaze focused on the sky for approaching helicopters and then aimed binoculars along the road. The pilot's gaze switched to the cockpit when Mason spoke over the radio, warning the team the Russians were almost here. Hornets indicated they would be arriving by helicopter.

*****

Frowning from Mason's message, Colbert replied, "Received and understood, Eagle 4. He then issued orders to Kelly. "Eagle 3 remain on post until advised and prep for a hasty EVAC with possible hurricane on our tail. Estimated safe distance, one click. Expected mission termination is currently thirty minutes, max."

*****

A little confused by what the American commander had just relayed to his men, Sven looked at the American as he sat opposite. "Your commander is mistaken. No hurricanes forecast this month."

Mason grinned at the Russian who had no idea hurricane in this context was code for a strong explosive blast. "Us Americans make our own."

Sven suddenly twigged what the American meant. "Oh." If it destroyed the alien monster that had killed his comrades, he was all for it. He then had another thought. "How big will be explosion?"

"Big enough that you don't want to be anywhere close by," replied Mason. "Does that motorbike outside work?"

Sven nodded.

"When the time comes, you'll need to ride it like the wind to escape what's coming."

Thankful the Americans weren't going to kill him when their mission was completed, Sven nodded vigorously. "I can do that, and I not mention you Americans were here. I could be punished for being captured if I did."

"Good," uttered Mason. "I'm certain that will be best for all concerned."

*****

Krisztina paused outside the control room, halting the team unexpectedly. "I need to let my superiors know I'm alive and warn soldiers coming here of imminent explosion. I might want to stop them from capturing alien, but I don't want them killed."

"Make it quick," consented Colbert, anxious to get his men clear of the facility as soon as possible. "Remember, you have no idea reinforcements are coming."

Krisztina entered the room. Glancing at the list of emergency numbers stuck to the wall, she dialed the facility's contact at the Kremlin. Her call was answered quicker than she expected.

"Da!" said a man's voice.

Krisztina answered in Russian. “This is Comrade Krisztina Sashura from The Kamera.”

“I was informed everyone there was dead,” replied the man on the other end.

Though the speaker failed to offer his name or title, Krisztina didn’t fail to recognize the voice of authority; whoever she was speaking to was used to being obeyed. “I barely survived when the alien creature overran Level 4. Our concern here was that it would make its way to the upper levels, which it might have already succeeded in doing, and escape from the facility.”

“That must not happen.”

“I agree, sir, as did my superior, Director Stanislav.”

“Is Director Stanislav with you?”

“No, sir. The last time I saw him he was going to activate the self-destruct protocols to ensure the alien didn’t escape.”

“Nyet! He doesn’t have permission for such a drastic measure. We need the alien alive to study.”

“I understand, sir, and I did try to talk him out of it, but he is my superior. We were chased by the creature and split up. That was the last I saw of him. I have tried reaching him over the internal intercom but have received no answer. He could be hiding from the creature or dead. I am also unaware if he has already set the self-destruct in motion, which is another reason why I am keen to leave.”

“I can’t hear a warning being broadcast through the facility, so it hasn’t been activated.”

“Correct, sir, there is no warning, yet,” confirmed Krisztina.

“Then not all is lost. Listen to me, Comrade Sashura, it’s imperative you keep trying to contact Stanislav over the intercom to set him away from his rash unauthorized course. If he is still alive and hiding, he might be able to hear you but not reply. Broadcast that he is forbidden to destroy the alien, or

the facility, and a team will arrive shortly to take control of the situation. Do you understand, Comrade?"

"I understand, sir. I will remain here and broadcast your orders until help arrives. However, if Director Stanislav disobeys your request and activates the self-destruct, do I have permission to vacate the facility and move to a safe distance?"

The man replied after a short pause. *"I suppose so, but only when you hear the alarm."*

"Thank you, sir."

When the man abruptly ended the call, Krisztina replaced the handset.

"The way you lie, you should have been a politician," said Colbert.

"No, thanks. Now I've covered my ass, let's destroy this place before creatures come."

Krisztina led them to Stanislav's office and gazed around the room Luka had ransacked during his search for the alien pistols. She crossed to the splintered doors of a wall cupboard and pulled one door open wider. Inside were files, stacks of papers, books and the alien pistol Vadim had started dismantling. Aware her superiors would be—to put it mildly—disappointed by its loss, and that it might encourage them to look on her more favorably after the facility and alien were destroyed, she gathered up the pieces and slipped them into her pocket.

"Have you found it?" asked Richard, breaking away from the men gathered in the hall guarding the corridor and entering the office.

Krisztina glanced at the Englishman, who seemed out of place. Obviously not a soldier, she wondered why he was here. "I look still."

As Krisztina returned to searching through the paperwork, Richard glanced around the room. Maybe there were some secrets he could steal and sell, but he soon realized as he couldn't read Russian it was pointless taking anything that might turn out to be a shopping list or a boring memo.

"Got it!" exclaimed Krisztina a few moments later.

Richard watched Krisztina break the seal on the plastic sleeve and remove two strangely shaped keys, which she put in a pocket, and a thin A4 pamphlet that she immediately started flicking through. After a few moments, he asked, "Can you operate it?"

Krisztina nodded without glancing up. "I think so. Just follow steps outlined in instructions."

Colbert glanced into the room. "Does it say where the self-destruct control is located?"

Krisztina looked at Colbert. "There's one on level 4. If dangerous substance leaked free, scientists below could set it in motion, sacrificing themselves to prevent it getting out."

"There's no way we can go back down there with those creatures running around," stated Dalton worriedly from the corridor. "We barely survived the last time."

"We won't have to. There is a secondary control to initiate self-destruct sequence by exit elevator on this level," explained Krisztina. "We go there, activate it and leave. Alien dies. We safe."

Dalton relaxed a little.

"Sounds like a plan," agreed Colbert. "How much time do we have when it's started?"

"Fifteen minutes."

Colbert stepped into the corridor. "You all hear that?"

His men nodded.

"Let's move," ordered Colbert.

"On me," said Sullivan, leading them along the corridor.

CHAPTER 24

dEV1Lment

When Boris arrived back at the elevator, he stared at the remains on the floor and then inside at the bones of the cow he had seen earlier. His search for his human friend or an exit to the outside had failed. He sensed something bad was happening and the strange, dark creature that had devoured the other animals and attacked one of the humans was responsible. Even more worrying was that it had grown and was now loose, roaming the corridors.

Noticing something on the floor sticking from beneath the bunched-up rug, Boris pulled it out. It was his human friend's lighter. Remembering the tasty treats they had enjoyed together, he struck it to flame. His head turned to the elevator. Clacking, clicks and slithering sounds headed his way. Something he didn't want to encounter was coming. His eyes focused on the elevator ceiling when it buckled slightly. A sniff of the air revealed the scent of the strange creature nearby, prompting him to flee along the corridor to look for somewhere to hide.

*****

EV1L reached the bottom of the elevator and slithered past. Arriving at the top of the shaft above the moving box and finding no avenue of escape around the winch motor, she dropped onto the elevator roof devoid of any means of access. Her form changed to a squat creature with powerful legs bent beneath its rotund body capable of propelling it great distances, but that was not why this form was chosen. A tiny, pointed head, its size out of proportion to its plump torso, emerged and turned its many-eyed gaze upon the arms stretching out from bony shoulder blades. When the arms were fully formed, she flexed the powerful limbs tipped with curved, hook-like claws. When she struck them together, a loud clack echoed down the shaft.

The small creatures clinging to the walls around the top of the shaft, watched their queen raise her arms and slam them into the metal box. Powered by muscular limbs, a metallic clangor rang out when sharp claw tips pressed through the metal.

Anchored by her rear limbs, Ev1L dragged her limbs forward. Metal shrieked, buckled and scrunched when it was ripped back. Releasing her grip on the flap of metal, EV1L shuffled to the hole and dropped through. Hanging on a hooked claw like an evil alien baboon, she roamed her eyes around the interior before focusing on the doors that slid together and reversed direction when they hit the obstacle preventing them from closing. She dropped to the floor, and as her minions poured through the hole in the roof and slithered around the walls, she hooked claws into the doors and yanked them inwards. The buckled doors became jammed partway into their frames and ceased motion.

Two small kangaroo-like springs carried EV1L into the corridor. After checking both directions and seeing no sign of the humans, she shrieked a command. Splitting up, her small army of viciousness morphed into their previous selected forms and while the majority moved off to search Level 3 for the humans, a few remained to finish off the bovine skeleton.

EV1L altered her appearance to mimic Svetlana and headed along the corridor. She observed small groups of her minions slip away from the main insidious mass to search each of the rooms they passed.

From his shadowy hiding place atop a cupboard, Boris watched the four dark creatures enter and cowered deeper into the dark corner. Aware that touching them would bring pain and death, fighting them wasn't an option. Hoping they wouldn't find him and leave, he anxiously watched them split up and begin searching the room.

One of the creatures jumped onto a workbench and scattered glass beakers, flasks, Bunsen burner tripods, test tubes and test tube clamps and other pieces of scientific equipment as it rushed along the top, its vicious head constantly swiveling, directing its evil eyes around the room in search of prey.

To the sound of glass crashing to the floor, another creature climbed a row of shelves. It halted at a line of large jars filled with human organs and animal specimens, some partly dissected from autopsies carried out after their experiments on Level 4. The creature nudged the jar containing a skinned rabbit and jumped back when its floating form gently struck the glass. Believing it alive, it attacked. The jar crashed into the one beside it and both fell. Exploding on contact with the floor, the specimens from each jar slid across the floor on a wave of formaldehyde.

Distracted by the loud crash, the other creatures looked at the two animals moving across the floor and rushed to claim their share. The creature on the shelf leapt onto the rabbit and wrapped it in a cloak of Black, absorbing what little nourishment the pickled corpse offered.

The first creature to reach the monkey brain, snatched it up and leapt onto the nearest workbench. The two creatures close on its heels set off in pursuit. Laboratory equipment crashed to the floor as the chase weaved through the lab. The creature with the prize doubled back and leapt onto the shelf unit. As it ran along it, spilling books, racks of test tubes and organ sculptures to the floor, it noticed the row of jars containing larger pieces of food than it possessed. It threw the spider monkey brain away and headed for the jars.

The two in pursuit leapt for the brain. One plucked it from the air and sprouting wings flew away with it and landed on top of a cupboard to devour the prize. It stared at its loser brethren who stared back for a few moments until it turned to another loud crash. When it also noticed the row of jars and the edible things inside, it bounded over to them and pushed them all off. The creature on the floor grabbed the human heart it had freed from its glass prison and leapt out of the path of a jar falling towards it. It climbed onto a workbench, oozed over the food and started its absorption process.

The final creature to claim a morsel, gathered the seven pieces of preserved organs into a heap and flowed over them.

Boris had observed all but now focused on the creature close enough to reach out and touch, perched on the edge of the cupboard where he had taken refuge. Acrid formaldehyde fumes filled the room, watering his eyes and burning his throat. He needed to leave. He cowered when the nearby creature moved away from the edge, nearer him, and then watched it melt and flow over the unappetizing food. This was his chance, while all the creatures were feeding. With his tearing eyes focused on the feasting Black, he placed his human friend's lighter in his mouth to leave his hands free and cautiously edged forward. The cupboard shifted slightly with a creak of wood. An eye appeared in the Black and looked at him. Boris rushed for the edge as the Black began to reform. He leapt, arms reaching for the nearest ceiling girder. He gripped it and swung for the next girder in line. The creature behind him screeched an alert to its brethren about the live prey in their midst.

All three creatures ended their feasting and reformed. Live prey would be much more sustaining, and the animal was big enough for them all to claim a share. Working together on the hunt, they converged on the fleeing primate.

Boris's fearful gaze flicked to each of the creatures in turn and then at the exit across the room. His escape route was about to be cut off. He quickly formed a plan. When his hand gripped the next girder, he changed direction and hanging from a foot, he swung down and snatched up a microscope. His momentum swung his hand back to the girder. He homed in on the nearest creature and dropped to the workbench below. In a sideways underarm movement, he hurled the microscope, turned on the two gas taps within reach and jumped onto the next workbench.

The creature easily ignored the missile by dodging around it and continued the chase. The microscope bounced off the edge of workbench and clattered to the floor.

After turning on three more gas taps, Boris leapt for a girder. He veered away from the two creatures blocking his exit route and headed back the way he had come. He dropped to the floor when the creature moving across the ceiling was almost upon him, grabbed the edge of the table and swung underneath as the creature landed on top. Slamming his feet against the floor, his arms lifted the table and threw it at another creature running along a workbench. The table twisted upside down and squashed both creatures. Boris bounded down an aisle between two workbenches. As he rushed past, he turned on the small levers from both benches. Soft hissing and gas fumes seeped through the room, mixing with the acrid stench of formaldehyde.

After climbing onto the top of the shelf unit, Boris glanced at the two creatures between him and the door. They seemed to have worked out it was his only means of escape. He needed to draw them nearer if his plan was to work. He swung along a beam and faked a fall, his hand slipping from the cold metal. He bounced off the workbench and dropped to the floor.

The gaze of the two creatures guarding the exit followed the animal's progress along the beam and watched it fall. When it didn't reappear, they looked at one another. One of them screeched instructions. They moved forward, splitting up to come at their prey from different sides.

While listening to the click of the creatures' approaching claws on the tiled floor, Boris turned his head to look at the gooey Black oozing from beneath the table and stretching to the floor. He didn't have much time. When the clicks reached the ends of the workbenches and the Black puddle on the floor began to reform, Boris slid back the door in the workbench, climbed inside and closed the door.

When the creatures appeared at either end and saw no sign of their prey, only their splattered brethren reforming, they screeched in frustration. One of them turned their attention to a partly open door and hooked a claw in the gap. It slid it open and peered inside at the racks of glass beakers and flasks. After gazing along the line of cupboards it screeched a series of short commands, and all three started searching the cupboards.

The fourth creature flowed from beneath the table onto the worktop and morphed into its previous creature form. Hearing the commotion nearby, it moved to the edge and observed its three brethren opening doors. Its head jerked up on hearing a sound and went to investigate.

The creature nearer the middle of the row of cupboards opened a door, and seeing the door opposite open, it scampered inside in time to see a hairy leg disappear around the end of the workbench. It screeched an alert and gave chase.

The other two raised their heads at the alert and jumped onto the workbench.

Realizing he had been spotted, Boris abandoned stealth and jumped onto the nearest workbench, almost colliding with one of the creatures. He scooped up a rack of test tubes and flung them at the creature. Surprised by the sudden encounter, the creature was slow to react. Unable to avoid the object, it softened its form. The wooden rack and test tubes sunk into its body.

Boris shot a glimpse back at the three creatures rushing him. He leapt high, grabbed a beam and swung from girder to girder towards the exit. When he was almost at the far wall, he dropped, turned in mid-air and landed sure-footedly on the last workbench. He spat the lighter from his mouth, and as soon as it was in his hand, he struck it to flame. He hooted at the creatures defiantly as he flung the lighter towards the far end of the room and then spun and bounded out the door.

As the creature pulled the objects from its body, the other three watched the flaming missile pass over their heads. Having no idea what it was, only that it didn't seem edible, they continued after their prey.

A loud whoosh signaled the coming together of flame and gas and turned the heads of the four creatures who were powerless to dodge the huge fireball that swept through the room and devoured them. The explosion that followed vaporized their burning forms and ended their high-pitched shrieks.

Boris glanced back at the flames shooting from the doorway he had just passed through and continued his dash along the corridor. Screeches from within the rooms he passed alerted him to more of the creatures nearby. He needed to find a way out or at the very least a safe place to hide. He knew if he could find his human friend, he would keep him safe.

CHAPTER 25

Self-Destruct

With flashlights lighting their way, the team arrived at the exit elevator. While Sullivan and Ramirez protected the corridor, Dalton took position by the elevator with Richard keeping the door open for their escape.

Lit by Colbert's flashlight, Krisztina inserted one of the strangely shaped keys into the matching hole in the panel and turned. The catch beside it clicked open. She pulled it down, releasing the top edge of the panel and lifted it out. She laid it aside and examined the controls that matched the images in the instruction manual.

After refreshing her memory with a flick through its pages, she turned the four levers positioned around the central panel made up of twelve square buttons, until they all faced in opposite directions. When the buttons glowed green, Krisztina flipped through the instruction manual to the correct page, and glancing from the book to the buttons and back again, she input the self-destruct sequence. Each green-lit button she pressed turned red. After inputting the correct sequence, a larger square button on the right flashed red.

Krisztina hovered a finger over the flashing button and looked at Colbert who had been watching her. "I press button and self-destruct activated."

Colbert glanced a short distance ahead where Dalton and Richard waited by the exit elevator, holding the doors open. Satisfied they were ready, he turned back to Krisztina. "Do it!"

Krisztina pressed the button. Something behind the panel clunked. The detonate button glowed red briefly and then flashed yellow. The red buttons on the center panel returned to their green status.

"Did it work?" questioned Colbert.

Krisztina cocked an ear for the emergency evacuation warning that remained silent. "Nyet. Something must be wrong. I try again."

Krisztina pressed the reset button and repeated the process, taking extra care to ensure she followed the instructions perfectly. When she pressed the activation button, the same thing happened. A clunk. Yellow flashing button. Red button lights reverted to green.

"It's not working," stated Krisztina, flicking through the manual again.

Colbert glanced at his watch. "Time is running out."

"Got it!" exclaimed Krisztina. She then let out a disappointed groan and looked at Colbert. "A flashing yellow activation button indicates device is disconnected."

"Damn!" cursed Colbert. "Can it be fixed?"

After consulting the manual again, Krisztina found the answer. "To get working, bomb must be reconnected manually. It was probably disconnected when they stopped using facility for dangerous and contagious substances."

"That's just great," said Colbert. Nothing about this mission had run smoothly. "How long will that take?"

Krisztina shrugged. "A simple matter of snapping together a couple of connectors. In ordinary circumstances, ten or fifteen minutes; however, that doesn't allow for lower levels overrun with aliens intent on killing any human they come across."

"Even ten or fifteen minutes would be cutting it fine. Your comrades will be arriving shortly, and the charges we've set will go off in..." Colbert glanced at his watch, "...thirty-eight minutes."

"Is any chance your explosions will set off nuclear device?" enquired Krisztina.

Colbert shook his head. "It doesn't work like that, unfortunately."

"Then someone must go below to reconnect bomb, because if not, those aliens will escape. I know we are long way from civilization, but we've seen what those things are capable of. They could change into alien flying creatures and reach nearest town in hours. Then is only hop, skip and a jump across Russia. If they keep on multiplying, they have whole world to expand and conquer. We can't let that happen, and the only time they can be stopped is here and now, by us."

"Great speech, and I agree with everything you say, but it's an impossible and suicidal mission with those creatures down there. We should leave. I will inform my superiors of the danger, and maybe they will nuke the site. I'm certain the President will do the right thing when he is informed of the threat."

"Maybe isn't good enough. I don't trust my own government to do right thing, so I not about to trust yours."

"Then what do you suggest?"

"I'll do it. If I can reach emergency escape ladder down to level 4, I should be fine as creatures seem to have moved up a level. I'll connect bomb, and if I don't return by time your charges are due to go off, you set self-destruct and leave."

"You don't even know if you'll make it past the upper levels to reach the escape ladder."

"Maybe, maybe not, but I'm willing to try. I think there is a second emergency escape ladder I can use to reach Level 3 and then make my way to Level 4 via the ladder I climbed before, but I must go check blueprint in control room."

"No need, I have it with me." Colbert pulled out the tablet, brought up the blueprint and handed it to Krisztina.

After scrolling across the map, she tapped a dotted line stretching from above ground to level three. "There it is. In backup generator room."

Colbert took the tablet and gazed at the screen. "It's still going to be a risky endeavor."

"I have no choice. With luck, maybe I succeed."

"I think you need more than luck to survive what's waiting for you down there.

Krisztina glanced at Sullivan and Dalton. "I know you and Dalton can't come with your injuries, but if one or two of your other men want to keep me company..."

"Actually, if you stand any chance of surviving I have the perfect person to accompany you." Colbert glanced over at Richard. "We just have to find some way of persuading him to do it."

Krisztina looked at Richard doubtfully. "But he not soldier."

"It's not a soldier you need. You need someone who is devious, quick-witted and willing to do anything to survive. Believe me, he's gotten out of worse scrapes than what you are about to face, virtually unscathed. He has also encountered the type of alien you have here and survived—and even managed to persuade it not to kill him. Yes, he risked a ship's crew to save himself, but he did survive. Watch him like a hawk, and you should be okay."

Unconvinced of the man's credentials, Krisztina studied Richard for anything that might alleviate her concerns.

Noticing the pretty Russian woman looking at him, which he took to be an expression of interest, Richard gave her one of his most charming smiles. Perhaps something pleasant would come from his abduction after all. He had never been with a Russian before.

With Krisztina following, Colbert approached the group by the elevator. "We have a problem."

"Now why doesn't that surprise me?" said Richard.

"The bomb has been disconnected, and someone needs to accompany Krisztina to Level 4 to reconnect it. Due to our injuries, Dalton and I can't go, and I want Sullivan and Ramirez to remain up top in case the Russians arrive earlier than expected."

A bad feeling swept over Richard when Colbert focused on him.

"That leaves the best man for the task in hand, you, Richard."

Richard shook his head. "Uh uh! No way I'm going back in there and especially not to the facility's alien-infested bowels."

"I understand your reluctance, but there is no one else," said Colbert. "As I just explained to Krisztina, if anyone can do the job and survive, it's you."

"Flattered as I am, I don't care. I'm not going," stated Richard adamantly. "I wouldn't set foot back in there for a million pounds."

Colbert appealed to Richard's vanity. "There's no money on the table, but there is your reputation."

Richard snorted. "What reputation? Your government shot that to pieces damn quick after Antarctica."

"What if you could get it back? Though for obvious reasons I'll be unable to mention your role here, if you do this I'll make sure everyone knows you are a hero who saved the world from an alien entity and that aliens do exist and you, Richard, battled with them on a spaceship in Antarctica, twice!"

Though Richard was tempted by the offer, it was too dangerous to go back in. "Won't do me much good if I'm dead, will it? No, thanks, I'll rather be alive with a bad reputation than dead with a good one. You'll have to think of a different plan."

"Your choice, Richard." Colbert glanced at Sullivan. "Shoot him."

Sullivan pointed his weapon at Richard.

Unconcerned, Richard looked at the rifle pointed at his heart. "Yeah, right, you're going to shoot me."

"Trust me, Richard, I will have you shot. I have the full authority of the President of the United States to do anything I see fit to complete this mission. You are one hundred percent expendable," stated Colbert. "The mission comes first, and if you're not part of the mission, you're a liability."

Richard began to worry. "You're bluffing. You wouldn't kill a civilian, and anyway, how will shooting me help? It doesn't make sense."

"We are wasting what precious little time we have. I need to go now," said Krisztina. "Alone, if necessary."

"Last chance, Richard," advised Colbert.

"Kill me then. A bullet will be a quicker and a less painful death than any I'd find down there."

Colbert nodded at Sullivan.

Sullivan lowered the rifle to aim at Richard's stomach. "I wouldn't be so sure about that, Richard. You ever see a man die a lingering painful death from a gut shot? It's not pretty, I can tell you."

Richard focused on Sullivan's finger moving nearer the trigger, resting against it and then beginning to squeeze. *Were they really going to shoot him? They wouldn't dare.* The trigger was depressed half-way now. Fear gripped Richard. Beads of sweat formed on his brow. The finger continued moving. Any moment now the bullet would pierce his flesh, and the agony would begin. He almost wet himself when the weapon clicked. There was no loud retort and no pain. Richard had called their bluff.

"You've more guts than I credited you with," praised Colbert.

Richard was just glad his guts weren't splattered on the floor.

"Tie him up," ordered Colbert. "We'll leave him here. If the aliens don't get to him first and he doesn't get vaporized by the bomb if Krisztina gets it working, the Russians can have him to torture for information when they arrive. If Krisztina fails, we'll have no option other than to abort the mission and hope the President will see sense and nuke this place."

Sullivan nudged Richard into a corner with the rifle, and after using plastic ties to bind his hands and legs, he forced him to sit on the floor.

"Whoa, hold on. You can't do this," pleaded Richard.

Everyone ignored him.

"Krisztina, let's get you up top and fitted out with some gear you might find helpful, and then you can start—or alternatively, you can leave with us?" said Colbert.

Krisztina shook her head. "You know I can't. I have to try and destroy it, them."

Colbert nodded. "If you fail, I'll do everything in my power to try and convince my superiors to destroy this place and everything inside."

Krisztina smiled anxiously. "Then it seems both our missions stand little chance of success."

"We're leaving," called out Colbert to Sullivan and Ramirez. As they stepped into the elevator, Colbert tapped his radio mic. "Mission aborted. Eagle 3. Power up. We're leaving in 5. Eagle 4, pick up in ten."

"*Powering up,*" replied the pilot.

"*Rodger that, pick up in ten,*" affirmed Mason.

As the rest of the team entered the elevator, Richard reluctantly called out, "Okay, okay, I'll go."

Either unheard or ignored, the others continued as if he hadn't spoken.

When the elevators doors began to close, Richard shouted, "I'll do it!"

Hiding a smile that his bluff had worked, Colbert slammed a hand against the door to prevent it closing, stepped out and glared at Richard.

"You'll do what?" asked Colbert.

"I'll go with Sweet Cheeks and help her connect the bomb."

"I no longer think you can be trusted," said Colbert. "You'll flee at the first chance and leave Krisztina in the shit."

"I must admit that did cross my mind, but the way I see it, if I return too soon and alone, you're going to suspect I double-crossed Krisztina and take appropriate action—like leaving me here again for the aliens, the bomb or the Russians. All three are obviously events I'm extremely eager to avoid. It's in my interest to help her in her foolhardy suicide mission that has little chance of either of us surviving, and slim though my odds are, they are a slight improvement over the former choices which offer me none."

"Fair enough," said Colbert. He pulled Richard to his feet and cut his ties.

Colbert updated his team over the radio. "Change of plan—we're staying a while longer."

"If we succeed in getting the bomb working and I live through this or not, you'll make sure people know what a hero I was."

Colbert nodded. "I will."

Richard turned to Krisztina waiting with the SEALs in the elevator. "Well, Sweet Cheeks, it seems we have our first date."

Krisztina glared at Richard. "My name is Krisztina, not Sweet Cheeks, and this isn't a date!"

Richard grinned, and turning to Colbert, he switched to survival mode. "This is what we'll need. Weapons, anything that explodes, like grenades, as it seems to be the only thing that causes the aliens any serious harm, a radio each and one of you in the control room watching the CCTV feeds to guide us past the creatures on the levels we can't avoid passing through."

Colbert nodded. "Anything else?"

Impressed by Richard's sudden change, Krisztina added, "Flashlights. It's dark down there."

Richard looked at Colbert's helmet. "And night vision goggles."

"Right, let's get you two equipped." Colbert glanced at his watch. "You only have twenty-nine minutes before the charges go off, so let's get a move on."

Richard and Colbert joined the others in the elevator and headed above ground to get geared up.

CHAPTER 26

Into Hell

Strolling through Level 3 in her human Svetlana form, EV1L glanced into the rooms she passed at her brood searching for the humans. A loud whump and pained screeches from some of her younglings filtering down the corridor quickened her pace to discover the cause. She entered the blackened room drifting with smoke and gazed around at the destruction and flames spouting from mangled pipes. Small chunks of hardened, brittle Black littering the room were evidence some of her brood had died here.

Assuming it to be the work of the humans, she returned to the corridor and gazed in both directions. Her face changed to a creature sporting a large sensitive snout that sniffed the air. She detected no recent human scent, only that of an animal similar to the kind she had devoured in the room of cages. That did not concern her. When her gaze fell upon the metal doors along the corridor, she reformed Svetlana's face and walked to them. It was another moving box.

Aware the humans could call the box and open the doors at will, EV1L searched for the means to do so. Discovering the button positioned to one side, she pressed it with a black finger. Nothing happened. She returned to the middle of the doors, formed hands into hooks, jammed them into the join and ripped them open. Poking her head inside, she stared up at the box high in the shaft and pondered the sounds of sliding doors moving back and forth on one side. She directed her gaze at the sliver of light seeping through the join of another set of doors halfway between her and the stationary box. Morphing into her many-legged insect form, EV1L screeched orders for her brood to follow and slithered up the shaft.

Arriving at the doors, EV1L formed two hooks and forced them apart. She glanced down when her offspring began pouring into the shaft. She screeched orders for half of them to search this level and for the remainder to follow her. She climbed the shaft.

*****

Returning to Level 1, Ramirez aimed his weapon at the gap between the elevator doors when they slid open. Wishing to be anywhere but here, he took a deep breath and peered around the edge of the frame. He doubted the darkness past the small patch of elevator light breaching the corridor could look more uninviting. Stepping out, he flicked down his NVGs and headed along the corridor. He cringed at the crunches of glass beneath his feet that he couldn't waste time avoiding; Krisztina and Richard had already started climbing down the upper escape ladder to Level 3.

Ramirez glanced behind at the sounds of the elevator doors swishing shut and the winch hauling it up. He had elected not to block the door because if he did and needed help, his buddies wouldn't be able to reach him. Dalton waited up above ready to send it down for his departure when he returned.

Pausing at the corner, Ramirez checked the offshoot was clear before continuing his harrowing journey. Hoping foul creatures weren't lying in wait for him, his weapon and head turned anxiously to every room he passed.

Blue light seeping into the corridor from the security office a short distance ahead indicated he had almost reached his destination. He froze when a shadow moved eerily through the light. Ignoring the beads of sweat forming beneath his helmet, he pushed back his fear and the strong urge to get the hell out of there and slowly moved forward.

He paused again when distant shrieks and echoing booms of something striking metal drifted along the corridor. The creatures were coming. Ramirez stared at the security office entrance when something again briefly blocked the light, heightening his anxiety further. He briefly considered leaving, but his training to complete the mission drove his cautious steps nearer the door. Pressing his back to the wall, rifle held close to his chest, he steeled himself for what he was about to face and peered around the frame. His gaze took in the small room thankfully free of creatures and focused on the draft from the oscillating fan flittering a poster, whose top edge had come loose from the wall and draped over a monitor.

Ramirez nipped inside, closed the door and barricaded the entrance with the chest high cupboard he dragged in front of it. Though, with the creatures transforming ability he doubted it would stop them for long, it gave him some semblance of security; he would take all he could get. He sat in the desk chair, wheeled it into position and glanced at each monitor in turn. He focused on the view showing a corridor on Level 2 as the doors of the internal elevator were forced open. He zoomed in on the vicious cat-size creatures that emerged and spread out across the level.

Wondering how Richard and Krisztina would survive their journey if they encountered the small army of horrors, he radioed them. “I’m in. Creatures have just arrived on Level 2 and are spreading out. I’m assuming they will make their way to level 1 shortly.” He scanned the Level 3 camera feeds. “No movement on Level 3, but there’s no assurance it’s unoccupied. For God’s sake hurry and good luck.”

*****

"Thanks, Ramirez. We don't plan on hanging around," Richard glanced at Krisztina as she stepped off the ladder in Escape Chute 1. "Showtime."

Apprehensive of what might be waiting for them on the other side, Krisztina anxiously looked at the small door hatch stenciled Level 3 as she slipped the assault rifle from her shoulder. "I guess."

Richard nodded at the weapon she held in hands that were as nervous as his own. "You're not going to panic if you see an alien and accidentally shoot me in the back?"

Krisztina shrugged. "Guess you be first to know if I do."

Richard flashed her a smile. "Let's get this done." He turned the wheel. The clunk of the seven bolts releasing from their locks sounded awfully loud within the confines of the chute.

*****

Eyes in the darkness shifted to the source of the clunks that resounded around the room and focused on the small door it hadn't noticed before. Wondering what was about to come through, it waited.

*****

After checking his nervous companion had her weapon trained on the hatch, Richard pulled it open. Both flinched at the screeches emitted by the long unused hinges forced into motion.

When nothing attacked and they heard no creatures nearby, they stepped into the storeroom and gazed past stacks of document and storage boxes at the light shining into the room through an open door. Unaware they were being watched, Richard and Krisztina trod softly towards it. Richard peered into the corridor. It was empty. He shifted his gaze to the red blinking light of an explosive charge stuck to the wall.

He walked over to the charge, read the timer readout and glanced at Krisztina. “Twenty-three minutes.”

Krisztina checked the time matched the countdown timer on her wristwatch. It did. “We need to get move on or we’ll never make it out.”

It was all the encouragement Richard needed. He pressed his mic button and whispered, “Ramirez, we’re on Level 3, any movement?”

*****

Fearing it was the creatures that were in the room earlier until a piercing screech had called them away, Boris cowered deeper into the shadows when the hatch screeched open. Though Boris recognized one of the humans, a female friend of his man friend he had failed to find, he remained hidden. They had already made too much noise; the creatures might already be on their way to find out what had caused it. No, best he remain here for now, hidden and safe. His eyes followed the humans across the room until they were out of his sight. Cocking an ear to their faint voices from outside the room, Boris focused his attention upon the dim light shining from the door through which they had arrived. He wondered where it led.

*****

With half her brood following, EV1L squeezed her pliable form between the elevator and the wall. She glanced at the chair blocking the doors when she entered the corridor. Changing into Svetlana again, she glanced in each direction and then at her offspring gathered around her waiting for their orders. Alien screeches from her human mouth sent them scurrying away in both directions.

Sensing their time to begin conquering the humans' world was drawing near, EV1L chose a direction and headed along it.

*****

In the control room, Ramirez glanced nervously behind at the small glass door panel when distant shrieks grew louder, nearer. His eyes flicked to the Level 1 screens and the small dark shapes moving rapidly through the rooms. *This isn't good.*

Concerned they'd be attracted by the glow of the CCTV screens seeping out, he pulled the poster he had stuck back in place from the wall. Hoping the sticky pads on the back were still tacky, he crossed to the door and stuck it over the glass.

"Ramirez, we're on Level 3, any movement?"

Ramirez rushed to his seat and quickly turned down the volume in case the creatures could hear. His gaze flicked across the Level 3 screens as he replied softly, "No movement on your level, but some of the creatures have just arrived on Level 1 and some are still on Level 2."

"Okay, we're heading for Escape Chute 2. Warn us if you see anything we need to avoid."

"Copy that."

Wondering how the hell he was going to get out alive and trying unsuccessfully to ignore the scampering of claws clacking on the hard floor and the sounds of rooms being ransacked back along the corridor, Ramirez concentrated on the Level 3 screens. He followed Krisztina and Richard's dash though corridors that, for now, seemed a lot less dangerous than those outside his door.

*****

Though they had already turned the volume low on their radios, their fear intensified senses caused it to seem louder than it was and prompted them to reduce the volume further.

"It will be faster if I lead instead of continually giving you instructions and also less talking to give us away," suggested Krisztina.

Richard waved an arm along the corridor. "Be my guest. Anything that gets me out of this hellhole sooner gets my vote." With his self-preservation senses on high alert for danger, he followed Krisztina.

*****

Krisztina and Richard's sprint through the corridors went unencumbered by any creature attacks, and they soon reached the room with the entrance to the Level 4 escape ladder. Remembering her last time at the hatch and the creature that chased her, which might still be in the chute, she pointed her weapon at the floor hatch and glanced at Richard. "Move the props and open it."

Richard knelt, freed the mop and broom and spun the wheel to release the locking pins. Krisztina tensed as he heaved it open. Nothing jumped out. Richard leaned into the hole and gazed down the ladder. "That's a longer climb than I expected."

"Getting down will be easy, climbing up, not so much. I've done it. Put your gloves on and copy me." Krisztina slipped the rifle strap over her head, fished gloves Dalton had loaned her from her pocket and slipped them on. Without hesitating, she crossed to the hole and climbed down the ladder until her head was below the floor. She looked up at Richard. "You will follow me, yes?"

Richard smiled as he pulled his borrowed gloves on. "To hell and back, Sweet Cheeks."

Krisztina rolled her eyes. She placed the side of her shoes, whose designer never imagined them ever being used in such an inappropriate fashion, against the outer edges of the ladder and released her hand grip slightly.

For a few indecisive moments, Richard watched her slide speedily deeper into the void, and sighed before climbing into the chute. Copying Krisztina's technique, he followed her down.

*****

Richard and Krisztina had become lost from the camera's viewing field when they entered the storeroom, so Ramirez focused on the other screens. Because Level 4 was in total darkness, he could do nothing until they returned, if indeed they did. He glanced at his watch. He had orders to evacuate at five minutes to the detonation of the charges they had placed throughout the facility. They didn't have much time. Come to that, neither did he. Though the creatures running amok through the rooms hadn't ventured as far as the security office yet, they were getting closer and would eventually cut off his only escape route.

*****

Krisztina gripped the sides of the ladder tighter to slow her progress when the bottom drew near and gently touched ground. Stepping back, she glanced up at her reluctant companion, who she had half expected to turn and flee. Though she would have carried out the frightful task by herself and Richard would not have been her first choice to accompany her, she was comforted by his presence.

As Richard approached, Krisztina readied her weapon and peered out through the open hatch into the darkness past the small patch of light spilling from the dimly lit escape chute. She briefly pictured the two tiny green indicator lights on the chugging generator's control panel as belonging to the eyes of some foul monstrosity staring at her. Startled by Richard's less than elegant arrival, which saw him spilled to the floor, she turned to check he was okay.

Recovering quickly from his rough landing, Richard climbed to his feet and gazed back up the towering ladder. It wasn't a climb he was looking forward to.

"You okay?" whispered Krisztina.

Richard nodded.

"Not far now." Krisztina flicked her NVGs over her eyes and stepped through the hatch.

Richard followed suit and gazed around the room at the generator tinted ghostly green and the small, bright light on the explosive charge before following Krisztina's spectral form into the corridor.

Recalling the map from the instruction pamphlet showing the location of the bomb, Krisztina hurried along the corridor past prison cells that emitted the lingering aura of misery suffered by their prisoners now long dead and into the hall.

Noticing the ripped-open elevator doors, she shuddered at the thought of what creature the Black had mimicked to rip them apart. She gazed ahead at what remained of the laboratories, the resulting damage of the explosion she had felt earlier.

Their footsteps crunched glass that sounded as loud as gunshots in the eerie silence prevalent throughout the level. Krisztina made her way forward, stepping over and around larger pieces of wreckage as her gaze took in the ghostly destruction. So much pain, suffering and death had gone on down here, it caused her no remorse knowing it would soon be vaporized, wiping clean the lingering souls of the tormented. To ensure she didn't suffer the same fate, she concentrated on her task that was made more difficult by the amount of debris everywhere. She swept her eyes over the floor while Richard kept lookout and roamed his rifle and senses around the darkness.

"I'm going to have to use the flashlight," Krisztina called softly after finding the NVGs light inadequate to pick out a single tile with four odd shaped keyholes in each corner from amongst the wreckage.

Richard gave her a thumbs-up signal and kept his NVGs pointed away from the bright light that invaded the edges of his limited vision. He cringed fearfully when the broken glass being swept aside shattered silence.

Aware the access panel she sought was in the middle of the hall, Krisztina used a foot to scrape away glass shards and other bits of wreckage from the area where she thought it should be. Bending over, she searched the cleared space with the flashlight and spotted the tile with four cross-shaped keyholes with a hexagon hole set in the center of each. She slipped the key from a pocket, crouched and inserted it into the first keyhole and turned until it clicked. She quickly repeated the process three more times. The final turn of the key in the fourth hole raised the tile. Krisztina slid her fingers beneath and hefted the large tile aside.

Krisztina's gaze roamed over the impressive but ominous shiny chrome device. It was surprisingly symmetrical, and if one ignored its deadly purpose, it almost beautiful in its design. Two shiny, chrome, elongated bulbous tanks at each end were stenciled with the universal three-pronged nuclear symbol. A smaller golden globe in the middle was attached to the outer tanks by arm-thick tubes. Cables circling the circumference of both end tanks led to the central globe. A control panel was positioned on the left side, and on the right was a raised indicator panel with various gauges, connecters and unlit colored lights that would, when powered up, show the operational state of the device.

The disconnected end of a red cable the width of a garden hose led from the control panel and hung beside the indicator panel on the left and another identical cable leading from the indicator panel to the center globe was draped over the device. It was a simple matter of reconnecting the two cables to bring the device back to operational status.

Krisztina picked up the end of the nearest cable and glanced at the nine protruding prongs set in two circular patterns that matched the holes in the female connector attached to the bomb's central golden globe. A protrusion on the outer edge ensured it could only be connected correctly. She nervously lined up the connector, inserted the prongs into their holes and pushed until it clicked into place. As she screwed down the outer sleeve that ensured it wouldn't come loose, her head jerked to the elevator when something metallic clattered noisily down the shaft.

Richard spun his fearful gaze and weapon at the sound and focused on the dark opening. When nothing appeared, he cautiously moved closer to investigate.

*****

The first of the creatures from the last three eggs to be laid, struggled from its slimy pod and formed into a creature plucked from its memory. It gazed around at the empty sacs before focusing on the two pods its brethren clawed their way out of. As they changed to mimic its own chosen form, its head darted around and stared towards the sound coming from nearby. Unsure if its kind had made the noise or it was something to be wary of or hunted, it shrieked softly at its two marginally younger siblings, and with them following, skulked from the room.

*****

Richard halted by the elevator door. Crouching slightly, he peered through the jagged hole. Stepping nearer for a better view, his vision picked out the metal debris at the bottom of the shaft. Sticking his head partway into the hole, he gazed up at the light spilling into the shaft from Level 3 and the bottom of the elevator stuck higher up on Level 2. The distant shrieks that floated down from the higher levels, though unnerving, seemed too far away to pose them any immediate threat. His gaze around the shaft's four sides revealed only electric cables and a maintenance ladder fixed to the wall; the shaft appeared to be free of monsters. He pulled his head back through the hole when a shadow interrupted the light on level 3.

Richard crossed to Krisztina. "How much longer?"

Krisztina picked up the last cable. "Ten seconds and I'm done."

Richard pressed the radio's talk button. "Ramirez, I just noticed movement on Level 3 near the elevator, and we're about to head back up. You seeing anything?"

*****

In the security office, Ramirez scanned the level three monitors and focused on the elevator corridor. "Nothing on the screens but suggest you proceed with caution."

"That's a given," replied Richard. *"Leaving radio open so you can lead us through."*

Ramirez turned his attention to Level 2 and the evil creatures moving through the rooms and corridors and then switched to the Level 1 screens. A group of small aliens had discovered the food stores in the kitchen and searched through them for anything edible. One moved to the large fridge, sniffed at the edge of the door and shrieked, the sound made dumb by the facility's cameras lacking sound capability. The four other creatures in the kitchen dropped the food packets and tins and excitedly crossed to the fridge. After detecting the scents of meat seeping from the old ill-fitting seal, they started shaking the fridge. Their frantic attacks sent the appliance toppling to the floor. The door flopped open when it crashed to the ground and rolled, squashing a creature and spilling out food items, bottles of milk, other dairy products and hunks of pork and other meats.

Equal parts horrified and fascinated, Ramirez watched them spread their melting bodies over the raw chickens, pork and slices of cold beef. The splattered creature seeped out from beneath the door as a greasy puddle, reformed and joined its brethren in devouring the cold meats.

Distracted by movement on the next monitor, Ramirez turned his gaze to the screen and froze at the sight of the figure walking through the corridor. It looked like a woman, but it wasn't. When he turned the camera and zoomed in on the Black figure, it directed its eyes to the camera. Shocked by the human creature's malicious stare that seemed to peer into his soul, Ramirez shot back in his seat. Certain that somehow it knew he was nearby and would come for him, he grabbed his rifle and was about to head for the door and flee before it found him when an alarm and a female Russian voice blaring from intercom speakers halted him.

*****

Krisztina plugged the second cable into its socket and was pleased to see the control and indicator panels light up. Richard raised the NVGs from his eyes and gazed at the deadly machine. "It's powered up. Let's go."

Krisztina climbed to her feet. "Better let Colbert know so someone can activate the self-destruct as soon as we're up top."

Before Richard had a chance to contact Colbert, a Russian female voice and an insistent repeating alarm erupted over the internal intercom speakers. Assuming Colbert no longer needed to be informed, he looked to Krisztina for confirmation; the dread on her face spoke volumes.

"The self-destruct has initialized," stated Krisztina. "Fifteen minutes before it detonates."

Though he had a few questions about how that was possible, Richard voiced the most important. “Can you stop it?”

She shook her head. “Not from here, only at a control point. There’s one on this level, but I don’t have the proper panel key to access controls. I left it with Colbert.”

Richard gazed around frantically. “There must be one around here with the instructions the scientists would have had to refer to in order to initiate it if needed.”

“I’m sure there is, but”—she waved a hand at the destruction—“do you want to waste what little time we have searching for it?”

Crunching glass directed their gazes and Krisztina’s flashlight. Caught in the beam, the three small creatures halted and stared past the dazzling light at their prey.

Richard raised his rifle, aimed and fired. Bullets raked a line of destruction in front of the creatures, spraying them with chunks of tile gouged from the floor. They turned pliant, absorbing the impacts without damage.

Richard turned and shoved Krisztina into movement. “Run!”

They ran.

CHAPTER 27

Going Nuclear

Colbert frowned when an alarm and a Russian female voice erupted from a speaker attached to the side of the main building. Though he couldn't understand Russian, the purpose of her message and the alarm was obvious. Krisztina's translation for Richard over the open radio he listened in on confirmed his fears. The self-destruct was active. The facility would be obliterated in fifteen minutes. Not wanting to distract Richard and Krisztina from their harrowing plight, he kept radio silence and crossed to the helicopter. After discussing their options, Colbert radioed Mason. "Eagle 4, evac in process. Fifteen minutes countdown. We leave in twelve. Do you have means of transport to rendezvous with us here?"

*****

Mason glanced through the window at the tanker that had arrived five minutes ago. The driver, puzzled why no soldiers had emerged from the hut to check his papers and open the barrier to let him pass, stared at the door. "Affirmative. See you in five."

Mason turned to Sven. "Time to leave, and I advise you hurry. Is there room on the motorbike for you and the driver?"

Sven climbed from his seat. "Da, but we can leave in truck. Is warmer."

"I'm not sure that antique will be fast enough to get you clear in time."

"Oh! Then we take bike."

Mason's rifle followed Sven to the door. "Inform the driver something has gone wrong at the facility, and a huge explosion is about to obliterate it and everything in about a kilometer radius."

Sven nodded. "I will tell him this but nothing else."

"Also tell him to leave the keys in the truck. Good luck, Sven."

"Good luck to you also, American." Sven closed the door behind him.

Mason observed Sven cross to the truck and speak to the driver. After a few moments arguing, the driver climbed from the truck, and both men vanished from his view. A few moments later, Mason heard the roar of the motorcycle before it appeared with Sven driving and the truck driver's large bulk balanced on the back. Skewing slightly when it turned onto the road, Sven steered around the barrier and roared away.

Mason exited the hut and climbed into the old truck. Wrinkling his nose at the lingering stench of body odor, he laid his rifle on the passenger seat and turned the key. The engine chugged a few times before it caught. Mason revved it, belching out dark fumes from the exhaust. He crunched it into gear and pulled forward, snapping the flimsy security barrier. Shifting through crunching gears, Mason drove to the facility.

*****

As they fled side by side, Richard, worried the light would give away their position to the creatures, snatched the flashlight from Krisztina's hand, threw it behind and flicked down hers and his own NVGs. He pressed his radio talk button. "Ramirez, we're heading to Level 3."

Rushing past the red LED lights of explosive charges stuck to the wall, which would be vaporized before they carried out their singular task, they soon reached the generator room. Richard shut the door and followed Krisztina across the room and through the hatch, which he closed and locked with a spin of the wheel. Confident the tight-fitting metal door would hold the creatures at bay if they breached the outside door, he turned to the ladder and climbed after Krisztina.

"Warning. Evacuation protocol in process. Thirteen minutes until detonation."

*****

"Ramirez, we're heading to Level 3."

Halfway to the security office door, Ramirez reluctantly returned to his seat at the monitors and ran his gaze over the Level 3 screens. Having completed their search of the rooms, many of the creatures had filtered into the corridors. Picking out the path Richard and Krisztina would need to take to reach the escape chute that would take them above ground, he saw it was an impossible task. It would take a miracle for them to survive the journey.

"Be advised your route is full of hostiles."

Richard's breathless reply was short and to the point. *"Then do your job, and find us one that isn't."*

Trying to block out the insistent, distracting alarm and the warning that counted down the minutes to detonation,

Ramirez took a red marker pen from a pot on the console and crossed to the large blueprint of the facility. Placing his finger on the room Richard and Krisztina would exit after their climb up Escape Ladder 2, he traced a finger along the corridors and connecting rooms between it and the exit escape chute. With glances back at the screens, he backtracked his finger and directed it down alternative routes until he had found their safest option, which really wasn't that safe at all with the creatures' constant meanderings.

After highlighting the route with the marker, he returned to the screens and pressed the talk button. "Okay, I have the best route available. Inform me when you're on Level 3."

*****

Breathless from her hurried climb, Krisztina paused at the top of the ladder and cautiously peered out. After checking her surroundings were clear, she climbed out and crossed to the door as Richard emerged from the chute.

Richard closed the hatch softly and spun the wheel before joining Krisztina. "We're ready, Ramirez."

"Route is clear, go now! Head left, turn right at first junction and enter first room on the left."

Ignoring the shrieks, clacks and growls filtering through the level, Richard and Krisztina followed Ramirez's instructions.

*****

Occasionally glancing behind at the route penned on the blueprint, Ramirez flicked his eyes over the Level 3 camera feeds as he followed Richard's and Krisztina's hurried dash through the corridors. When they reached the first room he issued their next instructions. "Head straight on through two rooms and then enter the corridor."

As they set off, Ramirez checked the corridor they were about to enter. His brow creased with worry when two creatures broke off from the pack that had, for some reason, gathered around the elevator, and headed along the corridor. His eyes flicked back to Richard and Krisztina. They were about to rush into the corridor and the creatures.

"Stop! Two creatures heading your way."

Ramirez's warning halted them.

*****

Richard and Krisztina pressed themselves against the wall beside the door and listened to the clacking of claws on the floor, barely audible above the alarm, coming closer.

"Warning. Evacuation protocol in process. Twelve minutes until detonation."

Constantly reminded their time was ticking down, Richard leaned towards Krisztina and whispered. "We don't have time for this. How far away is the escape chute?"

"Not far if there were no aliens to worry about."

"We have to risk it."

Krisztina nodded. "You lead. Head along corridor, turn first right, second left, take door at the end, and we are there."

With his weapon raised and his finger on the trigger, Richard stepped into the corridor and sprinted towards the surprised creatures. Bullets punched holes through their Black forms and sent them tumbling until they liquified to escape further injury. With Krisztina on his heels, he leapt over the black puddles and turned right.

*****

Ramirez's mouth dropped open when Richard and Krisztina stepped into the corridor and ran towards the creatures. Unable to hear the shots Richard fired, he watched the creatures suffer from the onslaught. He guessed lack of time had caused them to abandon his safe route for the more dangerous direct route. He hoped they made it.

*****

Richard almost faltered on seeing the large group of creatures gathered around the elevator ahead that turned their evil gazes upon them. "Grenades!"

He raised the rifle and raked the evil group with bullets.

Krisztina shouldered her rifle, pulled two grenades from her vest and holding down the arming levers, pulled the pins. "Two ready."

The creatures leapt for the walls when the first bullets struck and spreading out rushed at their prey.

Holding his nerve as they rushed nearer the oncoming creatures crawling and leaping from the floor, walls and ceiling in a macabre ballet of viciousness, Richard waited until they had reached the second left-hand corridor. "Now!"

Krisztina lobbed the grenades at the vicious onslaught of evilness and turned into the branching corridor close behind Richard. Shrieks and squeals followed the explosions that shook the walls.

Richard slowed when he reached the door at the corridor's end, and alert for creatures, he stepped inside and gazed around the room. It was clear.

Krisztina followed him through.

"Warning. Evacuation protocol in process. Eleven minutes until detonation."

As Richard shut the door, he glimpsed the survivors of the explosion, angry and snarling creatures thirsting for revenge and human blood, coming. Not confident the door would hold them at bay for long, he joined Krisztina climbing through the escape hatch. Richard closed and locked the hatch as soon as he was through. When he turned to the ladder he saw that though Krisztina gripped it, she hadn't started climbing; instead she gazed up.

"There's something up there."

Richard peered up, flipped his NVGs over his eyes and saw the focus of Krisztina's concern. A creature high on the ladder was silhouetted in the light shining through the top hatch they had left open for a quick retreat. Its eyes glowed bright, menacingly, in the NVGs spectral illumination when it looked down at them. He raised his rifle and took aim.

Krisztina pushed the weapon aside. "Not good idea. If any part of creature showers down on us, we're dead. I've seen drops of Black crawl inside my comrades and seep from their pores. It devoured them from inside out."

Richard sighed and moved to the hatch. "We'll have to find another way."

"But the creatures..."

"Trust me, when my life's in danger I excel at surviving," reassured Richard.

"Ramirez. Change of plan and warn Colbert he has an alien about to pay him a visit from the escape chute."

"Copy that," replied Ramirez.

"On it," replied Colbert, who had been listening in.

Richard exited the escape chute and crossed to the door the creatures scratched at, searching for a way in. The air tight seal held them at bay. His glance at Krisztina detected the fear in her eyes that for the moment self-preservation kept from his own. He also saw her determination. Like him, she was desperate to survive. "Do exactly as I say, and we might yet live through this."

With the insistent self-destruct alarm continually warning them of their imminent deaths if they didn't escape, Richard grabbed a glass flask from an open box and thrust it into Krisztina's free hand. "Throw it across the room when I open the door."

Shocked he would do such a thing but aware they needed to get past the creatures somehow, she joined Richard against the wall behind the door. She raised the flask as Richard reached for the handle and threw it when he yanked open the door.

Creatures eager to be first to reach the food, rushed in and headed for the sound of breaking glass. When the last of the small hoard had entered, Richard pulled Krisztina through the exit and yanked the door shut.

"What now," asked Krisztina, pointing her weapon along the dark corridor.

"The elevator. It's our only option."

Krisztina sprinted alongside Richard. "Isn't the elevator broken?"

"If it's the same as the other elevator on Level 4, there's a ladder in the shaft we can climb to Level 1 and from there we head for the exit elevator."

"Oh!" uttered Krisztina. "More climbing."

*****

"Are we clear, Ramirez?" asked Richard, rushing through the facility.

"I don't know how you did it, but it seems to be. Did I hear correctly, you're going to climb elevator shaft to Level 1?"

"Affirmative," replied Richard. "What's it like up there?"

"Crowded and I've been unable to find a clear path."

"Don't think we could afford the delay if you had. We'll have to fight our way through. Be grateful for any assistance you can offer from your end."

"I'll do what I can, which won't be much."

"Understood."

When they reached the corridor junction, their heads darted left at the sound of metallic clinks making themselves heard above the warning alarm. They briefly focused on the two creatures Richard had riddled with bullets a few moments earlier, reforming and shedding bullets from their small masses.

With no time to waste shooting them again, they sprinted for the elevator. Amongst the many brittle pieces of dead Black littering the floor, were splatters of fluid Black flowing towards one another and reforming.

Ignoring the danger that might be waiting for them inside, they climbed into the shaft and onto the ladder. Rung by rung they rose towards the elevator hanging high above them.

Richard notified Ramirez—the only person who might be able to help them—of their progress. “Climbing elevator shaft. Colbert, I know you’re listening. Don’t you dare leave without us.”

Colbert promptly replied. *“We leave at three minutes to detonation whether you’re here or not, and that’s cutting it fine to be clear of the blast. Good luck.”*

“We’ll be there,” said Richard with more confidence than he felt.

“Warning. Evacuation protocol in process. Ten minutes until detonation.”

“Ten minutes,” translated Krisztina, practically running up the ladder. “Seven until our ride to safety abandons us.”

“Then we don’t stop for anything. We blast everything that gets in between us and the exit. Understood, Sweet Cheeks?”

“Da. Whatever it takes, and I’m not Sweet Cheeks.”

Richard had a perfect view of Krisztina’s rear as he climbed. “You don’t have my point of view.”

*****

Peering through the wet streaks left in the wake of the juddering worn wiper blades, and snow whisked across the tundra by the biting wind, Mason noticed Sullivan sprinting for the smaller building attached to the side of the main construction, Mason steered the tanker into the compound and skidded to a halt beside the Russian transport truck. He killed the engine, climbed out and crossed to his commander.

"Good, you made it," greeted Colbert. "Go help Sullivan. There's something climbing the escape chute."

Not quite understanding everything that was happening here but certain he was about to find out, Mason held his questions in check and rushed across the compound to help Sullivan.

Sullivan entered the generator hut and moved cautiously to the open hatch his rifle pointed at. Gusts shook the heavily insulated hut and swung the single dim bulb hanging from the ceiling, which eerily moved the shadows it cast. Snow, more ice pellets than fluffy whiteness, pinged off its sides. He shot a glance behind at Mason when he entered and indicated the hatch with a slight movement of his head.

Mason switched on his rifle light and focused the beam on the hatch. He moved a few steps away from Sullivan and matched his footsteps moving nearer to the uninviting hole in the floor. When they were a single step away, both men darted forward and aimed their weapons into the hatch. Their twin beams probed the empty chute.

Mason glanced at Sullivan questioningly.

"One of those alien things was climbing up, but it looks like it went back down," explained Sullivan. "Probably hunting Richard and Krisztina who went below to reconnect the self-destruct bomb to get the device working, which they succeeded in doing, but when they reconnected it, the timer was initiated."

"*Richard* went below?" asked Mason in surprise. "Doesn't sound like the sort of thing he'd do."

"It wasn't entirely voluntary," informed Sullivan, roaming his weapon around the hut furnished with few places where something might be concealed. The swinging light imbued the inside of the hut with shadows that seemed to move as his eyes roamed over the large fuel tank and rested on the darkness behind the back-up diesel generator.

"Ah," uttered Mason. "Didn't think it would have been. Where are they now?"

"Making their way to Level 1. They were supposed to exit via this escape ladder but were unable to because one of the alien creatures was in it. Ramirez is also down there, on Level 1, presently clearing their route out to the exit elevator."

To check the alien wasn't hiding somewhere in the room, Sullivan pointed at the generator and signaled for Mason to work his way around the far end.

Mason nodded and moved into position.

Something leapt from the darkness, bowling Sullivan to the ground. His head struck the generator during his fall, dazing him. As he began to lose consciousness, the rifle slipped from his grasp, landing with its beam aimed across the floor.

The fast-moving creature jumped into the air. A limb slashed at the light, shattering the bulb. The thump of feet landing on the floor, a scampering, then stillness.

With his ears straining to pick out sounds of movement against the creaks of the hut, Mason's flashlight erratically roamed the darkness. When something swift, dark, little more than a blur, passed through Sullivan's dropped rifle beam, he fired. Bullets pinged off the floor, ricocheted off the metal hatch and struck the walls. Mason spun on hearing a noise behind him. Something grabbed his rifle and shoved the stock hard into his face. As he staggered back, the creature ran for the door and dashed through it. A little groggy from the blow, Mason set off in pursuit.

*****

Colbert glanced over at the generator building as shots erupted from inside. Hopefully that would be the end of the creature and they could now concentrate on their evac. Concerned that time was running out, he was about to contact Ramirez for an update when something burst from the hut—a chimpanzee. The primate glanced around the compound and then behind at Mason when he rushed through the door brandishing his weapon. The chimp rushed around the side of the hut and disappeared into darkness shed by the dark gray clouds filling the sky. When Mason set off in pursuit, Colbert called him to a halt.

"Let it go, Mason. It's only a chimpanzee."

Mason halted and looked over at his commander. "How do you know? I thought that the alien could change form?"

"It can, but the chimp is real," stated Colbert.

"How can you be so sure?"

"It wasn't black. "I don't think the aliens can do colors." Colbert glanced at the hut door when Sullivan staggered out rubbing the side of his head. "You all right, Sullivan?"

Sullivan winced when he nodded. "Throbbing headache, but nothing that will kill me."

Their eyes turned to the hut's doorway when screeches drifted out.

"You did close the hatch?" questioned Colbert.

Cursing, Sullivan and Mason rushed back inside.

*****

Sullivan and Mason crossed to the hatch and peered down. Beyond the reach of their flashlights, shapes darker than shadows shrieked amidst the clatter of small feet climbing the chute. They flipped down their NVGs and observed the spectral lit monstrosities climbing towards them.

"They look like giant alien centipedes," uttered Mason, shocked by their numbers.

"That's probably their least monstrous form," said Sullivan. "Let's shoot a few and then shut them in."

Their rifles spat short bursts of bullets at the oncoming hoard. Shrieks and squeals indicated some had found a target. Mason passed his rifle to Sullivan and slammed the lid shut. When he went to spin the wheel, it refused to turn. He increased his effort, but it still wouldn't budge. He raised it again and flipping up their NVGs, used their flashlights to examine the hatch lid. The root of the problem was a bent locking rod damaged by one of Mason's bullets striking it earlier. It no longer lined up with the hole it was meant to slide into.

"Hold the lid, and I'll try to straighten it," instructed Mason.

Sullivan gripped the lid with both hands while Mason kicked at the rod with the heel of his boot.

Sullivan glanced at the bent rod and then down the chute at the approaching hoard. "It's not working."

Mason joined Sullivan looking at the climbing creatures. "Any ideas?"

Sullivan pulled a grenade from his ammo vest. "Explosions kill them." He held the grenade over the chute, released the arming clip and counted to two before dropping it.

The two men stepped back from the hole to avoid the explosive blast that erupted from the chute. When it had settled, they returned to the hatch and aimed their flashlights inside. The swirling smoke slowly cleared. Their anxious gazes detected no movement and no sounds apart from the distant warning alarm drifting up from below.

"That seems to have done the trick," said Mason.

Though it couldn't be locked, Sullivan reached for the hatch to close it. He froze when a clacking drifted up the chute. The single clacking quickly changed to a cacophony of click, clacks, squeals and shrieks. Flicking down their NVGs, they gazed down at the army of small, rat-size ant-like creatures covering the circumference of the chute for as far as they could see and flowing towards them like an insidious oil slick.

"Now what?" asked Mason.

"Fire!" stated Sullivan. "We'll burn the evil fuckers." His eyes flicked to the diesel tank across the room. "I'll try and hold them off while you see if you can get some fuel out of that tank."

Mason glanced at the tank and the level indicator close to empty. "I have a better idea. There's a tanker full outside."

Sullivan nodded. "Let the commander know what we're doing, but hurry. I'm not sure how long I can hold them back."

When Mason rushed from the hut, Sullivan dropped another grenade into the chute.

Mason veered his sprint towards Colbert and before he reached him shouted out the plan. "Hatch is damaged, won't lock. Sullivan is holding back the creatures. Going to use fuel from the tanker to burn them."

Colbert nodded. "Do it!"

Mason headed for the truck, climbed inside and brought it to life. He crunched it into reverse and, narrowly missing the helicopter rotors, gunned it around in a semi-circle to the hut. He leapt out, grabbed a long thick hose from the side and attached it to the outlet at the rear. As gunshots rang out from inside, he opened the outlet valve. With fuel gushing from the end of the hose, he picked it up and rushed into the hut.

Eyes watering from the overpowering stench of noxious fumes choking the air and his lungs, Mason sprayed the volatile fuel around the sides of the chute and over the evilness intent on reaching them. When he was confident the creatures were covered, he dropped the diesel spouting hose into the hatch.

Mason dragged his tear-streaming eyes away from the hundreds of snapping mandibles and evil eyes looking up at him and turned to Sullivan standing by the fresher air at the entrance. "Light them up."

As Mason went outside to expel the fumes from his lungs with clean air, Sullivan pulled the pin from his last grenade and lobbed it at the opening. It bounced off the hatch frame and dropped into the chute. He joined Mason outside and they moved to a safe distance.

A loud whump announced the grenade's detonation and the igniting of diesel. A whoosh of flames shot from the chute, filled the hut and sprayed out the door, setting the spilt fuel around the tanker on fire.

Colbert joined the two men staring at the flames. "It probably would have been a good idea to move the tanker to a safe distance before lighting the fuel."

"We didn't have time, sir," answered Mason. "The creatures were almost at the top of the hatch."

To avoid the tanker's imminent explosion, they moved away.

Sullivan glanced over at the helicopter where Kelly had binoculars to his eyes gazing out at the horizon. "No sign of the others, yet."

Colbert shook his head. "Richard and Krisztina are making their way to the exit elevator where Ramirez will meet with them. Dalton is waiting in the building to send the elevator down when they are near it so it's ready for them to ride up. As soon as everyone is here, we leave."

They instinctively ducked when the tanker exploded, lifting the wheels off the ground and sending shrapnel and pieces of unrecognizable metal high into the air to rain down on the compound. When gravity had forced everything back to earth, the men looked at the burning wreckage, its large tank ripped open, the cab relatively intact. They turned their gazes to the partly destroyed generator hut when the roof collapsed.

"Hopefully that will be the last we'll see of the creatures," said Sullivan.

"Amen to that," said Colbert. Heading back to the main building, he contacted Ramirez for an update on the situation below.

CHAPTER 28

EVAC

The larger puddles of fluid Black, remnants of their kind decimated by the blasts from Krisztina's grenades, flowed together into an oily pool of sludge and pulled in its edges, bulging its middle. Fueled by Black seeping into its mass, it rose to form an irregular cohesive form that morphed into a creature with a stocky body the size of a Rottweiler. Double-jointed legs formed at its rear and folded beneath its haunch. Spindly arms longer than its body stretched from its shoulders and grew three long claws jointed like fingers. A head, elongated, pointed and sporting a jaw lined with short, dagger-sharp teeth, rose from middle of its back on a sinewy foot-long neck. Its eyes, small, red and sinful, glanced around at the brittle chunks of Black littering the floor, all that was left of its dead brethren.

Its head turned and observed two of its kind skulking warily along the corridor. It shifted its gaze to the elevator door and narrowed its eyes at the sounds coming from within. Growling a command for its two smaller brethren to follow, it rose on its haunches, poked its head into the shaft and gazed up at the humans responsible for the carnage the brood had barely survived. Its long slender arms reached for the ladder and hauled its body onto it. Letting out a low rumbling growl, it headed up the shaft.

The two smaller creatures leapt through the hole and reformed in flight, landing on the walls as the many-legged centipede creatures adept at climbing sheer surfaces. Fearing their vicious, larger brethren would perceive them as a threat for the food on offer and retaliate mercilessly, they were careful not to draw ahead of it and scampered up the shaft at a slower pace.

*****

The deep menacing growl drifting up the shaft sent a cold, clammy ripple down Richard's spine and filled him with dread. He glanced down. A strange creature poked its head into the shaft and looked up at him. As its long claw-tipped arms reached for the ladder, he returned his gaze to Krisztina. "We've got company. Move faster."

Krisztina glanced down the shaft and immediately regretted doing so. A fresh infusion of adrenalin recharged her tired body and spurted her up the ladder.

*****

Realizing there was nothing more he could do to help Richard and Krisztina from inside the control room, Ramirez grabbed his rifle and dragged the cupboard away from the door.

"Ramirez, what's your situation?"

Noticing his commander had dropped their call signs, he answered. "Up Shit Creek without a paddle in a boat full of holes and starving piranha in the water."

"We're coming to help."

"Not advisable, sir. I will clear hostiles from my end and head for the elevator corridor to wait for Richard and Krisztina. Be ready to send elevator down on my command."

"Understood. Dalton is waiting. Good luck."

Ramirez put an ear to the door. Frightening shrieks drew closer. He was running out of time. When he reached for the handle, the shrieks outside ceased. Straining to hear anything above the insistent alarm, he placed an ear to the door again. Nothing. He grabbed a corner of the poster covering the window and pulled it aside. Fear crept over him. Like faithful puppy dogs, the smaller creatures were gathered around the larger one currently impersonating a human female. All stared directly at him.

When Ramirez locked eyes with the female Black, the creature shot forward and stopped with its face almost touching the glass. He staggered back, barging into the cupboard he had moved a moment ago, and watched the face morph into his own. His eyes flicked to the handle when it turned. His finger moved to the trigger as he aimed his rifle at the door. Loud retorts reverberated around the room. Bullets punched splintered holes through the barrier holding the creatures at bay.

*****

Certain the alarm signaled the humans were up to something that posed a significant threat to her and her brood, and it would be advisable to kill them all before they completed whatever they had planned, EV1L halted at the door of the room she sensed the lone human was in. She turned to her excited brood gathered around her and hissed them to silence.

EV1L stared at the human when he peered through the door window at her. He would supply much needed sustenance to a few of her brood quick enough to be first to claim it. She darted forward and mimicked his face as she reached for the door handle. She didn't flinch when bullets gouged holes through the door and passed harmlessly through her body that she had turned malleable and then parted wide to avoid the following shots. When the firing ceased, she issued an order to her hungry offspring.

*****

As Ramirez frantically reloaded, gelatinous Black poured through the bullet holes and down the door. Before they had reached the floor, they began forming into vicious creatures. Aware there was no escape and his death was imminent, Ramirez chose a less painful demise that would take some of the aliens with him. He dropped the rifle and pulled the pins from the five grenades clipped to his ammo vest. He stared defiantly at the creatures reforming into hungry, malicious entities. Eager to feast, they leapt at him. Spreading on contact, they began their devouring process.

Ramirez screamed in agony as the Black claimed him. The door opened. The tall Black creature had discarded its female form completely. It was now the Black version of him. Horrified, Ramirez stared at his Black-formed self as it observed some of its brood claiming nourishment while more of its minions poured into the room. When his Black twin looked him in the eyes, Ramirez forced his pain-creased lips into a satisfied sneer.

When the human's smile replaced his agonized expression, EV1L sensed danger—a trap. She screeched a warning to her young as she collapsed into a pool of Black mercury.

The explosions killed Ramirez and every creature in the vicinity instantly. It bulged the surrounding walls before they disintegrated and sent wreckage flying out in all directions. The blast carried flame, smoke and debris along the corridor until its force dissipated.

"Warning. Evacuation protocol in process. Nine minutes until detonation."

*****

While Krisztina squeezed up between the elevator and wall, Richard glanced down at the large creature almost upon them. One of its long gangling arms reached up for him, its claws grasping air menacingly. Linking an arm around the ladder, Richard pulled Colbert's pistol from its holster and aimed at the creature's head. Six shots echoed loudly through the shaft. The creature screeched with each shot jerking its head back. The bullet holes blasted through it, but its face and body quickly reformed. Richard altered aim and fired at the claws wrapped around the ladder. Bullets sliced through its clawed fingers. It toppled back. Gripping on with its feet, it slammed back against the ladder. Its head merged through its body and grew out of its stomach. Its evil eyes looked at him. Its vicious lips snarled.

Ears ringing from the loud reverberating pistol retorts, Krisztina scrambled onto the top of the elevator, slipped the rifle from her shoulder and moved to one edge. She peered down between elevator and wall, took aim on one of the two smaller creatures and fired a short burst.

Flinching from the loud weapon fire, Richard watched one of the small creatures blasted from the wall. Short tentacles thrust from its body failed to find a purchase to halt its tumble down the shaft. Aware it would survive and return and trusting Krisztina had his back covered, Richard holstered the gun and climbed up to her.

To avoid the same fate as its brethren, the second smaller creature melted into sludge and slithered up the wall.

Krisztina turned her attention to the larger creature pulling itself upright on the ladder and fired a short burst. Believing her bullets had been responsible when it burst apart, she changed her mind when tentacles shot out and snaked up the side of the elevator.

"You coming?"

She turned to Richard's voice and saw him drop through the hole in the elevator roof. She hurried over, passed her rifle down to Richard and lowered herself into the elevator.

With weapons ready to repel any aliens they encountered, they stepped into the darkness shrouding Level 1 and flipped down their NVGs. Richard kicked away the chair preventing the doors from closing—a delaying tactic at most for the creatures in the shaft certain to follow—and joined Krisztina's rush for the exit elevator.

Richard and Krisztina heard the blast Ramirez had set in motion, twice. A brief boom over Ramirez's radio before it was obliterated and a longer, louder explosion that rumbled through the facility.

"What the hell was that?" asked Krisztina when Richard pulled alongside her.

"Hopefully Ramirez clearing us a path." Richard halted at a junction. "Which way?"

Krisztina jerked her weapon right. "That way to next junction, then left, right and at end left again, and elevator will be there."

"Let's hope Ramirez is waiting for us with the elevator ready to take us out of here."

"Warning. Evacuation protocol in process. Eight minutes until detonation."

They pressed on.

CHAPTER 29

Detonation

Turning a corner, Richard and Krisztina headed towards the gradually thinning smoke lingering in the corridor, evidence the explosion they'd heard a short while ago originated nearby. A few paces farther they stepped over debris and glimpsed the destruction the blast had caused. Through curls of swirling smoke, wrecked walls revealed themselves. Barely recognizable as its former self, it was only the smoldering shells of the CCTV monitors that identified it as the security office.

Richard ran his eyes over the destruction. "Ramirez sure did a number on this."

"Do you think he was attacked?" asked Krisztina.

"It's the only reason I can think of for him to have done it," reasoned Richard, his eyes searching through the choking, drifting smoke for signs of the Black. "Let's continue to the elevator, he's probably there waiting for us." He unnecessarily aimed his mouth towards his mic. "Ramirez, we're just passing what's left of the security office and will be at the exit elevator shortly. Colbert, power up the 'copter, we're coming."

Shifting wreckage a few paces away halted them and directed their eyes at the dark shadow rising from the floor.

*****

Wreckage that had rained down upon EV1L, shifted and clattered to the floor when she drew in the edges of the Black pool she had formed to escape death. Her increased mass progressively bulged and grew as she formed into a creature that would provide a defense against the humans she sensed nearby.

*****

Raising their weapons, Richard and Krisztina stepped back and fired at the shadow within the smoke. They ceased firing when the dark phantom disappeared.

Puzzled, Krisztina looked at Richard. “Where did it go?”

Richard shrugged. “Not far I expect.”

“Warning. Evacuation protocol in process. Seven minutes until detonation.”

“Seven minutes,” warned Krisztina.

Richard peered into the smoke. They needed to move, but the alien could be a puddle on the floor, a stain on the blast-blackened walls, a single monstrous creature or a hoard of tiny devils that would flow over them, and anything in-between. He needed to do something fast. *Think, Richard, think!*

A piece of wreckage fell from the ceiling and clanged to the floor in a nearby blast damaged room. Richard cast his gaze at the sound. The creature was creeping up at them from the side. He grabbed his last grenade from his vest, pulled the pin, showed it to Krisztina so she knew what was coming, and threw it at the sound. “Run!”

They sprinted through the smoke and along the corridor.

The blast wave funneled through the corridor pressed against their backs, almost toppling them to the ground. The already weakened ceiling crashed to the floor behind them. They kept running.

Spotting the elevator ahead and cursing Ramirez for abandoning them, Richard screamed into his mic. "Send the elevator down, now!"

"On its way," replied Dalton immediately.

Skidding to a halt at the lift, they rushed inside when the doors spread open. Richard thumped the up button, and both, expecting the Black to appear and rip them from the elevator, anxiously watched the gap between the doors get narrower until they met.

Relief flooded over them.

Krisztina turned to Richard when the elevator jerked into motion. "I don't believe it. We did it."

Richard shrugged and grinned. "Just another typical day for a hero like me."

"Every hero deserves a reward." Krisztina leaned toward Richard and kissed him on the cheek."

Richard smirked a little lecherously. "I'm hoping that was just an appetizer for what will follow."

Krisztina smiled. "Brave, resourceful *and* funny."

"Just a few of my many talents I'm eager to share with you."

"You may have impressed me, Richard, but I not sleep with you."

Richard shrugged.

The elevator trembled, re-awakening their fears.

Metal buckled above them.

Their anxious gazes lifted to the ceiling.

Krisztina looked at Richard for an explanation.

Richard shrugged. "Either the explosions have weakened the elevator, or one of those creatures is up there.

Krisztina wasn't certain what she feared most, but if the elevator broke and sent them back down, they were as good as dead. She experienced relief when the elevator halted, and the doors slid open.

"Warning. Evacuation protocol in process. Six minutes until detonation."

"Quick," urged Dalton. "We need to get out of here."

"Something we're well aware of," commented Richard. He was about to step out when an ominous sound halted him. He shot an arm across Krisztina's chest to halt her.

Dalton raised his eyes to the slithering at the top of the elevator doors. Fear spread across his face when a Black tentacle seeped out. Before he could react, the tentacle lashed out like a whip and wrapped around his neck. His mouth opened to scream, but the tentacle's choking grip squeezing ever tighter cut it off.

Horrified, Krisztina watched Dalton lifted into the air by his neck. She stifled a scream when his torso dropped and slumped to the floor. His head quickly followed.

Richard grabbed Krisztina's arm and dragged her out of the elevator as more tentacles slithered through the gap between elevator and doors. Dodging and ducking under the searching appendages trying to snare them, Richard snatched a grenade from Krisztina's ammo vest and pulled the pin. When a tentacle homed in on the schlik of sliding metal, Richard lobbed it in its path. The tentacle wrapped around it and smothered it.

Richard caught up with Krisztina by the exit door she yanked open. The blast slammed him against the door as shrapnel struck the walls. Feeling something strike him, Richard looked at the piece of Black on his chest. Without thinking, he instinctively brushed it off. It shattered on striking the floor. It was dead.

Richard glanced across the room at the Black pouring from the elevator roof like a waterfall formed of melted tar. When it started forming into a monstrosity he had no wish to see completed, he rushed through the exit.

Colbert, Sullivan and Mason sprinted over to investigate the explosion.

"What happened?" demanded Colbert.

"Good to see you, too," quipped Richard.

"The alien's here. It ripped Dalton's head off," explained Krisztina breathlessly.

Richard thought it was good that Krisztina wouldn't be reporting the man's demise to his family.

Saddened and shocked another of his men was dead, Colbert probed them for more information, "What do you mean it's here, and where's Ramirez?"

Richard headed for the helicopter and cocked a thumb at the building he walked away from. "Alien's in there, and you're welcome to it."

Though he didn't know for certain Ramirez was dead, he thought it probable. He couldn't risk Colbert delaying their escape while the man was searched for, so he added, "Ramirez is also dead." He glanced at Krisztina. "Come on, Sweet Cheeks, our work is done."

Krisztina shrugged at the shocked SEALs and followed Richard. She had done all she could.

"What do we do?" asked Mason, his eyes fixed on the entrance strange slithering sounds came from.

"Nothing we can do except continue with the EVAC and hope the blast incinerates the creature."

When they turned towards the waiting helicopter, the side of the building exploded outwards. A creature, black, bulbous, and with a body all mouth and teeth, thumped to the ground in a mass of tentacles between the SEALs and the helicopter.

Richard looked fearfully back at the alien. "That thing sure is persistent."

"What do we do?" asked Krisztina, wondering if they'd ever escape the alien's clutches alive.

"We get on the helicopter," Richard climbed aboard and looked at the pilot. "Time to leave. All your buddies are dead."

Kelly dragged his eyes away from the tentacle-waving monster his three teammates backed away from. "They're not dead. I can see them."

"Semantics. They soon will be, so let's leave while we still can because when it's finished feeding on them, it's going to come after us."

"A little over four and a half minutes to detonation," warned Krisztina, glancing at her watch.

"I'm not leaving my teammates while they are still alive," stated Kelly firmly.

Richard held up his rifle. "It would be merciful if I gave them a quick death."

Kelly leaned into the back and snatched the rifle from Richard. "I'll shoot you before I let you shoot my friends."

Richard humphed. "If that monster comes our way, I'll be begging you to."

"Why wait?" threatened Kelly, shooting Richard a frosty glare before directing his gaze back upon his buddies. "We have to help them."

Krisztina nudged Richard. "Go on, think of something."

Richard roamed his eyes around the helicopter. "Okay. I have an idea. Buckle up, Sweet Cheeks, it's going to get hairy. Kelly, get us airborne."

Kelly shot Richard a suspicious gaze. "I'm not leaving without them."

"Do as I say and we'll all be leaving together, or we'll all die here."

Indecisive as to what he should do, Kelly looked at his friends who desperately needed help.

"Trust him, he's good at this," advised Krisztina.

Having no ideas of his own to save his fellow SEALs, Kelly increased the power to the turbine and lifted the helicopter off the ground.

Richard shouted into his mic. "Colbert, I'm coming to save your ass, *again*."

Wondering what Richard was up to, Colbert glanced at the rising helicopter. “Then I suggest you do it fast.”

Gazing out the open door, Richard grinned at Colbert. “Get ready for the fastest EVAC of your life.”

“Put the headsets on, so you’ll be able to communicate more clearly,” instructed Kelly.

Richard and Krisztina picked headsets hanging from the ceiling and slipped them on.

“Where’s the abseiling ropes?” asked Richard.

“Under the seats,” replied Kelly, grasping an inkling of Richard’s plan.

Richard crouched and pulled a thick, black rope from beneath the nearest seat. While he hooked the locking clamp attached to one end of the neatly coiled ropes over one of the locking catches above the door, Krisztina pulled out another and passed it to him. When three ropes were attached, Richard gazed down at the men firing at the tentacled creature. To avoid the onslaught of bullets, it climbed over the top of the Russian transport truck and dropped to the ground.

“Do we have any more grenades?” Richard asked the pilot.

“You and Krisztina took the last ones,” replied Kelly.

Richard turned to Krisztina. “How much time do we have?”

Krisztina looked at her watch. “Three minutes and twenty-one seconds.”

“Kelly, how long to get us clear of the blast?”

“Three minutes, minimum.”

“Then we need to hurry. Take us around in a circle and approach them from the front so they can see us coming.”

Richard gripped the handle attached to the doorframe when the pilot swooped around the compound. He looked down as a grenade thrown by Sullivan at the creature atop the Russian truck, exploded. Tentacles swiped the air chaotically as it tumbled to the ground. Colbert, still limping from his leg wound, and Sullivan and Mason dashed for the smoldering remains of the tanker, probably planning to use the smoke to conceal themselves. Waving tentacles at the fleeing men, the creature emerged from behind the truck and gave chase.

"Colbert, I'm going to drop ropes for you three to grab when we pass. We don't have time for a second try or to hover, so make sure you grab them on the first pass."

"Understood," affirmed Colbert. "We'll be ready."

Richard kicked the three coils of rope out and watched them unravel. "Ropes are down," he informed the pilot. "As soon as we have them, lift up and get us out of here."

"It's already on my to-do list. Let me know as soon as they're on the ropes."

"Two minutes fifty," warned Krisztina.

"Crap," cursed the pilot. "It's going to be damn close."

"Seems to be the story of my life lately," commented Richard dryly.

*****

Colbert slammed fresh ammo in his rifle and glanced up at the helicopter moving into position. When ropes dropped, he turned his attention on the approaching monster and pulled the pin from last grenade they had. Giving it a kiss for luck, he released the priming clip and lobbed it at the creature.

Though she could survive being struck by bullets, EV1L feared the explosive things they threw. Seeing one sailing towards her, she quickly changed direction to avoid it. When it had exploded too far away to cause her any harm, she refocused on her hunt of the humans.

Cursing when the creature dodged the grenade and continued towards them, Colbert sprayed it with bullets.

"I'm out," shouted Sullivan.

Mason's weapon clicked on empty. "Me, too."

Saving what precious ammo he had left, Colbert stopped firing and directed his gaze at the helicopter that lowered until the ropes touched earth. “Get ready men. Here comes our ride out of here.”

Colbert kept his weapon trained on the creature and fired short bursts at intervals to slow its progress. Flicking his eyes from the creature to the ropes, when they were near enough, he shouted. “Let’s go.”

To leave their hands free, Sullivan and Mason stowed their weapons and ran.

When Sullivan glanced behind and saw Colbert hampered by his limp and shooting at the creature, he slowed and veered over to him. “Give me the rifle. Your wound is slowing you down.”

Aware Sullivan was right, Colbert handed over his weapon and continued his limping dash for the dangling ropes that were drawing nearer.

Noticing the creature look at the helicopter, Sullivan fired a longer burst of firepower to distract it. This time it didn’t try to avoid the bullets but absorbed them into its pliant mass. When it directed its gaze back upon the fleeing men, tentacles reached out for pieces of surrounding debris, plucked them up and threw them at the helicopter and them.

“Look out! Incoming!” warned Sullivan, discharging the remainder of the bullets at the creature.

Turning his gaze from the rope he had selected to grab, Mason ducked under a piece of flying metal, stumbled, regained his footing and continued his sprint for the rope.

Colbert ducked under, dodged around and leapt over the wreckage landing in his path.

Sullivan leapt over a piece of wreckage that struck the ground in front of him and toppled to the side when another piece glanced off his head. Unable to regain his balance, he tumbled to the ground.

Praying the wreckage striking his craft didn’t damage anything essential for keeping it airborne, Kelly held the helicopter steady and on course for his teammates' risky pickup.

Richard dodged back when a piece of metal clanged off the doorframe close to his hand.

"Two minutes," called out Krisztina, anxiously.

*****

Seizing her chance to catch one of the humans, EV1L rushed at the fallen man.

Shaking his head groggily to clear the fuzziness, Sullivan noticed a shadow sweep over him and looked fearfully at the tentacled creature leaning over him. He grabbed for his pistol that wasn't there; he had loaned it to Krisztina.

EV1l clashed its teeth together as it lowered its mouth towards the human feast.

*****

Mason grabbed at the rope when it was within his grasp and started climbing.

Colbert, a few steps behind, grasped a rope and groaned when the wound on his shoulder was ripped open. Ignoring the pain from his battered body, he hauled himself up the lifeline. When the roped twisted around, he noticed Sullivan had fallen and the creature was looming over him. Out of ammo and time, there was nothing he could do to help his friend.

*****

With teeth eager to sink into the human's flesh and her body anticipating the burst of nourishment about to surge through her, EV1L spread her jaws to receive the human and lowered its head. Defenseless against the Black he couldn't touch, Sullivan gazed at the tentacles surrounding him for an opening he might be able to escape through. There was none. The creature's glossy limbs trapped his as securely as any prison bars. He stared at the sharp black teeth around the widening mouth that emitted an acrid stench and accepted his fate.

EV1L jerked its jaws away when something bounced off her head. She gazed at the roundish object that thumped to the ground beside her and then at the hairy, human-like beast that had thrown it. She focused on the thing it held in its hand. It looked suspiciously like the exploding things the humans had thrown at her. Fearing the thing that had just struck her was about to explode, she rushed clear of the expected blast.

Though confused by the creature's sudden departure, Sullivan seized the opportunity and climbed to his feet. Dirt and snow picked up from the rotors' downwash, and wind whipped at him as the helicopter drew near. He turned as it flew above him and was slapped in the face by a rope. He stumbled backwards and almost tripped. Recovering quickly, he lunged at the rope pulling farther away. His grasp fell short, forcing him to run after it.

*****

"I can't believe a monkey just saved Sullivan," uttered Kelly, gazing below.

Krisztina leaned out the door and looked below in surprise at the scene playing out. "It's Boris." She watched the Black monstrosity climb the side of the building and move along the roof; it was creeping up on Boris. She waved a hand frantically at the chimp. "Move, Boris, move!"

*****

When Boris had seen the strange black creature that he blamed for his recent troubles and the absence of his human friend, he had jumped from the roof. He grabbed a couple of rocks from the ground and threw one at it. He bounced up and down and hooted in satisfaction when it hit. He was about to throw another when it darted away. Boris watched the human stand and looked at the noisy flying machine. Inside it were humans. He recognized the female, a friend of his human friend. *Was he also in there with the other humans?*

He scrutinized the faces he could see for his friend but couldn't pick him out. Hearing something, he turned his head to the roof behind him. The creature loomed over the edge with tentacles reaching for him. Boris spurted away.

EV1L gave chase.

*****

Aware there would be no second chances, Sullivan sprinted for the rope with a hand stretched to grasp it. His fingers curled around the lifeline and pulled it towards him. Gripping it with both hands, he started climbing. His glance up the rope picked out Colbert and Mason almost at the helicopter, and Richard and Krisztina focused on something behind him. He turned his head and was surprised to see a chimpanzee rushing towards him and behind it the Black, tentacled monster in pursuit.

*****

"Sullivan's on the rope, get us out of here," Richard ordered the pilot.

Kelly lifted his craft and increased power to the engine. "How much time do we have?"

Krisztina looked at her watch. "One minute twenty-five seconds."

"Fuck!" cursed Kelly.

When Mason's head appeared in the doorway, Richard helped him inside.

Colbert arrived on his heels and collapsed into a seat. Breathing heavily from the climb, he nodded at Richard. "Thanks."

"We're not out of trouble yet—just over a minute before the bomb goes boom!" said Richard.

Colbert smiled at him. "We'll survive, we have you, the man that should have died many times but miraculously, against all the odds, is still here."

Richard rolled his eyes. "Yeah, a lucky charm, that's me."

"I guess we'll find out soon if that's true," said Krisztina, looking down sadly at Boris. If the alien didn't get him, the explosion would.

*****

Boris's lumbering gait sped him towards the ropes speedily rising from the ground. He glanced behind at the creature, its floundering limbs propelling it swiftly, if not majestically, forward. Turning his attention back to the flying machine that had begun to turn, Boris veered to the side. Spurting forward he jumped onto the smoldering cab of the destroyed tanker and leapt for the nearest rope. As his momentum weakened and he began to head back to the ground, his hand grasped the rope.

Hanging on the rope for a breather, Sullivan glanced down when something jerked the lifeline and saw the chimp was responsible. It seemed he also didn't want to be left behind. His gaze flicked to the tentacled creature that seemed to roll in a mass of flailing limbs onto the burning truck. Thankful the rope was too far away for it to reach, he restarted his climb.

*****

With one last chance to claim the human nourishment, EV1L climbed onto the wrecked shell of the vehicle, and after withdrawing some of its limbs into its mass, it shot out a single long tentacle and wrapped it around a dangling rope. Yanked from the truck, EV1L dragged along the ground until the tentacle hauled its bulk onto the rope. As soon as its main mass was within reach, its other limbs pulled it up the rope.

*****

Kelly cursed when the helicopter tilted to the side. "What the hell was that."

Colbert peered down the ropes. "Shit! The alien's on the rope."

"Get rid of it or none of us will be leaving," screamed the pilot, turning away from the perimeter fence before Sullivan crashed into it and possibly snagged the abseil ropes.

Richard reached for the coupling securing the rope to the helicopter.

Colbert grabbed his arm. "What are you doing?"

"Getting rid of the monster."

"Sullivan's also on that rope."

"Then tell him to get off because if I don't cut the creature free, it will soon be in here with us. Then we all die!" Richard yanked Colbert's grip from his arm and continued unscrewing the coupling.

Colbert snatched a headset from the roof and slipped it on. "Sullivan. Get off the rope, we're cutting it free."

Still climbing, Sullivan tore his eyes away from the monster below and glanced up at Colbert looking down on him. "On it." He stretched for the nearest rope that was beyond his reach.

Colbert looked at the locking pin about to be freed from its thread. "Now, Sullivan!"

To avoid the reaching tentacles, Boris leapt for the nearby rope being whipped by the wind and the downdraft, grabbed it and climbed.

Heeding his commander's warning, Sullivan leapt as best he could from his unstable perch that offered no leverage to push off from and fell towards the creature's tangled limbs.

"He's falling," uttered Colbert.

As soon as Richard turned the screw free from its thread, the rope dropped. "Now can we get out of here?" said Richard.

Gripping the rope with three limbs, Boris grabbed at the falling human's hand reaching for the rope beyond his grasp and snagged it with his fourth.

Sullivan gripped the rope he swung towards. When he was securely on it, he nodded his thanks to his strange savior, but Boris was already climbing. Envying the chimp's climbing prowess, he looked down at the alien crashing to the ground. Having lost track of time, Sullivan wondered how long they had before the bomb detonated. With what little strength he had remaining, he restarted his climb.

Surprised by what he had just witnessed, Colbert informed the others. "He's safe. The chimp caught him."

"What about the alien?" asked Mason.

"Returned to earth," answered Richard. "And good riddance to it. I never want to see another alien creature for as long as I live."

"Living might not be very long," stated Krisztina. "Fifty-six seconds to detonation."

Colbert glanced at the back of the pilot's head. "Punch it, Kelly!"

"I'm punching! I'm punching!"

In a last-ditch effort to stop the humans from escaping, EV1L rushed for the fence, climbed it and shot out a limb that grew to an impossible length. Just as it looked as if it would grab the rope the human hung from, it was pulled from its reach.

Richard dodged back when the chimp bounded through the door and then returned to staring back at the alien creature watching them from its perch on the security fence. He pictured film footage he had seen on TV of nuclear explosions and thought they were still awfully close to be able to survive the blast. “Can’t this thing go any faster.”

“Only if we lighten the load,” replied Kelly.

“You want me to throw him out, sir?” asked Mason, smiling at Richard.

Colbert looked at Richard. “Before this mission I wouldn’t have hesitated, but he did save our asses.” He reached for Sullivan’s hand when he was near enough, and after hauling him inside, released the remaining ropes and slid the door shut. “You took your time.”

Panting, Sullivan sat on the floor. “Sorry, sir. Paused to play with the alien wildlife.”

Richard nodded at Boris on Krisztina’s lap. “What about throwing out the chimp?”

Boris pouted at Richard.

Krisztina grabbed Boris’s hand. “No one is throwing Boris out.”

Mason glanced at the countdown on Krisztina’s watch. “Forty seconds.”

“We’re not going to make it!” informed Kelly anxiously. “Hold on, it’s about to get bumpy.”

Those who weren’t buckled in, secured their harnesses and held anything solid they could find to cling to.

Sullivan slid into the co-pilot’s seat, strapped himself in and looked at Kelly. The worry etched on the pilot’s face increased his own. “Anything I can do?”

“Pray like you’ve never prayed before.”

The group fell to silence as the seconds ticked away.

Looking at her watch, Krisztina counted down. “Ten, nine, eight, seven, six...”

Those with their backs to the facility growing more distant with each second turned to observe the detonation.

"...five, four, three, two, one."

Nothing happened.

Richard sighed. "All that damn trouble for nothing."

"Why didn't it explode?" asked Mason.

"Russian engineering is probably to blame," offered Sullivan.

Krisztina was about to argue the slur against her countrymen when a bright flash followed by loud boom rolled across the sky. A mile-high mushroom of smoke, flame and debris rose into the sky above the facility. The shockwave sped dust and debris towards them. Richard gripped his seat when it was almost upon them. Picked up by the wave, the helicopter surged forward, jolting its fearful passengers.

The turbine whined in protest from the spinning craft. The tail rotor vibrated so violently it struck the fuselage. Torn violently from its mooring it whizzed along the side of the fuselage with a loud clatter until it shot off ahead of the craft. Fighting the excessive pitch and yaw as the helicopter spun in the opposite direction of the rotors the lost tail rotor no longer corrected, Kelly battled the G-force thrusting against him and activated autorotation. It was a lame attempt to bring back some semblance of control to lessen the impact with the ground that was coming close fast.

His face a mask of fear that matched some of the others who knew what was coming, Richard looked at Colbert. "How's your lucky charm working out for you now?"

Colbert grinned. "Ask me again after we've landed."

"We're going down!" shouted the pilot unnecessarily. It was the only thing presently occupying everyone's thoughts. "Brace for impact!"

*****

After watching the humans escape in their flying machine for a few moments, EV1L headed back to the building. She would collect the decapitated human corpse and go below to search for any of her surviving brood. After they had nourished themselves on the dead human, she would initiate a second birthing phase to boost their numbers. They would then leave this place and start their colonization of this human world.

As EV1L pushed through the hole in the side of the building, her plan to conquer Earth was brought to an abrupt end by the bright light that vaporized every molecule of her evil form.

CHAPTER 30

Crash Landing

In a frantic attempt to cushion the landing, Kelly flared the rotors just before machine met ground. Contact with the frozen tundra sent a powerful, metal-crunching jolt through the craft and everyone inside. The craft's forward momentum rolled the helicopter with accompanying sounds of crushing metal and fuselage. The rotor tips sheared off. One embedded in the fuselage, the end a finger-width from Colbert's face. The rotor stumps dug into the earth, sending the helicopter spinning across the ground. The engine, ripped from its mount, rolled over the craft. The spinning ends of the rotors ripped through the flimsy fuselage and passed between the horror-struck seated passengers with a terrifying whirring blur before rolling out into the tundra. Accompanied by the crunching and buckling of metal and the flimsy fuselage, as well as Richard's drawn out, hysterical scream, the occupants were tossed chaotically like laundry in a tumble dryer when the helicopter rolled over and over before coming to a stop.

Silence reigned as the cloud of dust thrown up by the rough landing settled. Groans filtered out from the battered passengers. Boris hooted in protest of the rough treatment.

Colbert glanced around at the faces at odd angles due the craft's listing position. He was pleased to see that though battered and disorientated, miraculously, all had survived. "If anyone is injured, call it out."

He received replies of all okay.

Colbert looked at Richard. "What about you? You must have a sore throat at the very least with all that screaming you did on the way down."

Richard glared at Colbert. "Funny."

"Everyone out!" ordered Colbert. "There might be leaking fuel which could ignite at any moment.

Spurred on by the thought of being roasted alive, everyone made a controlled but hasty exit.

With no scent of fuel in the air around the craft to indicate the imminent chance of an explosion, the group stared back at the mushroom cloud slowly beginning to drift apart.

After a few moments, Sullivan asked, "What's the plan now we've lost our transport, Commander?"

"We salvage anything that might be of use from the wreckage, place everything inside that might give away that we are SEALs—armaments, weapons, radios, etcetera—and destroy it all with the stowed charges we packed for such an event, including some thermite charges to ensure nothing is recognizable. We then head for the crater where we picked up..."

"Abducted!" reminded Richard.

"...Richard and contact HQ for an EVAC."

"That's a bloody long walk," said Mason, "with your leg and all."

"We're SEALs. We eat hardship for breakfast," replied Colbert, adding a smile.

Richard rolled his eyes at the macho bullshit. "What about me? I've not had your training."

Colbert turned to Richard. "We could be traveling across terrain infested with heavily armed Taliban, venomous snakes and starving man-eating tigers, and you'd still survive. I wouldn't concern yourself with a couple-of-hundred-kilometer trek."

"Kelly and I will set the charges," informed Mason.

The two men went to do the tasks.

"I'm going to head to the road and wait for my comrades to arrive," informed Krisztina.

"How will you explain the crashed helicopter if they spot it, as I'm sure they will when we destroy it?" asked Colbert.

Krisztina shrugged. "I've no idea."

"You could tell them you think it was a helicopter delivering supplies and equipment to the dig site at Batagaika crater," suggested Richard. "When I was brought here, the helicopter transporting me passed close to the guard post along the road, so they do come this way."

"Good idea," agreed Colbert. "Say it got caught in the blast and crashed. You noticed it go down and rushed over to see if there were any survivors, but all had perished."

Krisztina nodded. "I will." She looked at Boris. "Can you take Boris as I'm sure nothing pleasant is in store for him now his guardian Luka isn't about to protect him?"

"It's the least we can do," said Colbert.

"Thank you. Now, I must go before my comrades arrive."

"Us, too," said Colbert, holding out a hand. "Thanks for your help and good luck."

Krisztina shook his hand. "To you also." She crossed to Richard who was staring out into the tundra, dreading the long walk ahead. "Thank you, Richard. I doubt I would have survived and the aliens might not have been destroyed without your help." She held out a hand.

Richard pouted playfully as he took her hand. "No kiss?"

"You already had one, and I don't want make others jealous."

"Go ahead," said Sullivan. "I assure you none of us want a kiss from him."

Krisztina laughed. After saying her goodbyes to the rest of the team, she headed for the road a kilometer distant.

"All set?" asked Colbert when Mason and Kelly joined them.

Mason nodded. "Charges set for three minutes."

"Then let's move!" Colbert ordered.

After distributing what little gear they had salvaged from the wreckage among them, Sullivan checked the GPS reading on the tablet that had survived the crash and pointed out into the tundra. "That way."

As they set off, Richard touched the object in his pocket he had all but forgotten and looked back at Krisztina heading in the opposite direction. "I'll be back in minute." He rushed off to catch up with Krisztina.

"What's that damn fool doing now?" asked Colbert.

"Probably still after a kiss," quipped Mason.

Hearing running footsteps, Krisztina turned. Puzzlement crossed her face at seeing Richard heading towards her. "Richard?"

A little breathless from his sprint, Richard took something from his pocket and thrust it into her hands. "A present that might make what happened here a little easier for your superiors to accept."

Krisztina stared in surprise at the alien pistol. "Where you get it?"

Richard nodded towards the destroyed facility. "I found it back there. I was going to sell it for a huge amount of cash, but I now realize aliens and their technology have brought me nothing but hardship and close encounters with death. I don't want anything to do with either anymore."

Krisztina smiled at him. "Thank you, Richard. Now, for this, you deserve kiss." She planted a kiss on his lips.

"Hurry up, Richard, the helicopter's about to blow," warned Sullivan.

"Gotta go, they'll never survive without me. Goodbye, Sweet Cheeks." He turned and sprinted away.

Krisztina smiled. "Goodbye, Richard." She turned away and glanced at the distant speck in the sky growing larger, nearer.

Kelly had also noticed the distant speck. "Russians are coming."

As soon as Richard had rejoined them they sprinted across the tundra.

The helicopter exploded, sending fragments out into the landscape. At its heart an intense white light melted metal and everything else it came in contact with.

Noticing the Russian helicopter turn towards the black smoke whipped about by the wind, Richard and the SEALs lay down amongst a bunch of the shrub that thrived in the desolate wilderness. From their concealed positions they watched the helicopter swoop towards Krisztina when the pilot spied her waving at them. The helicopter landed near her, and two men climbed out. After conversing with Krisztina for a few moments they gazed towards the dissipating blast cloud over the facility and then over at the burning wreckage before all three boarded the helicopter. It took off and headed for the downed craft, where it hovered with a man leaning out of the open rear door scrutinizing the wreckage. Seeming to be satisfied with the explanation Krisztina had given for its presence, the man closed the door. The Russians turned and headed back the way they had come.

While waiting for the helicopter to fly far enough away to no longer be a danger, Mason spoke, "I've just thought of something. We've no rations, and it's a hell of a long walk to the crater. I'm already starving."

"Don't be such a pussy, Mason. You could do with losing some of that fat you've been collecting lately," said Sullivan.

Deciding the Russians were now far enough away, Colbert prompted his team to restart their long walk to Batagaika crater.

"Yeah, but," protested Mason, "after what all we've just survived, the aliens, the bomb and all, I'd hate to starve to death."

As he climbed to his feet, Richard smiled at Boris beside him. He reached down and squeezed his side playfully, feeling the meaty flesh beneath his hairy covering. "Oh, I don't think starving will be a problem we'll have to worry about."

Boris looked up at Richard and chattered at him.

As they headed across the tundra, Boris grabbed Richard's hand.

Richard looked down at the chimp. "Your lousy taste in friends could come back to bite you in the ass, literally."

Boris hooted and chattered at Richard.

Richard sighed. "No, I'm not carrying you."

Boris chattered again.

"Maybe you're right. Mason is chubbier and might be tastier."

Mason turned his head at Richard and glared.

THE END

Factual Places and Events mentioned in Ice Rift - Siberia

Kamera or "the Chamber"

The secret laboratory named Kamera is where the Soviet secret police invented exotic poisons used to kill dissidents in hideous and (mostly) untraceable ways.

The Soviet Union's secret poison factory was established in 1921, not long after an attempted assassination of Vladimir Lenin via poison-coated bullets. Originally dubbed the "*Special Room,*" it was later called Laboratory No. 1, Lab X, and Laboratory No. 12 before becoming known simply as the Kamera or "the Chamber" under Joseph Stalin.

It's no secret that the KGB used assassination, often by poison, to silence political dissidents who spoke out against the Soviet regime (known within the agency as "*liquid affairs*"). What remains shrouded in secrecy to this day, however, is the mysterious laboratory where the toxins were concocted.

The goal of the Chamber was to devise a poison that was tasteless, odorless, and, to protect the anonymity of the assassin, a substance that couldn't be detected in an autopsy. This led to innovations such as a cyanide that could be deployed as a mist, a poison that made the cause of death appear to be a heart attack, and a gas pistol that could shoot liquid up to 65 feet away. One politician was killed by a poison sprayed onto his reading lamp, which the heat from the bulb caused to disperse through the room with no trace.

As for the lab itself, very little is known to this day, including the exact location. KGB agents were forbidden to enter the lab and were never informed of its whereabouts; only Chamber staff and high-level officials were allowed in. Some disturbing details were revealed in 1954 by a KGB defector, who admitted that poisons were tested on political prisoners and described the lab as being near the secret police headquarters in Lubyanka.

The Soviet government, for its part, had just the previous year claimed that the lab was abolished. But many believe it may still be functioning in some form today, and the lethal innovations developed there still in use. Though it's been some 30 years since the fall of the Soviet Union, even within the last decade enemies of the Kremlin have been found dead in mysterious circumstances, including some, apparently, by poison.

Batagaika Crater – gateway to the underworld

Batagaika crater is a dramatic tadpole-shaped hole in the ground located near the Yana river basin in a vast area of permafrost.

The crater is also known as a "megaslump" and is the largest of its kind: almost 0.6 miles (1km) long and 282ft (86m) deep. But these figures will soon change, because it is growing quickly. A more recent report has it at 100 metres (328 feet) deep and continually expanding in size.

Locals in the area avoid it, saying it is a "*doorway to the underworld*".

For scientists, the site is of great interest. Examining the layers exposed by the slump can give indications of how our past climates of our world once looked. At the same time, the acceleration of the growth gives an immediate insight into the impact of climate change on the increasingly fragile permafrost.

The trigger that led to the crater started in the 1960s. Rapid deforestation meant that the ground was no longer shaded by trees in the warmer summer months. This incoming sunlight then slowly warmed the ground. This was made worse by the loss of cold "sweat" from trees as they transpire, which would have kept the ground cool.

As the ground surface warmed up, it caused the layer of soil directly above the permafrost to warm and thaw. Once this process started and the ice was exposed to warmer temperatures, melting escalated.

Analyzing the layers now exposed could reveal 200,000 years of climatic history. Continuous growth means that the crater gets deeper and deeper every year, exposing more of the past. Scientists have already found ancient forests and frozen remains of a musk ox, mammoth, and a 4,400-year-old horse inside the crater and believe there is much more to find.

Discovery of Ice Age Cave Lions

Two 12,000-year-old cave lion cubs preserved in remarkable detail have emerged from thawing ice in Siberia.

After thousands of years trapped beneath the ice, their young faces are still covered in fur. You can even make out the whiskers on their cheeks and the tips of their sharp retractable claws.

Named for the Siberian riverbank where they were found, Uyan and Dina are the most complete cave lion remains ever discovered. They could prove key to learning more about a species that became extinct over 12,000 years ago.

Over the summer of 2015, flooding along the Uyandina River exposed the ice lens where the cubs were buried. By a stroke of luck, a team of contractors was in the area collecting mammoth tusks. One sharp-eyed worker, Yakov Androsov, spotted the remains through a crack in the ice.

Until now, everything we knew about cave lions came from Stone Age art and fossilized bones. One of the largest feline predators of the ice ages, the cave lion made its way from Africa to Europe about 700,000 years ago, gradually spreading to most of North Eurasia. The size of a modern-day Siberian tiger, the cave lion once roamed everywhere from the British Isles to the Yukon in Canada.

In 2017 the frozen remains of another cave lion cub likely dating back to the last Ice Age was recently unveiled in Russia.

Local outlets reported that the remains of the roughly one-year-old cub were found in Russia's far northeastern Yukatia region this past September (2017) by a local resident. It's not the first time the frozen Siberian region has yielded prehistoric finds.

The area's permafrost, or permanently frozen ground, is capable of preserving animals like cave lions and woolly mammoths, even tens of thousands of years after their species went extinct.

The new cub comes just two years after two similarly frozen and intact lion cubs, named Uyan and Dina, were found. Dated to around 12,000 years old, Uyan and Dina were the first prehistoric cave lions found in such a well-preserved state.

Unlike the 2015 cubs, who died at around two to three weeks of age (before their teeth came in), the new cub appears to have died when it was roughly a year old. Because it was old enough to grow teeth, scientists may be able to get a fairly accurate estimate of the cub's remains.

The new cub's good condition has refueled hopes that the remains could be used for cloning. In 2016, Korean and Russian scientists told Interfax they would attempt to clone a cave lion cub. What becomes of this new cub remains to be seen, but bringing extinct animals back to life, or de-extinction, has been a pursuit rife with debate among scientific communities.

De-Extinction

Thanks to ongoing advances in DNA recovery, replication and manipulation technology, as well as the ability of scientists to recover soft tissue from fossilized animals, it may soon be possible to breed Tasmanian Tigers, Woolly Mammoths and Dodo Birds back into existence.

Communications Security Establishment Canada (CSEC)

The Communications Security Establishment (CSE) is one of Canada's key security and intelligence organizations, focused on collecting foreign signals intelligence in support of the Government of Canada's priorities, and on helping protect the computer networks and information of greatest importance to Canada. They also provide assistance to federal law enforcement and security organizations in their legally authorized activities, when they may require our unique technical capabilities.

Note from Author

Thank you for purchasing and reading my book. I hope you found it an enjoyable experience. If so, could you please spread the word and perhaps consider posting a review on your place of purchase. It is the single most powerful thing you can do for me. It raises my visibility and many more people will learn about my book.

If you would like to send feedback, drop me a line, or be added to my mailing list to receive notifications of my new books, receive limited free advance review copies, and occasional free books, send feedback or drop me a line, please contact me at: benhammott@gmail.com

ICE RIFT & ICE RIFT - SALVAGE

In Antarctica everyone can hear you scream!

Something ancient dwells beneath the ice...

Humans have always looked to the stars for signs of Extraterrestrials.
They have been looking in the wrong place.
They are already here. Entombed beneath Antarctic ice for thousands of years.
The ice is melting and soon they will be free.

Sarcophagus

Their mistake wasn't finding it, it was bringing it back!

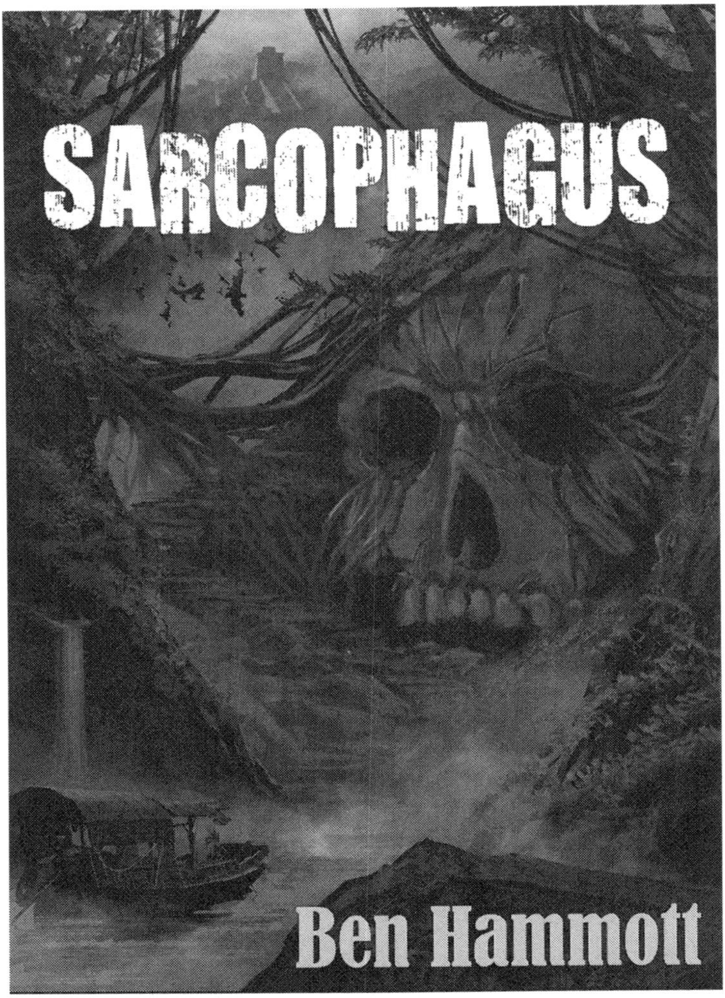

"The Mummy, meets Relic, meets Alien in this scary action driven horror thriller."

Action adventure horror set in the Amazon jungle and London, England.

Concealed in a remote area of the Amazon jungle is something the Mayans thought so dangerous they built a secret prison to entomb it. It remained undiscovered for centuries.

When a maverick archaeologist hears rumours of a mysterious lost city, he heads into the Amazon jungle, determined to find it.

He soon learns that some things are best left unfound. The dangerous past the Mayans tried so hard to bury, is about to become our terrifying future.

Extended book blurb:

When an archaeologist stumbles across a mysterious Mayan city in a remote part of the Amazon jungle, he informs the British museum funding his expedition of the discovery.

When fellow archaeologist, Greyson Bradshaw, receives news of the discovery, he jumps at the chance to travel to the Amazon jungle to collect artifacts for the forthcoming Mayan exhibition he is arranging.

The two archaeologists explore the city's subterranean levels and enter Xibalba, the Mayan underworld. In a secret chamber they discover something hidden away for centuries; a sarcophagus. Realizing its potential as a centerpiece for his exhibition, Greyson transports the sarcophagus and other artifacts back to England. The past is about to come alive.

"Hammott is fast becoming the master of monster horror. Read his Ice Rift books and you'll know what I mean. Fantastic escapism."

"The author has such a creative mind it's scary. The monsters he brings alive in his books are simply terrifying. Add atmospheric locations, characters you root for, racked up tension, a thrilling plot that forbids you to stop reading, and you have Sarcophagus."

The Lost Inheritance Mystery

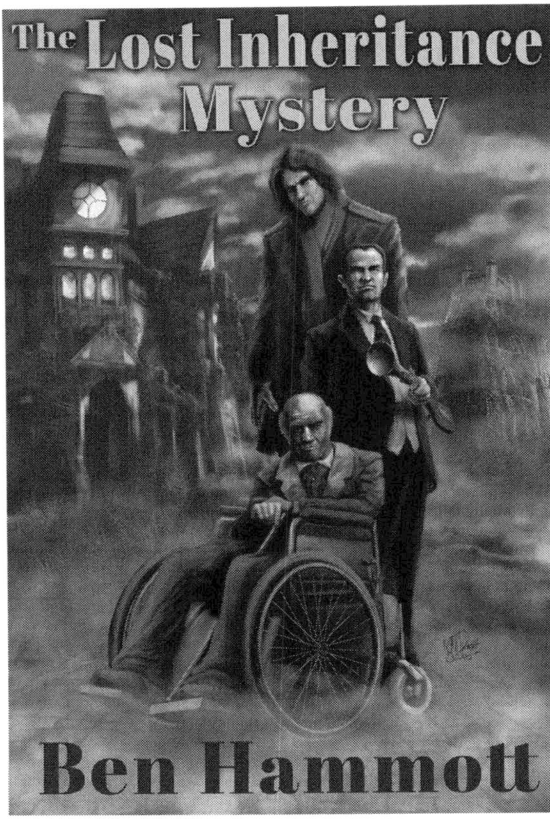

A Victorian mystery adventure revolving around the search for a lost inheritance worth millions. The two rival miserly Drooge brothers, a butler, a murderous hunchback, a shadowy assassin, a fashion senseless burglar, a beast named Diablo, strange henchmen, an actor who once had a standing ovation, and many more oddball characters, all conspire in ways you couldn't possibly imagine to steal two paintings that contain clues to the long lost inheritance of Jacobus Drooge.

This is a complete standalone adventure.

SOLOMON'S TREASURE 1
BEGINNINGS: A Hunt for Treasure
and
SOLOMON'S TREASURE 2
THE PRIEST'S SECRET
(The Tomb, the Temple, the Treasure Book 1 and 2)
An ancient mystery, a lost treasure and the search for the most sought after relics in all antiquity.

An exciting archaeological thriller spanning more than 2000 years.

Beginning with the construction of Solomon's Temple, the Fall of Jerusalem, the creation of the Copper Scrolls and the forming of the Knights Templar and their mysterious tunnelling under the Temple Mount. The story then takes us into the trap-riddled catacombs beneath Rosslyn Chapel, on to Rennes-le-Chateau, into the Tomb, Jerusalem and its secret tunnels and beyond.

*****

The Lost City Book Series

EL DORADO Book 1: Search for the Lost City - An Unexpected Adventure

EL DORADO - Book 2: Fabled Lost Treasure - The Secret City

One of the world's most legendary and elusive treasures, sought after for centuries.

An ancient mystery

A Lost Treasure

A Hidden City

An impossible location

An unimaginable adventure

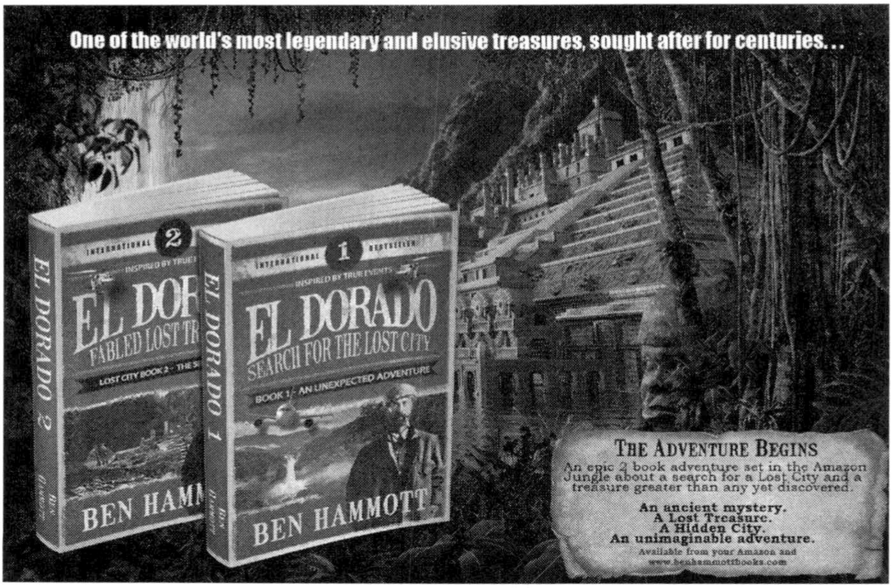

Included in Aztec and Mayan legends, Conquistadors had heard rumours of its existence when exploring the New World, but never found it.

During World War 2, Nazi inspired archaeologists were convinced they had pinpointed its location. They packed a U-Boat with supplies and set a course for the Amazon Jungle. They disappeared!

Many adventurers eager to claim the legendary gold as their own entered one of the most inhospitable places on earth, the Amazon Jungle. Most were never seen again!

And yet the exact location of El Dorado and its fantastic hoard of Mayan, Aztec and Inca treasure so many have dreamed of finding, remains a mystery. Any who may have stumbled upon it never returned to tell the tale. It was as if someone, or something, was protecting it...

An Insatiable Thirst for Murder Serial Killer Henry Holmes

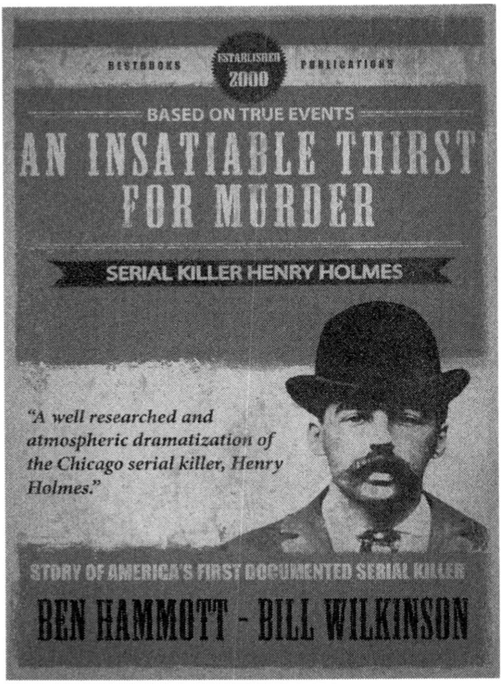

This book contains the shocking dramatization of real events carried out by the serial killer, Henry Howard Holmes.

STORY OF AMERICA'S FIRST DOCUMENTED SERIAL KILLER. (Fiction)

America's first documented serial killer, Henry Howard Holmes, holds a dubious and ghastly record that few serial killers in history have surpassed. The 19th century killer is thought to have committed over 200 murders, but, for unexplained reasons, appears to have been overlooked by many true crime enthusiasts. Set partly in the era when "Jack the Ripper" was terrorizing the foggy streets of London with his gruesome slayings in the 19th century, Holmes was committing his nefarious crimes in America, undetected.

Holmes, a handsome, well dressed gentleman with high intelligence, was a murderer and accomplished con-man. Charm and trust were his most effective weapons and he welded them as expertly as any surgeon would a scalpel.

To achieve an easy way to entrap and dispose of his intended victims, Holmes constructed a huge building that when his crimes were revealed, the newspapers of the time named the "Murder Hotel." And this is a fair description as there can be no doubt the building was constructed for the sole purpose of killing his victims and the disposal of their corpses. Though the majority of his victims were women he charmed and ensnared in his murderous grasp, he also murdered men and children.

As the trial judge said when charging the jury responsible for convicting Holmes: ***"Truth is stranger than fiction, and if Mrs. Pitezel's story is true—(and it was proven to be true)—it is the most wonderful exhibition of the power of mind over mind I have ever seen, and stranger than any novel I have ever read."***

After 2 years of research and consultation with modern day serial killer profilers, I believe this to be the most accurate dramatized account of America's first documented serial killer, H. H. Holmes.

If you hear him lock the door, you are already dead!

"Insightful thoughts of some characters during their impending death make it too easy to identify with the horror of what they experienced. By the time I got to the end of some parts, I was out of breath, literally!"

***

"Grabs your concentration by the throat with every horrific and appalling act carried out by Holmes and never lets go. The scenes are so well written that you find yourself witnessing everything as if you were there."

***

"An atmospheric dramatization of a true crime mystery using source documents and the investigations carried out by detective Frank Geyer to portray a believable and disturbing account of the heinous murders and crimes of the serial killer, Henry H. Holmes."

***

"This well researched dramatization of the Chicago serial killer, Henry Holmes, because is based on actual events, isn't something that's always easily digestible; it sits in your gut and gnaws at your insides. It becomes part of your subconscious. You think of it long after you have laid the book aside. No punches are pulled to describe the horrendous crimes carried out by this cold hearted killer."

***

"Hammott's writing is easy to read. He has a real knack for creating great descriptions of scenes, characters, and murderous action."

***

"Absorbingly horrific. As if it were a plane crash that you just can't look away from, because you're intrigued as to how and what will happen next."

"As fascinating as it is shocking.

Dead Dragons Gold - Book 1
A Gathering of Dwarfs

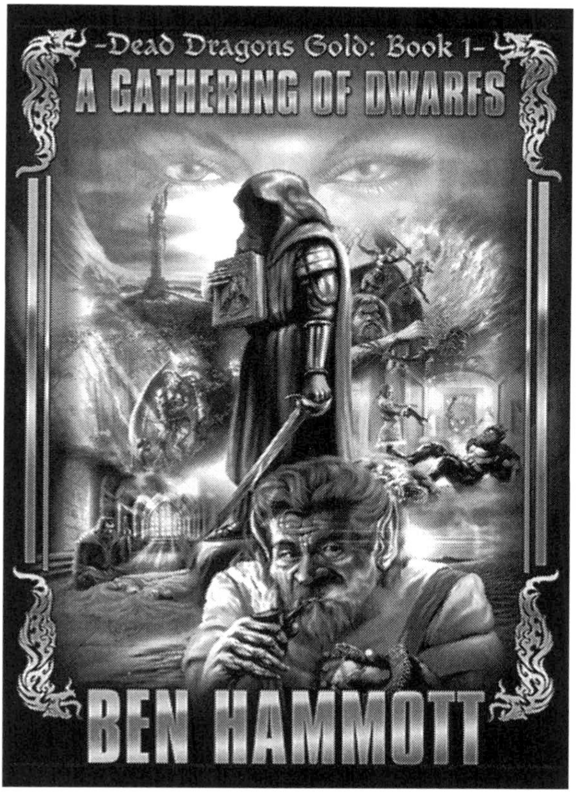

"This book will appeal to fans of Terry Pratchett's Discworld Sagas."

"An exciting humorous fantasy adventure which reveals what happened to the 7 dwarfs after Prince Charming had claimed Snow White as his bride."

"A dark fantasy tale interjected with humour interwoven in an original plot that will change your view of Snow White's seven dwarfs."

"If you like your fantasy stories full of originality and humour, this is the book for you and one for Pratchett fans of all ages. Highly recommended."

Not every Fairy Tale ends happily for all...
A dauntless young hero.
An impossible quest.
A Hunt for Dead Dragons Gold.

We all know Snow White lived happily ever after, but what happened to the seven dwarfs?

When their diamond mine becomes choked with the barbed roots of the thorny hedge the wicked queen erected around their land the dwarfs are forced to split up and survive using their various talents of Assassin, Thief, Bounty Hunter, Medicus, Pirate, Inventor and Priest.

After many years their lives change with the appearance of an unlikely young adventurer whose plan is to plunder the treasure hoards of the many long dead dragons. However, to achieve this he needs the foremost book on dragons containing a map depicting every location of the deceased dragons lairs. A snag in his plan is only one copy of this book exists, and it's in possession of the wicked queen who was not killed as the popular story would have everyone believe but is very much alive. Banished to the top of a lonely mountain she will only relinquish her ownership of the book if he can set her free.

All he has to do is track down the seven dwarfs scattered across the kingdom and convince them to have the wizard lift the curse from the one they most hate. It will be a far from easy task.

For the first time, the fate of the seven dwarfs is revealed in an exciting, original story of heroic adventure, strange lands, terrifying creatures, death, dangerous deeds and dead dragons gold that takes place ten years after Snow White leaves with her not so charming prince.

A fantasy adventure about what happens when someone who isn't destined to be a hero slaps fate around the face and tries to be one anyway.

Reviews

"I enjoyed this read. It was funny, exciting action and adventurous."

***

"...had me laughing out loud, what an enjoyable read."

***

"A great twist on a well-known fairy tale."

***

"Bloody, Bawdy and Funny, it's not fairy tale for children."

Non-Fiction Books by Author

Also available is the best non-fiction account of Holmes Crimes, frauds, capture and trial:

The Hunt for H. H. Holmes and Trial of America's First Serial Killer

Holmes Pitezel Case - History of the Greatest Crime of the Century and the Search for the Missing Pitezel Children by Frank P. Geyer 1896.

(Illustrated - complete and unabridged)

4 Books in 1 Edition

Detective Frank Geyer, the author of one of the included books, was the man responsible for bringing H. H. Holmes to justice and revealing some of his atrocious crimes.

Bonus material includes:

HOLMES CONFESSIONS With Moyamensing Prison Diary Appendix - Burk & McFetridge Co. 1895

(Illustrated - complete and unabridged)

HOLMES CONFESSES 27 MURDERS

THE MOST AWFUL STORY OF MODERN TIMES

TOLD BY THE FIEND IN HUMAN SHAPE.

Every Detail of His Fearful Crimes Told by the Man Who Admits He Is Turning Into the Shape of the Devil. THE TALE OF THE GREATEST CRIMINAL IN HISTORY

Copyright, 1896 by W.R. Hearst and James Elverson, Jr.

(Illustrated - complete and unabridged)

HOLMES' MURDER CASTLE

A Story of H. H. Holmes' Mysterious Work By ROBERT. L. CORBITT. COPYRIGHT, 1895 (Illustrated - complete and unabridged)

WAS HOLMES JACK THE RIPPER?

The hunt for H.H. Homes (Real Name, Herman Webster Mudgett) by Detective Frank Geyer is a fascinating read. With hardly any clues to help him, except for Holmes first confession, which Geyer believed was mostly lies, and the Pitezel's children's letters to their mother, Geyer sets off on a hunt across America on the trail of the missing children.

If it was not for Geyer's unrelenting persistence, the outcome he achieved would never have been reached.

Though it reads like a work of fiction, the Holmes murder case is real and will be enjoyed by anyone who likes a good murder mystery or detective story.

This is the complete and unabridged version of 1896 publication, **The Holmes Pitezel Case - A History Of The Greatest Crime Of The Century and the Search For The Missing Pitezel Children by Detective Geyer.**

*****

90950610R10168

Made in the USA
Middletown, DE
27 September 2018